Capitol
Murder

Madison Parker's ad agency wins the large USMed Healthcare business. USMed will bring total healthcare coverage to all Americans – if congress passes the bill. But powerful people want to kill the bill … and Madison's best friend.

Capitol
Murder

A suspense thriller.
MIKE BROGAN

Lighthouse Publishing

ISBN: 978-1-7338037-3-1 print

ISBN: 978-1-7338037-4-8 ebook

ISBN: 978-1-7338037-5-5 ebook

Library of Congress Control Number: 2021936424

Printed in the United States of America
Published in the United States by Lighthouse Publishing

Cover design: Vong Lee

First Edition

This book is dedicated to the doctors, nurses, hospital workers, and all medical personnel who each day risk their health to protect ours.

It's also dedicated to bringing better health and healthcare to all Americans, including the 40 million who can't afford health insurance and the thirty million who have insufficient healthcare.

Acknowledgments

To my terrific doctors for reminding me to keep six feet apart to avoid six feet under.

To my parents for bequeathing me healthy DNA.

To my family for tolerating my 5 a.m. jogging on our noisy treadmill.

To my fellow novelists and colleagues for their helpful thoughts and recommendations that made this book much better.

To editor-translator, Brendan Brogan, for his insightful improvements to the rough draft.

To wife Marcie for her helpful suggestions and improvements to the manuscript.

To author, Rebecca M. Lyles, for her comprehensive and invaluable final edit of Capitol Murder.

ONE

"I don't believe you!" Madison Parker said to her executive assistant, Christine.

"It's true. A woman woke up with her shirt soaked in blood. She was bleeding from her nipple and terrified. She rushed to the emergency room where doctors found she had a benign tumor that needed surgery. Her health insurance agreed to pay the $3,000 bill. But after the surgery, the insurance company changed its mind-and sent *her* the bill for the $3,000."

"That's outrageous." Madison said. "Why?"

"Her insurance said she should have realized there was no emergency."

"She was bleeding from her breast for God's sake!"

"Didn't matter, they said."

"So bleeding from the breast means she's fine? No problem?" Madison said.

"I guess."

Madison couldn't believe it. She'd heard similar horror stories of health insurance companies agreeing to pay their members emergency room bills, then refusing to pay later and sticking the patient with the bill.

"Please tell me the insurance company wasn't *our* agency client, HealCare?" Madison said.

"It's not. It was another national healthcare provider."

Madison exhaled in relief. As CEO of Turner Advertising, she'd been working on a new campaign for HealCare, which had excellent heart and cancer centers nationwide.

It also had excellent corporate profits, a necessary and reasonable goal. But not, she felt, when high profits resulted in outrageously high-priced prescriptions and hospital services that more and more American families could not afford.

Madison looked at her family photo on her desk: her husband, Kevin, their baby daughter, Mia, and her. Their first family photo. Mia was six hours old, sprouting stalks of Kevin's copper-red hair above cobalt-blue eyes.

Now Mia was two years old, marching around barking orders like General George S. Patton, and spending lots of time with Kevin's mom, whose apartment, thank God, connected directly to their Manhattan apartment. His mom, Kate, was a gift from the childcare gods. With their unpredictable travel schedules, she made both of their lives so much easier.

Madison's office door opened, and Christine hurried back in.

"Senator Jonathon Nelson is on line one. Maybe he has news about that advertising assignment for USMed."

"It's too early. The winning agency won't be selected for two months. And we don't have a prayer."

"Why not?"

"HealCare might be seen as a conflict with USMed. And the USMed selection committee will assume we're in favor of maintaining America's present multiple managed healthcare systems. Also, Senator Nelson has an executive friend at a much bigger ad agency."

"But you're friends with his daughter, Ellie."

"Great friends."

"Only one way to find out what the Senator wants." Christine pointed at Madison's phone.

Madison crossed her fingers and picked up Senator Nelson's call.

"Senator, it's nice to hear from you. How are you and your talented daughter, my favorite college roommate?"

"Your *only* college roommate as I recall."

"Who else would put up with us?"

He laughed. "We're both fine, but Ellie's working too hard."

"She tells me you are too. Is hard work a Nelson DNA thing?"

"A defect. But this call is easy work. Our committee liked your proposal for our national USMed campaign. Your strategy and TV advertising concepts are excellent. We chose three agency finalists. Yours was one."

And you're calling to say you're giving the business to a bigger agency? Madison thought.

"A few hours ago our committee voted and made a final decision."

Her heart pounded. Despite her impossible chance to win, she'd really love to win this assignment.

"We decided to go with a non-favored agency."

"Who?"

"Yours."

Madison coughed coffee onto her desk and shouted, *"AWESOME!"* as coffee dripped from her nose.

"The committee liked *your* agency's campaign a lot, Madison. Congratulations."

Madison caught her breath. "Thank you very much, Senator."

"You guys earned it. But we want to get the campaign going ASAP. So I need to brief you soon. When can we meet?"

"I'll fly down to Washington tonight."

"No need to. I'm in Manhattan at the Plaza. Can we meet briefly this evening say around six o'clock in the Rose Club?"

"See you there."

TWO

Madison felt like she had stepped into the *Great Gatsby* movie as she walked into the magnificent lobby of the Plaza Hotel. She loved the huge, brilliantly lit chandeliers, the gilded ceiling, the gleaming floor, the soaring palm trees, and the long auburn window drapes that for some reason always reminded her of giant Creamsicles.

She explained to a young receptionist that she was meeting Senator Nelson.

"He's expecting you in The Rose Club. You know the way?"

"Yes, thank you."

Moments later, Madison stepped down the polished wood staircase into the Rose Club. She loved the plush red chairs, the rose-flower carpet, and the small tables with glowing red lamps. She felt comforted by the room's cozy, turn-of-the-century ambiance.

She saw Senator Nelson sitting at a table, talking on his phone. She's met him years ago at Ellie's college graduation. She and Ellie graduated together and had remained best friends despite their Manhattan-to-DC distance.

She walked over as he hung up. He smiled, stood up and they hugged.

"Senator, it's so nice to see you again."

"You too, Madison. You look as gorgeous as the day you and Ellie graduated."

"Thank you. And you look just as dashing."

"Don't I wish. I can still see you and Ellie flaunting your diplomas as you strutted across the stage—"

"—until I stepped into the fountain pool and Ellie yanked me out."

"You recovered gracefully."

"With squishy shoes."

He smiled.

They sat down.

"You mentioned she's working long hours at the law firm," Madison said.

"She is. But she manages to help me a bit with USMed. So maybe you two can work together on the ad campaign."

"Nothing would make me happier."

His phone rang, he checked the caller ID, and turned it off.

"So here's the deal. As I told you, the National Institute of Health committee reviewed ten ad agency proposals to develop the USMed and social media campaigns. They tested all ten campaigns and selected three finalists. Bottom line? Your campaign tested highest in *credibility,* something Congress badly needs."

She nodded.

"So officially … the committee is asking your agency to handle the advertising and social media campaigns for USMed when and if Congress passes the USMed legislation."

Madison could barely contain her excitement.

"Thank you, Senator. We're honored to support USMed, since it provides healthcare for all Americans. Especially for those who couldn't afford it before. When do you want us to start?"

"As soon as possible. You'll get official notification tomorrow, and your contract as soon as possible. You'll also get our research on the failings of today's healthcare quagmire. If you have questions Madison, just call me or my office." He handed her his card.

"Thank you, Senator. But I'm afraid your USMed assignment will concern one of our agency clients."

"Who's that?" he asked.

"HealCare."

He nodded. "A well-managed, very profitable healthcare company."

"They are. But I'm sure they'll declare a conflict of interest for us handling HealCare *and* USMed. They'll likely release our agency or ask us to resign their business. Both are acceptable to us."

"Whatever they or you decide, Madison, I'd estimate that USMed's revenue to your agency could more than triple your lost revenue from HealCare."

"That's hallelujah time!"

THREE

Surrounded by the sleek teak-paneled DC law offices of Little, Asher and Smythe, Associate Ellie Nelson, worked on business for her Bernardo Sports Center client.

Her firm's senior partner, Lester Little, walked into her office and smiled.

"Hey, Les, what's up?"

"Your billable hours, I see."

"Up six percent this month," she said, feeling good about it.

"Thanks to Bernardo Sports Equipment?"

"Mostly!"

"Why up six percent?"

"Simple. Mr. Bernardo keeps arguing with the city council about which colors they'll let him paint his new sports building downtown. He wants *hot sporty* colors. The city demands distinguished *calm* tones."

"Calm like what?"

"Off-gray."

"What the hell is off-gray?"

"Butt ugly," she said.

"Well, the more they debate butt-ugly colors, the more beautiful hours you bill, right?"

"Yep."

Les smiled, then frowned at a file on the corner of her desk. "You reading about USMed?"

"A bit."

"Helping your father, the Senator?"

"Only at home, Les. Here, I'm reading how USMed could affect *our* healthcare client, LifeLocke."

"Think tsunami effect," Les said. "If USMed becomes law, LifeLocke and the thousands of other individual managed healthcare plans will shrink faster than the buggy whip business."

"I agree."

Lester's secretary walked in and called him to an important phone call.

"Let's talk later about this, Ellie."

"Okay."

He smiled and left.

Ellie felt relieved that Les wasn't complaining that she was helping her dad a bit on USMed since this was a potential conflict for LifeLocke.

She looked down at the proposed USMed bill, a national healthcare and pharma plan that covered *all* Americans. A smart single-payer plan. And the single payer was the American government.

Her dad, Jonathon Nelson, an MD and US Senator, led the senate charge for USMed. He'd seen too many women, men, and children die from curable diseases simply because they could not afford health insurance or treatment.

Her phone rang. She smiled at Caller ID and whispered, "Speak of the devil."

She picked up. "Hi, dad."

"How's the law treating my favorite daughter?"

"And only daughter. I'm still slogging my way through eighty-hour workweeks. How's your USMed bill moving along?"

"Slogging its way through boring Congressional committee meetings."

"Didn't Churchill say democracy is the sloggiest form of government except for all the others?" Ellie said.

"Sounds like him."

"You still coming for dinner tonight?" she asked.

"Is 7:00 okay?"

"Perfect. I'm making your favorite. Mario Lasagna."

"I salivate! See you later."

"Love you, dad."

"Love you."

They hung up and Ellie leaned back and took a deep breath. It would be great to have dinner with dad. He'd buried himself in work since her mother's death four years ago. He worked 24/7 on USMed and other legislation. And he'd been alone too much.

Tonight, she'd try to relax him. Remind him again to ease up, enjoy his Mario Lasagna like her mom made, and slow down a bit.

No, he wouldn't slow down.

But at least he'd have a nice home-cooked family dinner.

FOUR

In her apartment, Ellie replayed the audio recording of her Bernardo's Sports client's argument with the City Councilman, Durwood Akerley III.

Akerley said, "Mr. Bernardo you may paint your new sports and hunting equipment building any of these four captivating colors: Off-Gray, Subtle-Beige, Pale-Butter, or Mirage-Hue."

"Boring. Boring. Boring. Boring. How about leopard?"

"Heavens no—all those obnoxious black spots!"

"Tiger stripes?"

"Prisoners wear stripes. Ugly. Dreadful!"

"I got it."

"What?"

"Baboon-butt fuchsia."

"Get serious, Mr. Bernardo."

And so it went. Ellie tried to suggest compromise colors and hues, but these men couldn't agree on what day follows Friday. And the less they agreed, the more agreeable hours she billed.

Ellie turned off the recorder and checked her watch. 7:40 p.m. Her dad should have been here forty minutes ago. Her Mario Lasagna's mouth-watering scent filled her apartment.

She called him. No answer. His message box was full. She texted. No answer.

He always calls if he'll be this late. What's going on?

Then, like magic, her phone rang. *Finally!*

"Ellie … ?" Her dad's assistant, Estelle.

"Your father … he … "

"What—?"

Estelle was breathing heavy. "He's being rushed to-"

Ellie felt faint.

"… MedStar Georgetown University Hospital. Please hurry Ellie!"

* * *

Blinking away tears and fears, Ellie raced toward MedStar Georgetown University Hospital. She parked in the Emergency lot, rushed inside past the gleaming white walls and sliding glass doors, and hurried over to a female receptionist monitoring three large computers.

"My father, Senator Nelson, was just—"

"—he's in Emergency," she said, pointing down a hallway.

"*Ellie!*" someone shouted behind her.

She turned and saw Estelle, red-faced and panicked, rushing toward her. Her eyes were damp.

"This way, Ellie. Down here."

They hurried down the hallway and stopped at the door to a glassed-in Emergency alcove that appeared connected to the much larger Emergency area.

She looked through the small glass window and saw her father on what looked like a respirator. A mask covered his mouth and nose. IVs dripped into his body, masked doctors and nurses hovered over him.

Her heart pounded against her ribs. Tears blurred her vision. She felt lightheaded and had to steady herself on Estelle's elbow.

"What happened?" Ellie whispered.

"He has a lot of trouble breathing. The doctors don't know why yet."

The ER alcove door opened, and a tall doctor with thick blond hair hurried out of the room and over to her.

"Are you the Senator's daughter?"

"Yes."

"I'm Doctor Tom Lyons."

"What's his status, Doctor?"

"Serious. We can't determine what's causing his breathing difficulties. Tests should soon tell us what—"

"—Doctor!" A nurse waved him back into the emergency room.

He turned to Ellie. "I'll be back."

Dr. Lyons raced back into the room.

Ellie noticed her dad's normal healthy complexion was now pale. *My God, he's fading.* It made no sense. Three weeks ago, his doctor said his annual exam revealed the test results of a healthy man twenty years younger. Heart, lungs, kidneys, and blood pressure—all excellent. He still jogged and exercised five days a week.

The doctors were bent over her dad's body, checking vital signs and monitors and issuing rapid instructions every few seconds. She couldn't read the monitors from this distance.

But she could read the doctors' faces.

All wore grave expressions.

Moments later, Dr. Lyons stopped giving directions, took a deep breath, stared at the monitors, and leaned against the gurney.

The medical team looked at the monitors, then at Dr. Lyons. He looked at the wall clock, said something to the nurse beside him. She nodded and wrote something down.

Dr. Lyons turned, walked slowly from the room, and headed toward Ellie, his light-blue eyes telling her what she already knew.

"I'm very sorry," Dr. Lyons said.

FIVE

MANHATTAN

Her alarm clock news jolted Madison awake like a Taser.

The announcer said Senator Jonathon Nelson died last night.

She collapsed back on the bed and felt tears spill onto her pillow.

Not possible! He looked in terrific health at the Plaza just days ago. She reached over to tell Kevin and remembered he was still filming car commercials in the Mohave Desert.

Ellie must be devastated. Her mother passed away a few years ago and she has no brothers or sisters. An invalid aunt lives somewhere in Idaho. Ellie is alone.

I've got to be there for her ... like she was there for me when my mom died.

Thank God, Kevin's mother is here to take care of Mia.

* * *

Madison flew to DC to attend Senator Nelson's funeral. But mostly to comfort Ellie.

During the funeral, Madison watched Ellie's eyes fill with tears. She seemed overwhelmed by grief, despite being consoled by friends, Congress members, and even the President.

After the funeral, Madison helped Ellie hold a reception at her father's home in Georgetown. Ellie tried to put on a good face, but she kept staring out the window as though expecting her dad to walk up to the front door. She and her father had always been close, and grew even closer after his wife, Ellie's mother, died.

Madison saw a small gap in the condolence line and hurried over to Ellie.

"Hug re-boot?" Madison said.

"Please."

Madison hugged her.

"Thanks, Maddy."

"Anytime."

As Ellie greeted an older couple, Madison looked around at Senator Nelson's fellow Senators and Congress members, political pals from both parties, and pals from Indiana.

Her father's sixtyish assistant, Estelle Tompkins, eyes moist, walked up and embraced Ellie. "Anything you need, Ellie, *anything*, just ask."

"Thanks, Estelle. This is my good friend, Madison."

"Nice to meet you," Estelle said.

"And you," Madison said.

"Estelle, do you recall what my dad was doing in his office before he collapsed?"

"Working on USMed. Like always. I told him to ease up, but he kept working, writing and texting. At 6:15 I put some mail on his desk. He looked fine. Said he wanted to rest a bit before going to your apartment for dinner." She wiped away a tear.

"Then what?"

"About 7:20 I walked into his office and found him lying on his sofa. I couldn't wake him." She closed her eyes and took a deep breath. "The ambulance arrived within three minutes and rushed him to MedStar."

Another tear spilled down her cheek.

"I should have checked him sooner."

"It's okay, Estelle."

No one spoke for a while.

Estelle said, "Ellie, I Fed-Exed you his latest USMed files. He was going to show you something to see if you picked up on what he suspected."

"What?" Ellie asked.

"He didn't say."

Madison asked, "Did he suspect some *thing*?"

"*Someone*, I think. Or maybe both."

"Any idea who?"

"Sorry, no."

Estelle saw she was holding up the condolence line "If you need anything, call me."

"Thanks, Estelle."

Madison said, "Ellie, your father told me you're finishing up some USMed work for him."

"I am."

"He suggested it might make sense for us to work together on the USMed ad campaigns."

"I totally agree," Ellie said.

"But more importantly, we can catch up on our vile college classmates gossip."

Ellie managed a smile. "Like weird Flora's Annual Navel Jewelry Awards?"

"Flora could hide a battleship in her navel."

They smiled but stopped as Ellie turned to accept the condolences from the Vice President, followed by several Senators from both parties.

Madison saw Ellie nod at someone she obviously knew, a tall, attractive man in his mid-forties with thick black hair and shiny black leather cowboy boots walking toward Ellie.

Ellie turned to Madison and whispered, "Meet Senator Loren D. Estleman from Michigan, one of dad's favorites."

"Ellie, my deepest condolences," he said.

"Thank you, Senator. This is my good friend, Madison."

"Nice to meet you, Madison."

"And you, Senator."

"Ellie, your dad was special to me. He mentored me even though I'm a shameless Independent. He also gave me the best advice I ever got in this town."

"What advice?"

"That ninety percent of the politicians in DC give the other ten percent a bad reputation. Harry Truman said it first. Harry was right."

Ellie said, "Harry also said, "If you want a friend in Washington, get a dog.""

"Right again."

They smiled, and as Estleman started to move down the condolence line, he turned back and said, "Ellie, have you heard anything about your dad's interim replacement in the Senate?"

She shook her head. "No."

"This morning I heard some rumbling that the Governor of Indiana might consider a surprise choice."

"Who?"

"I'm talking to her."

"*Me?*" Ellie smiled. "Impossible!"

"Why?"

"I don't have the patience to handle all the political games and backstabbing. And I don't own a Kevlar vest."

Estleman smiled. "Still, maybe give it some thought. Your dad thought you'd be great in the Senate." He smiled and moved on down the condolence line.

Ellie as interim Senator. Madison thought it was a terrific idea.

"Maybe you should talk to the Indiana Governor. If he suggests you might finish your father's senate term, consider it. You could guarantee your dad's vote for USMed."

Ellie seemed to accept the logic but didn't look persuaded.

"Your dad told me he wanted to cast the USMed vote more than any other vote. Imagine how honored he'd be if *you* cast it."

SIX

Senator Clete Ruskin settled into his office chair in his forest cabin … his cozy getaway when Washington got too crazy. Like from Monday to Monday.

Clete, a seventy-seven-year-old West-By-God Virginian, nursed his nightly Jack Daniels and tapped his Cohiba cigar ashes in the tray as he reviewed the proposed USMed bill.

A life-long Republican, Clete, and his long-time pal, Senator-Doctor Jonathon Nelson, an unashamed Democrat, worked well together. Always had. They drafted most of the USMed legislative language and felt proud of their resulting bill.

But now Nelson was gone. Deceased. The news hit Ruskin like a semi. It made no damn sense. *Doc Nelson was a thousand times healthier than me!*

Ruskin sipped more Jack as his phone rang. He checked Caller ID: a reporter he'd promised to give a brief interview.

He picked up. "Ruskin."

———

"Senator Ruskin, it's Luke Lapointe with *Washington NewsTime*. You mentioned we could chat today."

"Sure, Luke. Chat away."

"Thank you, Senator. First off, thank you for this chance. I've been on the international news desk for a long time. So healthcare is new editorial territory for me as my questions will probably reveal."

"No problem, Luke."

"Thank you, sir. Last Thursday, you said that our present healthcare system is broken for many millions of Americans. Why is that?"

"Because America's healthcare is not based on better healthcare for *all* Americans."

"What's it based on?"

"Better profits for the healthcare, pharmaceutical industries, and special interest groups."

"Any example?"

"Lots. Take the drug industry. It made billions in profit last year, and donated two hundred and seventy million dollars to the election campaigns of Congress members. Why? Simple. To pressure Congress members to vote for laws that protect their high drug prices."

"Any high-priced drugs come to mind?" Luke said.

"Hundreds. Like NARCAN. It saves the lives of overdosed addicts. Without it, they can die. It used to be cheap so they could afford it. Then the company raised the price to $575 per prescription."

"Wow! But I read NARCAN is free in some countries."

"It is. In many it costs only $20–$50 bucks. But a while ago, Congress passed new legislation that allowed the drug maker to raise its price even higher than $575, so they did."

"To what?"

"$4,500 per prescription."

"*WHAT?*"

"As a result, thousands of American addicts likely died because they didn't have the jacked-up price of $4,500 to go buy NARCAN?"

"That seems cruel, immoral."

"So does Acthar," Ruskin said.

"Acthar?"

"A drug for babies with seizures. Also, for adults with multiple sclerosis. It requires doses twice daily for a few weeks. Multiple sclerosis patients require doses for two to three weeks."

"What's Acthar cost?"

"One dose costs $8,124. Two doses daily cost $16,246. A two-dose daily for a full month costs you around $457,800."

"Who in hell can afford that?"

"Bill Gates, Elon Musk, Mark Zuckerberg, Michael Bloomberg. But they don't need it."

"I read that 58 million American adults can't afford the drugs they need," Luke said.

"It's true."

"Why don't Congress members *force* drug companies to reduce their outrageous prices so normal people can pay?"

"Because Congress members need drug company donations to fund their election campaigns."

"What about managed healthcare plans? And big hospital networks?"

"Same story, Luke. Managed care and hospital networks donate gazillions to the election campaigns of Congressmembers so they'll pass laws that protect high-priced healthcare and hospital pricing."

"The old *quid pro quo.*"

"Yep."

"How much do these drug and healthcare industries donate to Congress members?"

"Over the last ten years-*five billion dollars!*"

"Jesus H. Christ!" Luke said. "I also hear that *un*insured people who get treated in hospital have to pay outrageous prices."

"You hear right," Ruskin said. "True story. An *un*insured man walking in Central Park tripped and broke his ankle. A nearby hospital put his ankle in a cast and couple hours later, as he hobbled out on crutches, they handed him the bill."

"How much?"

"Eighty thousand dollars."

"You're joking."

"I saw his hospital bill."

"That's incredible! Can I use this example?"

"Absolutely."

"Senator thank you for your time. And thank you for your candor."

"You're welcome, Luke."

They hung up.

Clete Ruskin puffed his cigar, sipped more Jack Daniels, and checked his watch. His wife of forty-six years would arrive here any minute and give him bloody hell again for smoking and drinking. He'd remind her of his belief that … "To keep one's sanity in DC, a Senator needs a vice or two."

"So why do you have fourteen?" she'd say.

Ruskin's phone rang again. He saw it was a reporter he did not want to talk to, so he let it ring. A minute later, another ring-Caller ID said *Private Caller* and he picked up. Might be a donor. No one came on the line, so he hung up. The phone rang again. His aide calling. He picked up.

"Don't forget your 10 a.m. meeting with Finance," the aide said.

"I'll be there."

They hung up.

Ruskin yawned. He'd been up for fifteen hours. He felt old, he felt tired, he felt a nap coming on.

He drank the rest of his Jack Daniels, snubbed out his Cohiba cigar, closed his eyes, and drifted off.

SEVEN

MANHATTAN

Madison's office phone rang, and she saw it was Ellie.

"What's up?" Madison asked.

Ellie took a deep breath.

"Senator Clete Ruskin just passed away."

Madison slumped in her chair. "My God! He seemed fine at your dad's funeral."

"He did. But last night he died at his cabin."

"From what?"

"They suspect heart attack. He had a heart condition. Loved his cigars and whiskey."

"He and your dad co-authored much of the USMed bill, right?" Madison said.

"Right. They worked well together on bills like John McCain and Ted Kennedy used to."

"Who's replacing Ruskin as interim Senator?" Madison said.

"His Governor just named a man who's against USMed."

"So, we've lost another pro-USMed senate vote."

"We also lost one more in the House."

"Who?" Madison said, growing concerned.

"Congressman Bob Maybin."

"But last week Maybin said he was voting for USMed," Madison said.

"Not anymore. Dad called him Congressman Maybe ... maybe he'll vote for a bill, maybe against."

"So, we can't count on his vote?"

"We can't. Also, Estelle rechecked all votes: the sure votes, not-so-sure votes, the no votes, and possible flip-flopper votes in both the Senate and the House. She figures there are four or five undecided or unconfirmed voters in the Senate at present."

"How many undecideds in the House?"

"Nine to eleven," Ellie said.

"More than enough to defeat USMed."

EIGHT

WASHINGTON

Madison flew back to DC and met Ellie in a conference room at MedTech Labs. They hoped to learn the cause of death for Ellie's father. A very healthy man whose sudden death made no sense.

Madison liked the murals of famous turn-of-the-century scientists: Charles Darwin in his London study, Madame Curie in her small French workshop, and Alexander Fleming in London's St. Mary's Hospital where he accidentally discovered penicillin.

Madison felt fortunate that she and her family lived now, when medicine and healthcare offered more ways to heal people—*if* they could afford the medicine and healthcare that would heal them.

But Senator Nelson's research found that forty-four million Americans could not afford any health insurance at all. Another thirty-eight million could only afford inferior low-grade insurance.

In other words, one out of three Americans get up each morning not knowing if adequate medical care will be available to them and their families when they need it.

Ellie stared at a case history in her briefcase. "True story. Jennifer got pregnant at nineteen. She had a low-paying clerk job. Couldn't afford health insurance. Her hospital birth would cost her $20,000. She told the hospital nurse she couldn't afford that. So the nurse suggested she apply for Medicaid. She applied, but Medicaid denied her coverage."

"Why?"

"Because her annual income was fifty-six dollars over the annual income level to qualify for Medicaid."

"What'd she do?"

"The nurse suggested she *quit* her job, so she'd automatically qualify for Medicaid."

"Did she quit?"

"No. She couldn't quit. She needed her *Stop-n-Buy* clerk job to pay for food and rent. The baby's father had deserted her."

"So, what happened?"

"Her *Stop-n-Buy* boss was smart. He cut her pay by a few cents an hour. That lowered her annual income by fifty-nine dollars which qualified her for Medicaid!"

"And?"

"Baby Jenna was born in the hospital."

Madison smiled, then shook her head. "Welcome to American healthcare—where a poor woman is forced to quit her job to have her baby born in a hospital? What kind of healthcare system that does that to its poorer citizens?"

"A heartless, ruthless system," Ellie said.

"And deadly," Madison said, "if you can't afford your life-saving surgery."

"And Dad's research said that one in four Americans delay medical treatment for a serious illness due to the high costs of treatment."

A petite young Asian lab assistant with long black hair walked in. "I'm Maeko. Dr. Browner's assistant. He'll be with you very shortly."

"Thank you, Maeko," Ellie said.

Maeko left.

"Let's hope he learned what caused my Dad's death."

"Did he give you any hint?"

Ellie shook her head. "He knew Dad was in good health. So he was quite shocked."

"What do you think happened?"

Ellie shrugged. "Possible heart attack."

"Why?"

"His mother died from one at eighty-three."

"Did he, or do you, have any genetic markers for a heart problems?"

"I don't know. And maybe I don't want to know."

The door opened and in walked a white-coated, sixtyish, rosy-cheeked doctor with gray hair and a stethoscope dangling around his neck.

"Your big brown eyes suggest you might be Ellie Nelson," Dr. Browner said, smiling at her.

"Yes, I'm Ellie. And this is my friend, Madison Parker."

"Nice to meet you both. I'm Bill Browner. We just got back your father's preliminary report."

They waited.

"It's somewhat incomplete because we're waiting for a *final* toxicology report."

"Anything you can share now?" Ellie asked.

Dr. Browner scratched his bushy eyebrows. "Well, we know he experienced sudden-onset severe breathing difficulties and nausea. He died soon after from cardiac arrest. We don't know what caused the breathing difficulties and cardiac arrest. I'm hoping the final tox test will tell us more."

"When do you expect it?"

"Later this afternoon or tonight."

"Dad's mother died of a heart attack," Ellie said.

"His heart was in excellent condition. So was everything else. He was in terrific shape. A very fit man. So this is puzzling."

Ellie nodded.

"Do you know what your father was doing right before he collapsed? Anything strenuous? Jogging, lifting weights?"

"No. His secretary said that he was working in his office. Reading files, texting colleagues, reviewing legislation. I talked to him earlier and he sounded fine. Maybe a bit stressed by all the political nonsense."

"Understandable. Did he handle stress well?"

"Yes. He said years as an ER doctor taught him how."

Dr. Browner nodded knowingly.

"When the lab report comes in, will you call me?"

"Of course, I'll ca—"

"—no need to call her later, Doctor," Maeko said, hurrying in. "We just got his final lab report."

She handed it to Dr. Browner.

"Thank you, Maeko."

He scanned the pages, his eyes locking on the last page for several moments. "Well now, this is unexpected."

Ellie and Madison waited.

"Your father's lab report indicates he came into contact with some kind of powerful chemical toxin. A toxin strong enough to trigger his respiratory difficulties and subsequent cardiac arrest."

Ellie was stunned. "You mean like a dangerous poison?"

"Possibly. Did he visit any chemical plants?"

"Not that I know."

"Any military hospitals or bases recently?"

"I don't think so. He visited regular hospitals to meet with doctors, and administrators about healthcare."

"No military hospitals?"

"Pretty sure he didn't. He said active military personnel are often covered by the Department of Defense insurance plans like TRICARE and others. But I can double-check with his assistant right now."

"Please do."

Ellie dialed Estelle and asked about military location visits, listened a while, and hung up.

"He visited no military hospitals, or military bases, or chemical factories in the past year."

"Could his assistant send me a list of all hospitals and industrial locations he visited in the last month?"

"I'll ask Estelle to send you that list."

"Thank you."

"Doctor," Madison said, "why are you interested in military installations?"

Dr. Browner paused as though unsure what to say. "Well, there's a remote possibility that the chemical toxin that caused his breathing difficulties might have been a lethal nerve agent."

"A nerve agent?" Ellie looked stunned.

"Are you sure?" Madison grew alarmed. She'd read about nerve agents.

"It's possible. A follow-up tox report will confirm it. So, if he visited a military location, especially the labs, there's a very remote chance he breathed in a lethal toxin."

Or maybe, Madison thought, *someone made him breathe in a lethal toxin.*

NINE

Tall, blonde, athletic Congresswoman Anne Wilson parked in the garage of her DC apartment complex. She grabbed her briefcase and took the elevator up to her third-floor apartment. She loved her apartment's large bedroom and living room, even its tiny study that forced her to keep it neat.

She especially loved her kitchen's stainless-steel counters, and center-island with flip-down stools for quick meals, all she had time for working fourteen-hour days for USMed.

But getting enough votes to pass USMed was proving more difficult each day. Death just claimed two USMed voters: Senators Nelson and Ruskin. Still, she felt they should have the votes to pass the USMed bill in the Senate and the House—but *just barely.*

Just barely wasn't good enough. Because the drug and healthcare lobbyists were increasing their campaign donations—she called them *bribes*—to Congress members.

But her new PAC alternative-funding approach was also starting to work. This week she persuaded two Congress members, long addicted to pharma and healthcare donations, to accept comparable PAC donations with no request to vote for or against USMed. The Congress members could vote their consciences and what their constituents wanted.

Her phone rang and she recognized the caller: Madison Parker, a close friend of Ellie Nelson.

"Hi Madison, what's up?"

"I wondered, Anne, if you could confirm a scary story about a young girl named Natty from your district. I may want to use her in our ad campaign for USMed."

"What's Natty story?" Anne said.

"Natty was a fourteen-year-old with leukemia. And after her bone marrow transplant, her leukemia went into remission thankfully."

"That's great!"

"Yes, but then her liver failed, and she needed a liver transplant fast. But her health insurance company denied her liver transplant."

"Why deny it if they just covered her bone marrow transplant?"

"They said a liver transplant was "experimental, investigational, and unproven," Madison said.

"*What?* Thousands of successful liver transplant survivors prove otherwise. So, what happened?"

"After dragging their feet with denials for several weeks, the insurance company finally agreed to cover Natty's transplant cost. Just one problem."

"What?" Anne said.

"Natty died the night before."

Anne grew angry. "Makes me wonder if the insurer knew Natty was dying and stalled to save money. If so, it makes me furious!"

"Me too. Madison said. "Some insurers replace their heart with a slab of granite."

* * *

Through the thin opening of a closet door, Archie Braun had an excellent view of Congresswoman Anne Wilson hanging up and walking into her bathroom.

She stripped down.

Now he had an excellent view of her body. Very nice. Wilson was a stunning woman. Beautiful breasts, perfect figure, long legs.

She filled the bathtub with steamy water, grabbed her laptop, and plugged it into the wall outlet.

Then to his amazement, she placed the laptop on a small metal stool just an inch from the bathtub.

She put on her ear pods wired to the laptop, slid into the water, leaned back, closed her eyes. He heard her humming along with Sinead O'Connor's *Nothing Compares 2U.*

Archie couldn't believe how close the laptop was to the bathtub water. An accident waiting to happen.

Could this be any easier?

She settled in. He allowed her to relax a few seconds, and soon she closed her eyes and seemed to doze off. Then, from behind, he inched toward the back of her head.

He gazed down at her magnificent body. She reminded him of his ex-wife, Lurleen, a topless dancer in a Baltimore club. Anne Wilson was stunning.

He felt himself getting aroused. But no, this had to be an *accident.* No sex. No DNA. No evidence.

He stepped closer. The wood floor squeaked, but she didn't hear it, thanks to the music thumping in her ears.

He lifted the laptop, paused for one last glorious gaze.

Then slid the laptop into the water.

The laptop sparked, hissed, sank onto her breasts.

Suddenly, her body jerked and flailed about like she was being Tasered non-stop. The massive volts of electricity shook her violently. Her arms and legs thrashed about like a Raggedy Ann doll. Her eyes bulged as though escaping her skull.

He watched hypnotized.

Soon he realized the electricity was vibrating a corpse.

The fuse blew and the bathroom light went out.

So did the light in her eyes.

TEN

Ellie Nelson sipped green tea in her office at Little, Clement & Smythe Law Offices.

Her boss, Lester Little, walked in as she worked on a minor contract for their LifeLocke client.

He frowned. "What's up with LifeLocke?"

"Their sales!"

"Great!" he said, "But not if USMed passes, right?"

"Right, but sadly true. USMed will cover most of what LifeLocke now covers. But for much, much less cost."

Lester nodded, but seemed troubled about something.

"Ellie, you mentioned you're following up with some of your father's USMed work at home."

"Just a bit." She'd promised her dad she'd finish a few things.

"Somehow our LifeLocke clients learned you're his daughter and that you assisted him on USMed."

"Yikes!"

"Yeah, and obviously they feel LifeLocke's goals conflict with USMed's goals."

She nodded. "They do conflict. But I don't let my Dad's USMed work affect my LifeLocke work here."

"I know you don't, Ellie."

"And I appreciate our firm's patience with me as I finish his work. Frankly, Les, I've felt somewhat conflicted working on our LifeLocke plan here at the office—*and* on USMed work a bit at home. I've been meaning to talk to you about whether a leave of absence until after the USMed vote would be best."

Lester nodded, but still looked troubled. "Actually, our board of directors asked me to talk to you about this."

"About a leave of absence?"

He paused, looked down. "I tried that, Ellie. But our LifeLocke client CEO doesn't want a leave of absence."

"What's he want?"

He walked to the window and looked out. "He wants you to leave our firm."

She felt like she'd swallowed ice. "As in fired, canned, sacked … ?"

"He'd prefer *resigned*." He and other LifeLocke executives are putting heavy pressure on us, Ellie. They respect you, and your work, and really like working with you. But when they learned you were Senator Nelson's daughter, and that you helped him with USMed a bit, they panicked, got very concerned. They think it's inappropriate for you to work on their business and his."

"The appearance of conflict," she said.

Lester nodded.

"What if you transfer my LifeLocke legal work to another attorney here in the firm?"

"We suggested that. No luck."

"I see."

"Good, because the client gave us an either or."

She waited.

"Either you leave our firm—or they leave our firm."

She swallowed again.

"As you know, Ellie, we absolutely need the LifeLocke revenue."

"I understand, Les."

"Thanks. But they're so concerned they'd like you to leave *today.*"

She was stunned by the *today* demand but tried to hide her hurt.

"If I can find a big cardboard box, I'll disappear like Tinker Bell."

Les nodded, his eyes downcast, clearly unhappy being the bearer of bad news.

"I'm very sorry, Ellie. But if USMed passes, maybe LifeLocke will no longer exist. In that case, we'd welcome you back with open arms."

"Thanks, Les."

"In the meantime, we'll pay your salary and healthcare for the next six months."

"I appreciate that. Thank you, Les."

She really liked the man. And leaving felt odd.

No. Not odd. It hurt like hell.

This was her last day in a job she really liked—at a firm she really liked—with people she really liked.

Then she reminded herself of Rule One in law firms:

Clients Rule.

ELEVEN

The Guardian turned off his seat-massager in the Mercedes Maybach GLS as his chauffeur opened the door. He stepped outside and strolled beneath the art deco front portico of the luxurious Jefferson Hotel in Washington.

He entered the elegant lobby as the sun's rays poured through the huge skylight and warmed his face. The manager nodded to him.

A bellhop walked over and whispered, "Your colleagues await you, sir."

"Thank you."

He boarded the elevator, removed his sunglasses, and headed up to the sixth floor. He got off, walked down to the conference room door, knocked four times, and said, "Did Elmer take his medicine?"

A voice in the room said, "Elmer took his medicine at precisely 9:16 a.m."

The door clicked open, the Guardian stepped in, and looked at the men seated around a gleaming oak conference table, awaiting him.

"Is the room clean?" he asked his pudgy technician, Seth.

"Yes. All clean."

"Rooms on both sides?"

"Clean. We occupy both."

"What about all of us?" He nodded to the men around the table.

"All clean."

"And me?"

Seth ran the scanning device over the Guardian's clothes.

"Clean," he said.

The Guardian nodded and stared at the men. Top executives from major managed-care healthcare companies, pharmaceutical corporations, hospital networks, testing facilities groups, 24-hour emergency walk-in outlets, ambulance and MedEvac helicopter fleets—all very profitable. Healthcare industries that pumped billions of dollars into their corporate bottom lines, and millions into the pockets of everyone sitting here, including many millions into *his* pocket.

With many more millions donated to members of Congress. Donations for their elections. Money to persuade members to preserve the present health systems.

The Guardian scanned his group. Their goal was simple. Protect America's existing healthcare structure at *all* costs. And destroy anything and anyone that threatened it.

Like USMed.

The Guardian turned to Donald Bennett, his number two, the silver-haired CEO of massive worldwide drug manufacturer Paragon Pharmaceuticals. The ruddy-faced, three-hundred-ten-pound man had obviously failed to use his own company's very successful weight-loss drug.

"What's your assessment, Don?" the Guardian asked Bennett.

"Our chances to defeat USMed just improved," Bennett said, tossing cashews into his mouth. "Two pro-USMed Senators have recently died."

The Guardian knew *how* they died. And *why*.

"I knew Senator Jonathon Nelson well," the Guardian said. "Excellent doctor and Senator. But terribly misguided about our present US healthcare systems. So was Senator Ruskin."

"So is Senator Nelson's daughter, Ellie Nelson," Bennett said. "I just heard a crazy rumor about her. The Indiana Governor might consider her as her father's interim Senator to finish his term. If he names her, she'll vote for USMed like her father."

The Guardian had already heard the rumor. "We'll address that possibility if necessary."

Carl Shuster, the CEO of a major drug company, nodded. "And if USMed is passed, the federal government will negotiate and coordinate the purchase of *all* pharmaceuticals in the country, like most other countries do! They'll slash our prices down to dirt-cheap prices. Peanuts. What the rest of the world pays for drugs."

"Our bonuses will shrink faster than our profits," someone said.

Worried faces grumbled agreement.

"Same thing would happen to all hospital prices nationwide," said Ben Bannister, the cadaverous-faced CEO of a major nationwide network of hospital chains.

"USMed would slash *uninsured* surgery prices down to the Medicaid surgery prices or maybe even lower! Our basic cost for a baby born in our hospital would drop from twenty-five thousand dollars or more to a lousy thousand bucks or so."

"Same with our managed healthcare plans," another executive said. "USMed would be a financial Hiroshima. USMed would consolidate the country's thousand or more healthcare plans under *one* umbrella plan. An everybody's-covered-for-everything plan. A disaster! We'd be left with insuring tummy tucks, cosmetic nose jobs and butt lifts."

"Administrative positions would shrivel up like bacon. Ten jobs would become one," a director said.

Donald Bennett said, "We can't let that happen. *Won't* let that happen. Our health care systems nationwide already run flawlessly."

"So how do we stop USMed?" Bannister asked the group.

All eyes turned toward the Guardian.

The Guardian stood up, walked to the door, faced them, and said …

"USMed. Won't. Become. Law."

Then he walked out of the room.

* * *

In the hallway, the Guardian entered the stairwell, walked down two floors, and inserted a key in a corner suite - his annual lease. He entered, sat in a leather chair, opened his phone, and checked messages.

Two minutes later, Donald Bennett left the upstairs meeting, came downstairs with a man named Archie Braun, and entered the suite with the Guardian. These three men knew things the men upstairs would never know.

The Guardian watched CEO Donald Bennett lean back and stretch his white shirt over his massive stomach. The buttons looked ready to blast into orbit. His black-rimmed glasses hung on a gold chain that disappeared under his double-chin.

Beside him sat Archie, wearing jeans and a short-sleeve shirt that flaunted his muscles and tats. The ex-SEAL's main talent, thanks to his two hundred ten pounds of weightlifter muscles and eighteen-inch neck, was persuading people to do things. When logic failed, his 9 mm Beretta proved persuasive.

The Guardian looked at Bennett. "What's the vote count?"

Bennett checked his laptop screen. "The recent Senators' deaths and others helped our senate vote numbers.

"Your best calculation?" the Guardian asked.

"We need three more votes in the Senate," Bennett said.

"Even with the deaths of Nelson and Ruskin?"

"Yes."

"Which three Senators might be persuaded to vote against USMed?"

Bennett named them.

"How can we persuade them?" The Guardian asked.

"We have many ways," Bennett said.

The Guardian nodded. "And how's our House vote?"

"We need four more votes to be sure," Bennett said.

"Do you have candidates?"

"Yes."

"Can we persuade them?"

"Yes," Bennett said.

"How?"

"Leverage on them."

"What kind?"

"Dirt. Hidden felonies. Insider stock buying. Sexual perversions. And more," Bennett said.

"And what if those don't work?" The Guardian asked.

"They all have kids," Bennett said.

TWELVE

Wendy Shuman, an aide to Senator Nelson, had a tough job: find wealthy individuals or PAC groups who would make campaign donations to Congress members—*but without insisting how they vote.*

She did her job well.

Too well, complained pharma and healthcare executives. She was upsetting their system. For decades, lobbyists for the pharma/ healthcare and other special interests gave Congress members large campaign donations. The donations came with strong suggestions, demands, and in some cases clear mandates that they vote to protect pharma/health care and special interest businesses that donated to them.

But now, Wendy's new "No-Strings-Attached PAC" could offer Congress members comparable donations that let members vote how they and their constituents wanted.

Wendy's phone rang. Nellie, her research assistant calling.

"What's up, Nellie?"

"Remember my neighbor who was insurance-approved and scheduled for an immediate double mastectomy?"

"Yes."

"Her health insurance company called her and said they would not pay for the surgery."

"Why not?"

"Because years ago her dermatologist made a note about treating Nellie's *acne*. Her insurance company misinterpreted acne treatment as a pre-cancerous condition. "It was only *acne!*" the dermatologist insisted over and over. But the insurance company denied the surgery. By the time the issue was finally resolved, Nellie's tumor had doubled in size and she had to have all the lymph nodes removed in her arm!"

"The bastards!" Wendy said. "Tell her to get a lawyer."

"She did. But I've gotta a call coming in. Let's talk later."

They hung up.

Feeling discouraged about healthcare's unfairness, Wendy stepped into a Subway, ate a tuna sub, grabbed a taxi, and headed toward her office.

The taxi stopped in front of her office building. She stepped from the icy taxi into hot humid DC air, and then into the icy lobby. She felt exhausted from working too many hours, sleeping too little, and hearing too many depressing healthcare horror stories.

She sat in a lobby chair to rest a bit and check her phone messages before heading up to her office.

Her phone rang. She picked up, talked to a colleague for a minute, hung up. Another call came in. She answered but no one spoke, so she dialed her sister and told her she'd be a little late for dinner tonight. Then she called her assistant and confirmed their meeting at 4 p.m. and hung up.

She checked her messages for a while, then closed her eyes. A minute later, she had trouble breathing. Soon her lungs felt like steel bands were squeezing them.

What's happening?

Panic seized her. She grew breathless and nauseated. She stood to walk to the restroom, felt dizzy and started to collapse. The lobby security guard caught her before she fell, eased her back down in the chair, and called 911.

Three minutes later, the ambulance arrived.

Six minutes after that, Wendy Shuman was pronounced dead.

THIRTEEN

Ellie raised her StairMaster level to 10 and her pulse level to 138. She sucked in air faster, pumped her heart faster, and burned calories faster so she could finish six minutes faster. Enough time to grab a fast lunch.

Resigning from her law firm didn't bother her as much as she feared. In fact, she felt liberated. She missed her colleagues and clients, but not her conflicted stress working on LifeLocke and finishing up her dad's USMed tasks.

After the USMed vote, she'd see if the firm wanted her to return. And whether *she* wanted to return. In the meantime, she was okay financially. She had her salary and health insurance for six months. She also had her father's inheritance. It would make her life comfortable for many years if she invested wisely.

Meanwhile, she'd finish up her dad's USMed tasks.

She cranked her StairMaster up to eleven.

Her phone rang. Madison calling.

"Hey ... Maddy," Ellie huffed.

"You climbing Mount Everest?"

"Mount StairMaster."

"Wonder Woman lives! After StairMaster what are you doing?

"Reviewing medical horror stories that show how unfair American healthcare is to Americans who can't afford it."

"Forty million Americans can't afford it. Kevin and I are also looking at the horror stories," Madison said.

"Why?"

"Maybe dramatize them in television commercials."

"Makes sense."

Madison said, "Here's a disgusting example: Harvard Research found that *forty-five thousand* Americans, including infants and children, *DIED* last year because they didn't have, or couldn't afford coverage, or else were denied coverage because they had a pre-existing condition. Forty-five thousand moms, dads, kids, grandparents—*died*."

Ellie said, "Like my former neighbor with treatable cancer. She and her daughter were driving to sign up for health insurance early in the morning on the last sign-up day. A drunk driver blindsided their car and put them in the hospital ER that morning and afternoon. Late afternoon they were released and drove over to sign up. They showed their hospital doctor's note but were refused—because they missed the final sign-up time by forty-one minutes."

"But they were in the *hospital* for God's sake!" Madison said, angry as hell.

"Didn't matter, she was told. "Weeks later, the mother couldn't get insurance because her cancer was preexisting. Ten months later, she died from her untreated cancer that could have been treated."

Madison grew angrier. "I just saw a CNN report of a eleven-month-old baby named Zoe. She needed lifesaving heart surgery. Her parents were drug addicts. No insurance. No money. No home. They left her in a cardboard box in a Walmart baby department. She was taken to a hospital. Two weeks later, while still awaiting surgery approval from a healthcare company, she died.

"Yeah, but the insurance company probably saved around $200,000 in hospital surgery costs," Ellie said.

Madison felt nauseated.

"How the hell can the world's wealthiest country allow these deaths to happen, when two hundred other advanced industrialized countries do not?"

"Simple," Madison said. "American healthcare is not about saving lives."

"It's about saving money," Ellie said. "Or making more money."

Madison nodded. "Health insurance executives who deny coverage for babies should be required to attend their funerals."

"And dig their graves."

They hung up.

Ellie's StairMaster slowed to a stop. She rested her head on the handlebars, saddened by how cruel Baby Zoe's short life had been.

Ellie showered, left the gym, and grabbed a lunch with several other USMed campaign workers. As she left the café, she got a call from Estelle.

Ellie couldn't believe Estelle's news and immediately called Madison.

"What's up?" Madison said.

"One of Dad's key aides just died."

"Who?" Madison asked.

"Wendy Shuman. I talked with her this morning and she sounded fine. She was terrific campaigner."

"What happened?"

"She just collapsed. She'd been working long hours, ate lunch at Subway, taxied back to her office building, walked in the lobby, and apparently felt tired. She sat in a lobby chair to rest and felt sick. The EM team got there in minutes. But they couldn't save her."

"What did she die from?"

"They have no idea. They're doing an autopsy."

"How old?"

"Thirty–six."

"My God … "

Ellie paused. "There's more … "

"What?"

"Another key USMed campaigner died yesterday. LaTisha Darnell."

"The tall, attractive woman we met at your dad's funeral reception?" Madison said.

"Yes."

"My God, she looked in her twenties."

"Twenty-nine."

"What happened?"

"LaTisha was waiting for her Metro train at Union Station. A woman said LaTisha suddenly collapsed on the platform and died minutes later on the spot."

"What the hell's going on, Ellie?"

"I don't know. But I'm alarmed. We've lost two Senators who would have voted for USMed. One healthy. One had a heart condition. And now we've lost two young, healthy, very effective USMed campaign workers. LaTisha and Wendy. Even though they couldn't vote for USMed, they persuaded members of Congress to vote for it."

"When will we know their cause of death?" Madison asked.

"The toxicology tests are being rushed."

"Please let me know," Madison said.

"I will. But … "

"But what?"

Ellie paused. "Something is causing too many USMed Congress members and their aides to get sick and die!"

"Or *someone* is," Madison said.

FOURTEEN

Congressman Ethan Anderson, a former college hockey power forward, parked his Chevy Tahoe in the underground garage of his apartment building, *Le Residence*, on Biltmore Street in DC. He grabbed his briefcase, stuffed with USMed files and half a chicken sandwich.

After being elected, he dedicated himself to passing USMed as a tribute to his deceased parents. His dad, who never smoked, died of lung cancer because he couldn't afford the necessary chemotherapy, surgery, and radiation treatment. His mother's life-saving surgery was approved, then denied, then reapproved, but the reapproval authorization was lost in computer system glitches for several weeks. During that time, her condition deteriorated, and she died.

Many healthcare professionals told him that as much as 70% of online medical records have incorrect information, in some cases making them prone to errors that could lead to patient accidents and deaths.

Anderson stepped from his Tahoe and walked toward the elevators at the end of the garage. As he passed a rusty Econovan he didn't recognize, he sensed movement behind it. He turned and saw two ski-masked guys emerge from the shadows, aiming silenced handguns at him.

"Toss your wallet over here on the floor! Real slow." the larger man said.

Anderson removed his wallet and tossed it at their feet. The larger man picked it up, opened it, and seemed to study his driver's license. He showed the driver's license to the shorter masked man, who read it and nodded.

Thieves don't check IDs!

They're after me! Why?

But then the shorter man took cash and credit cards from the wallet and tossed the wallet on the floor, making it *look* like a robbery.

They stared at him again.

They're hitmen!

"Turn around and walk toward the elevator."

Anderson turned and walked slowly toward the elevator, hoping someone would drive in the garage or step off the elevator and see what was happening.

As he walked, he glanced in a car's side mirror and saw the man with the gun following him.

The man slowly raised his gun and started to aim at him, but Anderson spun around and karate-kicked the gun.

His shoe hit the gun barrel as it fired.

The bullet grazed Anderson's right shoulder. The gun scattered onto the floor.

Anderson reached over and touched the gun handle, but the second man kicked the gun away.

Then he turned and shot Anderson in the chest.

Anderson collapsed and watched the two men run back to their Econovan, jump in, and race toward the exit.

Anderson knew he was hit badly. His upper shirt was already soaking with blood. Did the bullet hit an artery? He felt weak, his vision spinning.

He grabbed his phone, dialed 911, said he'd been shot, and mumbled his address.

Blood spilled from his lips.

The phone fell from his hand.

FIFTEEN

Madison walked out of Washington National Airport into a refreshing cool breeze, relief from the hot stuffy aircraft and the obese salesman beside her who smelled like a urinal cake.

Her phone rang. Caller ID read: *Ellie Nelson.*

"Hey Ellie."

"Hi Maddy. When are you coming back to DC?"

"Just landed. I'm staying at the Marriott, working on the USMed social media campaign. What's up?"

"We might lose another USMed Congressman."

Madison felt her stomach flip.

"Who?"

"Ethan Anderson."

"Isn't he young?"

"Forty-one," Ellie said.

"What the hell happ—?"

"—shot and robbed in his apartment building garage. Video shows two masked men take his wallet, study his ID, take his money, and shoot him."

"*Study* his ID?"

"Making sure they had their target."

Madison paused. "How is he?"

"Critical."

Madison felt nauseated. "Any chance he'll survive?"

"50-50, doctors say."

"Is he for USMed?" Madison asked.

"Yes. And he persuaded several fellow Congress members to vote for USMed."

Madison said, "Why does this feel like another attempted assassination of a USMed voter?"

"Maybe because it was."

Madison nodded. "Too damn many USMed voters and supporters are dying in a short time period, Ellie."

"But dying in different ways," Ellie added.

"Still, we should talk to the police."

"I agree. My father's good friend, Mack McCall, is a DC Detective. I'll ask him if we can meet. I'll call you right back."

As Ellie called the Detective, Madison tried to remember how many *pro*-USMed voters had died, or been incapacitated, or retired from Congress in the last six months or so. She wasn't sure, but it seemed the number of USMed voters was much higher than she'd realized.

Ellie called back. "Detective McCall will meet us in your Marriott lobby in thirty minutes."

✳ ✳ ✳

Madison watched Ellie walk in the Marriott lobby beside a tall, fifty-something man wearing a navy-blue sport coat, white shirt, and tan trousers with a crease sharp enough to slice bread. Tortoise shell glasses framed his large blue eyes. As he walked, his DC police badge hung from his coat pocket.

Ellie turned and greeted him.

"Madison, meet Detective Mack McCall of the DC police."

"Nice to meet you, Detective."

"And you, Madison."

He looked at Ellie. "I'm so sorry I missed your father's funeral. I was in LA when I got the news."

"I understand."

"I'll miss him. And our bridge games."

"They were his escape from DC madness."

"And mine."

They walked over and sat in comfortable lobby chairs.

"Any more on his cause of death?" McCall asked.

Ellie shook her head. "The medical examiner is still trying to determine that. He suspects some chemical agent."

"Chemical agent?" McCall's eyes widened.

"He thought so."

Madison watched Detective McCall flip open a small notebook and make a note.

"Any idea what kind?"

"Not yet."

"You mentioned something else earlier that caught my attention."

"What's that?" Ellie said.

"You and Madison were worried about how many pro-USMed voters and activists had died, resigned, or became incapable of voting for various reasons over the last several months. Is that right?"

"Yes," Ellie said.

"That seems to be the case," Madison said.

"Both Senators *and* House members?"

"Yes," Ellie said. "Also, some Congressional aides."

"Do you have all these names?"

"Most." Ellie handed him a list of *pro* USMed Senators, Congress members, and aides who'd died, resigned, retired, or were hired away in the last nine months."

McCall looked at the list. "Why did some activists resign?"

"Probably got better-paying jobs," Ellie said.

Madison wondered if they were bribed away with better-paying jobs to stop them from promoting USMed so well.

"Better paying jobs from who?" McCall said.

"I don't know. But we can find that out."

"Okay. At a quick glance, this total … all these USMed deaths and departures … it seems like a large number."

"Some died in their thirties, early forties," Madison said.

"Really?" McCall made more notes. "But we should also check out how many *anti*-USMed Congress members died, resigned, retired, or were hired away in the same time period."

"Our agency researchers just compiled this rough *anti*-USMed list," Madison said. "So far they found only four *anti*-USMed voters died or retired, plus two who took another job. Only a third as many as the *pro*-USMed voters and aides and campaigners."

Detective McCall shook his head. "I'm no actuary, but this high *pro*-USMed number, three times more than the *anti*-USMed number, really concerns me. So does this chemical toxin possibility."

Madison and Ellie nodded.

"*Where* did USMed voters die?"

Ellie said, "My dad was in his office. Ruskin was sitting in his cottage. Also two young, healthy female USMed campaign workers just collapsed and died. Anne Wilson was electrocuted in her bath. Congressman Ethan Anderson was robbed and shot in his apartment garage. He's critical and may not recover in time to vote."

Detective McCall made a note. "Did the autopsies of these two young campaign workers also indicate the presence of a chemical toxin like your father's?"

Ellie shrugged. "We don't know yet. We plan to ask the MEs who did those autopsies."

"I can also get that ME's autopsy information," Detective McCall said.

Madison said, "So you agree something might connect all these deaths?"

McCall paused, looked at his notes, then closed his eyes for several moments. "Very possibly. They're all working *for* USMed. But also my gut instinct."

Madison sensed he believed the deaths were connected.

Detective McCall's eyes narrowed "I'll check all this out and get back to you."

"Thank you, Detective."

He got up to leave. "When the doctor identifies the chemical that caused your father's death let me know immediately."

"You'll be the first."

SIXTEEN

The Guardian sipped his fifteen-year-old Glenfiddich single malt as his chauffeur drove the Mercedes through DC, and then onto Route 7 heading toward Potomac Falls, Virginia.

They passed malls showcasing his new *Walk-Right-In* medical clinics, a division of his consortium of healthcare companies. The *Walk-Right-In* parking lots were filled with cars. Filled meant fat profits.

A few miles farther, they parked in the Guardian's private garage at his *Potomac Healthcare Research Center*, a six-story, white-brick, chrome and glass structure.

The chauffeur jumped out and opened the Guardian's door.

"This meeting will be brief, Leland. Just stay here."

Leland nodded.

The entrance door opened, and the Guardian walked in. He nodded to Mavis, the bleached-blonde security guard. He liked her dangling earrings, tiny Colt 45s with long barrels, pointing down at her most engaging attributes. Mammoth breasts.

How they hangin'? he always wanted to say, but said, "Afternoon, Mavis."

"Good afternoon, Mr. Chairman."

He walked down a long marble hall, then down a narrow passageway to a steel door. He leaned close to an eye-scanner, and the door disappeared into the wall. He entered and sat down opposite Donald Bennett and Archie Braun.

"Everything on schedule?" the Guardian asked Bennett.

"Yes."

"Good. But one thing is not," the Guardian said.

"What?"

"Optics!"

"What's optics?" Archie said.

"What people *see.*"

"See where?"

"On TV, online, on social media, on the front page of the newspapers."

Archie clearly needed more explanation.

The Guardian said, "What people are seeing now is that far more *pro*-USMed voters and aides are dying or leaving Congress than *anti*-USMed voters and aides. These lopsided numbers-optics make them suspicious. And suspicious creates investigations."

"But that old Senator, Cyrus Drummond, a strong anti-USMed critic died just three months ago," Bennett said.

"That's just *one* anti-USMed vote."

Bennett named a couple more anti-USMed voters and activists who'd retired or left in the last three years.

"Still not enough," the Guardian said. "There are far more pro USMed voters and activists who've died or left recently than *anti*-USMed voters and activists who've died or left."

Bennett nodded he understood.

"This disparity of numbers has caught the attention of Senator Nelson's daughter, Ellie. She and Madison Parker, the USMed advertising woman, are suspicious. They're working with a DC detective."

"Which detective?" Archie asked.

"Mack McCall."

"Fuck!" Archie groaned.

"What about him?" Bennett asked.

"McCall's a smart cop. Bastard never lets up."

"But the USMed deaths were mostly different," Bennett said. "Different causes of death. Nothing connects these deaths. No single death pattern."

"Their pro-USMed voting intentions connect them. So, we need to *balance* the *numbers* better. The optics. We need another *anti*-USMed senate voter to go away. Pick an old one with health issues. And one more in the House. Also, an *anti*-USMed non-voting aide or activist."

"Starting when?"

"Now."

* * *

"How far apart are your contractions, Betty Lou?" said midwife Karen Mayfield.

The seventy-three-year-old nurse-midwife delivered babies in her small South Dakota village home when a mother couldn't afford a hospital birth.

"About six minutes apart. And gittin' stronger," Betty Lou Simmons groaned. She was single, poor, twenty-two, and in her ninth month.

Another strong contraction grabbed her, then a sharp cramp and another contraction.

"Betty Lou, did you visit an obstetrician in the last six months?"

"No, ma'am. I cain't afford no doctors, no hospitals. No health insurance. Can barely afford food, gas, and rent since Eugene run off on me."

"Your contractions are strengthening, and you're dilated to seven. Your baby's getting ready to come out!"

A hard contraction gripped her again. It hurt more! Betty Lou moaned and grew more frightened.

"Keep pushing, Betty Lou."

She pushed, and minutes later, she felt an odd shifting movement.

"You're dilated to nine … nearly there now …"

Betty Lou pushed harder, but it hurt again. "Something don't feel right."

"*Wait!* Stop pushing Betty Lou!"

"Why? What's wrong—?"

"—Your baby … may be …"

"What?"

"Breaching.*"

Betty Lou heard breach babies were a problem. She grew more terrified. "Can you do that kind?"

"I could twenty years ago. These days, breach babies are delivered by Caesarian in hospitals. But this baby might come out before we'd get halfway to Sioux Falls General."

"Don't matter. I can't afford no twenty-thousand-dollar hospital birth bill for this baby."

"Betty Lou, this baby *is* breached. That means it's upside down. Stuck in the canal. The fetal heart rate is fast. And the umbilical cord seems tangled around the left leg and might cut off the baby's oxygen."

Tears flooded Betty Lou's face. "I want this baby so bad, Karen! And now I'm losing it."

"I can't get the head facing down."

Nurse Karen's phone rang.

"*Not now!*" Karen said to her phone. Then suddenly remembered something.

She grabbed the phone and speed-dialed a number.

"I'm calling a doctor I know. I'll Zoom him into us."

Twenty seconds later Dr. Alex Dubin, an obstetrician, appeared on her iPad screen holding a putter and golf ball.

Nurse Karen described the baby's apparent breach position. Dr. Dubin asked several questions that Karen answered, then gave her instructions that she completed.

"Now place the mom on her left side again," he said.

Nurse Karen did.

Minutes later, after more of Dr. Alex's instructions, Karen felt the baby's body shift around, and begin to ease downward.

Seconds later, Karen slid the head out … slowly … followed by the left arm and shoulder … and the rest of the body.

"She's out and breathing fine!" Nurse Karen said. "And screaming like a cheerleader!"

"A girl?"

"A *beautiful* little girl, Betty Lou! She's *beautiful!*"

"Everything looks fine," Dr. Dubin said. "Well done, Betty Lou! Well done, Karen!"

Karen clamped the umbilical cord and collected the placenta, then wrapped the baby in a clean towel and handed her to Betty Lou.

Betty Lou wept with joy. She wanted a girl so much.

* * *

Then reality hit Karen.

What if I didn't come home and find Betty Lou already in labor, waiting for me in her pickup? What if Dr. Dubin had not been available? Betty Lou's beautiful baby likely would have died.

Karen wondered how many babies died in childbirth this year because their mothers couldn't afford a hospital birth?

SEVENTEEN

In her Marriott hotel room, Madison Zoomed with Detective Mack McCall in his office and Ellie in her home.

"My agency just sent me more analysis on the deaths of pro-USMed voters and anti-USMed voters," Madison said. "Can you see them?"

"Yes," Ellie and McCall said.

Madison paused to let them read the statistics.

"These stats," Detective McCall said, "confirm three times more pro-USMed people have died, retired, or stopped campaigning than anti-USMed people in the last eleven months. Just like you thought."

"But the causes of death vary," Ellie said. "A lethal chemical toxin, heart attacks, old age, a robbery gunshot victim, electrocution in a bathtub."

McCall said, "Even so, the same person or group could be orchestrating all these deaths."

"I agree," Madison said.

McCall said, "The doctor thinks some kind of a spray *device* released the lethal chemical agent that attacked Ellie's father. Can we go check your dad's private office now for the device?"

"I'll be there in fifteen minutes," Ellie said.

"Me too," Madison said.

Ellie gave them the address. "See you both there."

✱ ✱ ✱

Madison's taxi let her out in front of the modern three-story office building on 19th Street near Dupont Circle. DC's humidity was climbing fast.

She saw Detective Mack McCall park right in front of the building and put his police pass in the windshield. Nice perk. But the police need more than parking perks these days. They need bulletproof cars and full-body armor. Too many crazies are out to shoot them.

Madison greeted McCall and they entered the tall gray glass office building where Ellie met them. She wore dark gray slacks, a smudged blue sweatshirt, and old Nikes. Madison knew she'd been cleaning her father's office.

Ellie escorted them down to the two-room workplace.

Madison saw the large mahogany desk Ellie said came from his medical office days, and big brown leather chairs with matching leather sofa where Ellie said he sometimes slept overnight when his workloads overwhelmed him. The walls showcased family photos: Ellie's grandparents, his med school diploma, Ellie's law school graduation picture, and signed pictures of her dad with two Republican presidents and two Democrat presidents.

"Your dad was always the political bridge builder," Madison said.

"But he said it got more difficult each year," Ellie said.

"Why use this office if his official Senate office is in the Rayburn Building?" Madison asked.

"This was his *getaway* office," Ellie said.

"Getaway?" McCall asked.

"From the Rayburn Building. It gets noisy and hectic with reporters barking questions and accusations. So he escaped here to his quiet work office."

"What was he doing here the last night?"

"The usual, Estelle said. Working on legislation, drafting memos, writing letters, emailing, texting, persuading people to support USMed. After a while, he told Estelle he felt a little tired and would rest a bit before coming to my apartment for dinner."

"Then what happened?"

"Sometime later, Estelle walked in and found him lying unconscious."

"Did anyone visit him in this office earlier."

"Not according to Estelle."

"May I see the files he was working on and his daily planner?" McCall asked.

"They're right over here."

She walked them over to his desk and pointed. "Those are his files. The planner's open to his last day."

"his last day" jolted Ellie, Madison noticed.

"The names on his planner are political colleagues he worked with that day and evening."

Madison looked at the names. None raised any immediate suspicion. "He worked with some pharmaceutical executives."

"Why them?" McCall asked.

"Probably to negotiate. Get them to reduce some outrageous drug prices," Ellie said.

Madison nodded. "I hear pharmaceutical guys don't negotiate much."

"Like Congress," Ellie said, smiling.

They searched the office and small bathroom, examining everything again.

Ten minutes later, McCall said, "I see no device here that might have released the chemical agent that triggered his heart attack."

"Nor do I," Ellie said.

Madison agreed.

"Have they identified the chemical toxin yet?"

"Not yet. But Doctor Browner just texted that he'll have the final tox results in about a half hour at his lab. Can you go with us?"

"Yep," McCall said.

* * *

Ellie drove Madison toward the DC Medical Laboratories complex on Nebraska Avenue near American University.

Madison hoped Dr. Browner's toxicology test revealed what caused Ellie's father's severe breathing difficulties and the resulting heart attack that led to his death.

"I like Detective McCall," Madison said.

"Me too. So did Dad. He met him years ago when McCall arrested some Congressmen."

"For what?"

"Greed. They bought tons of stock through Caribbean shell companies for a new cancer drug they learned the FDA would approve in four days. Their stock rocketed in value. They made millions. Insider-information trading. Felony crimes. Jail time."

"Greedy Congress members? Who knew?" Madison said.

"Yeah, most Congress members leave Congress much better off financially than when they arrived. Over fifty are multi-millionaires."

Madison nodded. "Sounds like drug executives who jack up prescription prices, then give themselves millions in bonuses."

"Prescriptions like Luxturna," Ellie said.

"What's Luxturna?" Madison asked.

"A new eye-gene drug. Actually *cures* blindness in some children."

"*Cures* blindness?" Madison said, stunned.

"Yes. But at a steep price."

"How steep?"

"Sit down first."

"I'm sitting beside you."

"Tighten your seatbelt!"

"How much?"

"$850,000 dollars!"

"Bullshit!"

"Look it up."

Speechless, Madison stared at her.

"My dad showed me an article about a former blind kid who now *sees* thanks to Luxturna and his very rich parents."

"Any *poor* blind kids get cured?"

"At that price?"

Madison sensed Luxturna might make a good TV commercial explaining how USMed will eliminate outrageous drug costs and the unfairness of prices for poor people.

"Reminds me of Firdapse," Madison said, "the drug my friend needs for her muscle and nerve disease."

"What's the price?" Ellie asked.

"Firdapse was once *free*."

"And now?"

"$375,000 a year."

"You're joking," Ellie said.

"Nope."

"No wonder many Americans can't afford health insurance or their prescriptions," Ellie said.

"No wonder so many force themselves to take less than their prescribed dose—and die early."

"No wonder high medical costs forced over 500,000 Americans to declare bankruptcy last year."

Ellie parked in the DC Medical Laboratories as Detective McCall pulled in two slots away. They walked together toward a modern four-story glass and steel building with two long attached laboratory annexes.

Inside, they were led to the conference room where Dr. Browner was waiting. He smiled and shook hands with them.

"I just this minute got your dad's final toxicology report." Dr. Browner held up a sealed envelope.

He pulled off the tape, lifted the flap, took out the report, and flipped through numerous pages. He froze on the last page and continued staring at it. Madison watched his eyebrows rise.

"Well, I didn't expect this."

They waited.

"As I mentioned earlier, your father had a deadly toxin in his system. The lab is reconfirming it, but they're certain it's a *nerve agent!*"

"Nerve agent?" Ellie said.

Madison couldn't believe what he'd said. She'd read how deadly nerve agents were.

"Maybe a variation of VX. But different."

"Different how?" Ellie asked.

"*Much* faster-acting."

"But who has access to this kind of nerve toxin?" Madison asked.

"Our military. Foreign militaries. And very probably some terrorist groups."

Ellie and Madison stared at Dr. Browner.

"But we saw nothing in his office where he might come into contact with this nerve agent," Detective McCall said.

Dr. Browner nodded. "And his assistant Estelle confirmed he didn't visit any military facilities or military hospitals."

Ellie nodded.

"So maybe," Dr. Browner said, "someone or something dusted him with it in his building lobby. Like Kim Jung Un's half-brother was dusted with VX by two women in the Kuala Lumpur airport. He died quickly."

Madison said, "Could the agent have been discharged by a time-release mechanism in his office?"

"Very possibly. And it could be quite small."

Detective McCall said, "We'll have our tech people, and your experts recheck his office for minute traces of the agent."

"Good idea," Dr. Browner said.

McCall said, "We'll also check Senator Clete Ruskin's cabin for traces of the agent."

"I'll call Ruskin's ME for that info," Dr. Browner said.

McCall said, "Ellie, did your father plan to meet someone before coming to your place for dinner?"

"Not according to Estelle."

"Maybe a surprise visitor?"

"Estelle said no. But she left her office to go to the restroom for maybe two minutes."

"So someone *could* have visited him and exposed him to the nerve agent in those minutes," Madison said.

Dr. Browner shrugged a maybe.

"Did CCTV video show anyone visit his office during two minutes?"

"His private office doesn't have CCTV."

Ellie opened his agenda planner. "This planner says he worked from home in the morning. Arrived at the office at noon. He scheduled no visitors that afternoon, or the evening he died."

Detective McCall said, "So the agent might have been planted in his office and programmed to release at a specific time when he was there."

"Very possible," Dr. Browner said.

EIGHTEEN

Eighty-year-old Ernest Woodwillow III, a distinguished Congressman for the last thirty-nine years, sat alone in his Congressional office, reading a proposed international trade bill that would probably lead to a trade war.

Doesn't Congress realize that trade wars hinder global trade?

But his mind was on another bill where all Americans are winners. USMed. He'd worked hard for universal health care with John Dingell, Ted Kennedy, Bernie Sanders, Hillary Clinton, Barack Obama, Reagan, both Bushes, and others who tried to create better healthcare for all Americans.

Then came the Affordable Care program and its amendments that made parts less affordable, less caring for some, and only slightly less comprehendible than quantum mechanics.

Now, finally, comes USMed. It gives *all* Americans healthcare coverage. A universal plan like USMed should have become America's universal healthcare plan fifty years ago but didn't. Why?

Because Congress members were hooked on big donations from pharmaceuticals, healthcare, and special-interest groups. In return, the members helped healthcare and pharmaceuticals prices remain very profitable: that is, very high priced.

The *DC Quid Pro Quo* ... you help me, and my vote will help your business.

Ernie's phone rang. Caller ID: Senator Dale Barnstable, a Republican pal and poker buddy.

Ernie answered. "Hey Dale, what's up?"

"My cholesterol."

"That's all?"

"My poker winnings!"

"Because your thick cigar smoke hides your cheating!"

"Fix your cataracts," Dale said, "so you can see me vote *for* USMed."

"What? *You're* voting for USMed*?*"

"Yep."

"Why'd you flip?"

"I'm softening my views as I get older."

"Shit, Dale, you're old enough to be carbon-dated. Why the hell are you really voting for USMed?"

"My constituents want me to."

"Never mattered before."

"True, but my bladder is voting to pee right now! See you tonight, Ernie. Bring lots of money."

They hung up.

Ernie looked forward to this get-together of Congressional poker players. They often achieved more bi-partisan compromises with Jack Daniels and seven-card-stud than with eight-hour committee meetings.

He phoned his aide, Kenny, and asked him to set up a breakfast meeting. Then he called another poker player to be sure he was coming tonight.

Ernie's phone rang again. He didn't recognize the number, but it might be a campaign contributor. He picked up but heard nothing. So, he hung up and phoned his brother. They talked a couple minutes about their family reunion. As usual, he wondered if it would be his last.

He hung up and yawned. At eighty Ernest Woodwillow got tired earlier. He ate the rest of his mac-and-cheese and chugged down the rest of his whiskey.

A minute later, he yawned again and felt his eyelids droop.

* * *

Madison couldn't believe what she'd just heard. She grabbed her phone and called Ellie.

Ellie picked up on the first ring.

"Hey Maddy, what's up?"

"I'm at *VideoTroniks Studios* working on USMed commercials. A Congressional aide just ran in and said another Congressman has died."

"Who?"

"Congressman Ernie Woodwillow."

Ellie sighed. "Oh no—he was a terrific guy."

"And a terrific USMed campaigner."

"How'd he die?"

"I don't know," Madison said. "But he was eighty. His aide said he had a mild heart condition and inhaled cigars. We should let McCall know."

"I'll call him," Ellie said.

* * *

As he drove, Detective Mack McCall wondered what caused Congressman Ernest Woodwillow to pass away? His heart condition? Stroke? Old age?

Or the mysterious nerve agent that killed others?

McCall pulled into a parking spot reserved for police cars near the Rayburn Office Building on Independence Avenue. He saw a parked ambulance and some medical personnel leaving the building.

He flashed his credentials at the security guard in the lobby and hurried down the long hallway to Woodwillow's office. He focused on a family photo: Ernie, his deceased wife, three adult children, and several smiley-faced grandchildren at a lake. Fewer smiles now.

In the office, McCall was relieved to see Molly O'Brien MD, the Medical Examiner, hovering over Ernest Woodwillow's body. Molly was a smart, no-nonsense ME, and great to work with.

"Hey Molly."

Molly looked up and smiled. "Mack McCall Himself! What brings the likes of you here?"

"The facts, Doctor."

"Facts about Mr. Woodwillow here?"

He nodded. "Any idea yet about what caused his death, other than living for eighty years? Any hint of foul play?"

"Not yet. But something serious hit him hard and fast. Maybe heart attack or stroke. He seemed to be reading in this chair, stood, then collapsed to the floor. Do you really suspect foul play, Mack?"

"Maybe ... "

"Why?"

"We've had a number of Congress members drop dead in the last few weeks. Some were young and healthy, some were older, like Ernest Woodwillow."

"Have you found a connection between them?"

"Just one so far. All were working very hard to pass the USMed bill."

"Did Congressman Woodwillow also plan to vote for the USMed bill?"

"Yes. And that's why I'm here."

"How did the other victims die?" she asked.

"Various causes. A laptop apparently fell into a bathtub and electrocuted a Congresswoman. A young USMed worker dropped dead in the Metro station. Senators Nelson and Ruskin both died sitting in their offices. Ruskin had heart problems; but Nelson was healthy as a horse, and his tox report suggested a nerve agent killed him."

"Nerve agent?" Dr. O'Brien seemed shocked by the possibility. He nodded.

"That's a lot of different ways to die. What was Ernie Woodwillow doing here just before he collapsed?" McCall asked.

"Apparently reading his committee files and sipping whiskey."

McCall stared down at the whiskey glass. "You'll test the whiskey for poison and a nerve agent."

"Absolutely."

He nodded. "We'll compare Ernie's tox report with the tox reports of other victims."

"Did they all die in DC?" she asked.

"No. Virginia, Maryland, and DC. Since the crimes cross state lines, I'm bringing in the FBI."

She nodded. "Are all victims buried?"

"Some. But we may need to exhume more bodies," McCall said.

"Why?"

"To see if their blood contains the same deadly nerve agent as Senator Nelson's."

NINETEEN

M adison followed Ellie into her father's private office.

"A few days ago," Ellie said, "Estelle told me my dad discovered something that concerned him."

"What?"

"He said, *something that appeared good … but might not be.*"

"Some *thing*?" Madison said.

"Or some *person.* He suggested the person might be *a wolf in sheep's clothing.*"

"Maybe he wrote down the wolf's name. Let's look around."

Forty minutes later, after reading every paper and file on his desk, they paused and stared at each other.

"I found no wolf or sheep reference," Ellie said.

"Nor did I. But I did find your dad's amazing estimate."

"What?"

"That USMed could *save* the average American family about *$3,000 dollars* a year in healthcare costs."

"$3,000 is a family vacation. Or some school tuition."

Madison nodded, but felt her anger rise. "So again—if USMed universal healthcare would save each family three thousand dollars a year, why the hell haven't Congress members passed it?"

"You know why. They want and need the big healthcare and pharma donations for their election campaigns."

"The donations smell like bribes," Madison said.

"If it smells like a bribe and works like a bribe ..."

"... it's a bribe,"

"Yeah, but we the American people pay for the bribes. Outrageously high prices for healthcare insurance, prescriptions, testing, and extremely high hospital surgical costs."

"If the surgery doesn't kill you," Madison said, "the bills will."

* * *

The Guardian walked into a small soundproof conference room to meet with Donald Bennett and Archie Braun.

Bennett's phone rang and he answered. His brow tightened and he looked troubled. He hung up.

"What's wrong?" The Guardian asked.

"An *anti*-USMed Senator just flip-flopped. Bastard plans to vote *for* USMed!" Bennett said.

"Who?"

"Jesse Lee Howell."

"The Southern conservative?" the Guardian said.

"Yeah."

"But he already took our very generous pharma donation!"

"I know," Bennett said. "But now the bastard claims his constituents *demand* that he votes for USMed."

"His constituents are fuckin' red-necks," Archie said. "Half of them can't read!"

"They read well enough to vote for him!" the Guardian said.

Silence.

"Handle Congressman Howell now," the Guardian said.

"Make it … a believable accident."

Archie snapped his fingers, looked at the Guardian, and smiled. "I know a very believable accident for Howell."

The Guardian sensed Archie had a feasible plan. "What is it?"

Archie explained the accident in detail.

"Why's this accident believable for him?" Bennett asked Archie.

"Because he had two similar accidents. One in college and another three years ago. Didn't learn his lesson. Last accident almost killed him. Could happen again, right?"

The Guardian stared at Archie. "Make it happen."

TWENTY

T he next day, Madison and Ellie walked toward the Medical Examiner's building on E Street. The large modern glass and steel building occupied the entire block and handled thousands of autopsies a year.

Including its latest arrival.

Senator Jesse Lee Howell.

Madison had met Senator Howell and liked his honesty.

A police car rolled up. Detective McCall stepped out.

Ellie said, "I told Detective McCall we're meeting with Dr. Browner here."

They greeted McCall.

Madison said, "I talked with Senator Howell a few days ago and he sounded almost like he was rethinking his anti-USMed vote."

"Interesting," McCall said.

"So what happened to him this morning?" Ellie asked.

McCall said, "Jesse Lee Howell is a sculler. He rows in the Potomac at seven o'clock most mornings. The currents can get tricky, even treacherous like this morning. He was sculling and had an accident. But no witnesses."

"Then what?"

"A jogger found his body and scull flipped over and tangled up in a dock. "Apparently, the choppy Potomac current pushed him too close to the dock. But he didn't realize it because he was rowing backwards fast in the fog. He didn't see metal rod sticking out from a dock. His oar probably hit the rod, flipped his scull over, and the rod ripped into the back of his head."

Madison took a breath. "But I read he was an Olympic-class sculler who knew sculling safety."

"He did," McCall said, "but he'd had accidents before."

Ellie's phone rang, she answered and hung up looking surprised. "Last night, Jesse Lee told a colleague he planned to switch and vote *for* USMed. My source says CNN will confirm it."

Detective McCall shook his head. "This looks like an accident, but his decision to switch and vote for USMed suggests the bad guys might have arranged his accident."

Madison nodded. "Where's Jesse Lee Howell's body now?"

"Downstairs. Dr. Browner from MedTech labs is downstairs here handling the autopsy."

They followed Detective McCall down to the medical examiner's autopsy rooms.

Madison shivered when she hit icy air conditioning and saw some pale corpses lying on nearby gurneys. The scent of decomposing bodies nauseated her, like rotting raw garbage left to ferment for days in hot summer sun.

She spread minty balm on her upper lip, but it didn't help much.

They walked past a wall of large stainless-steel drawers. One small drawer was pulled out. Beneath the sheet lay a tiny child's body. A little foot stuck out beneath the sheet. Her tag read: *Sophia Tanner, Aged 2.*

Madison's heart stopped and she felt queasy. She closed her eyes. *How did Sophia die? Disease? Neglect? Drive-by shooting?*

Same age as Mia, our beautiful daughter.

Madison's eyes moistened. She couldn't begin to imagine the pain Sophia's parents felt.

Mia was safe and happy when I talked to her a few hours ago. Maybe I should call Kevin's mom now and check. No, it's Mia's naptime. I'll call later.

Madison turned and saw Dr. Browner walking toward them.

"Ellie, Madison, Detective, nice to see you all again," Dr. Browner said.

Madison smiled, but it was difficult surrounded by corpses. She felt if she smiled too much, the vile stench would stick to her teeth.

Detective McCall said, "Doctor, we're here regarding Senator Jesse Lee Howell's autopsy."

"We just finished it," Dr. Browner said.

"Did you determine a cause of death?"

"Blunt force trauma to the head. His skull flipped over, and his head appeared to have hit an iron rod sticking out from the dock pole he was wrapped around. But that didn't seem right to me."

"Why not?"

"Because the shape of his head injury did not match the shape of the iron rod. The head injury suggests a small flat *round* metal object caused it. But the iron rod pole has a bigger flat *square* surface. Our associate ME just reconfirmed that the metal rod does *not* match the head wound."

"What does he think caused the head wound?" Madison asked.

"He *knows* what caused it."

They waited.

"A large 16-ounce Stanley hammer. They found it a hundred yards down on the riverbank. Whoever tossed it in the river there didn't know the Potomac has tides. The tide went out and left the bright yellow-handled Stanley hammer sticking up in the muck like an award-winning Dutch tulip. The hammerhead matches the

Senator's head wound dimensions precisely. And the fresh blood on the hammer should soon give us the Senator's DNA match."

"So homicide," McCall said.

Dr. Browner nodded.

"It's FBI time," McCall said.

"Why?" Madison asked.

"Because Jesse Lee's body was found in Prince George's County, Maryland, and other deaths were over in Virginia and in DC. Our perpetrators are crossing state lines. That's FBI time. I'm calling my Special Agent colleague."

* * *

Madison and Ellie walked toward the entrance of Washington Police Department Headquarters on Indiana Street. Madison was impressed by the massive six-story structure that sprawled over the entire block. In front, thick concrete abutments defended against vehicle suicide attacks. Two tall pillars, American Eagles, stood like giant guardian angels.

Police need guardian angels these days, she reminded herself. *Radicals and terrorists have police locked in their cross hairs.*

Detective McCall greeted them and led them to a small conference room with large-screen television monitors.

"Our FBI colleagues will be here any minute."

"Good," Madison said, "Here's an updated copy of my agency report on the USMed deaths. Would they want it?"

"They will. And thanks, Madison."

His phone beeped with a text.

"FBI's here."

Madison watched the door open and a tall, late-thirties man and a thin, mid-thirties blonde walk in. He wore a dark suit, blue shirt and red-blue tie. She wore dark slacks, blue blouse and Navy blazer, and thick-soled shoes. Both flashed friendly smiles, then defaulted to serious expressions.

McCall said, "Meet FBI Special Agents Tim Stanford and Kate Carras. They've saved my bacon many times."

"And you've saved ours," Stanford said with a smile.

Detective McCall gave the agents a quick overview of the abnormally high number of pro-USMed voters and supporters who'd died.

Agent Stanford nodded. "All victims supported USMed?"

"All," McCall said. "Madison collected some information about them. Age ... title ... location of their death ... their general health ... manner and apparent cause of death."

"Here," Madison handed him the file.

"Thanks, Madison. This will save us time."

"Where did they die?" Stanford asked.

Madison told them the different locations.

Special Agent Stanford nodded. "So, you suspect someone who's against passing the USMed bill is responsible for all their deaths?"

McCall nodded. "It makes sense, Tim. But the problem is—*many* are against USMed. Big pharma, the healthcare plans industries, and many special interest health groups. And probably some radical unhinged individuals in those groups."

Agent Stanford nodded. "And you're right—these report numbers show many USMed voters and supporters died in a relatively short time frame, compared to anti-USMed voters and supporters. We'll recheck CCTV videos where these victims died. Maybe identify some attackers."

"The USMed vote is in a few days," Madison said. "We should try to find some way to warn pro USMed Senators and House members. Tell them what to be on the lookout for."

Agent Stanford said, "I agree. But the attacks are so different what do we warn them to be on the lookout for?"

TWENTY-ONE

"**M**ost pro-USMed Senate votes seem solid," Ellie said,

Madison nodded agreement as they sat in Ellie's apartment.

"But two are known flip-floppers."

"Who?" Madison asked.

Ellie named them. "They often flip their vote at the last minute. One Senator sits and adds up his donations from pharmaceuticals, healthcare, and other special interest lobbyists, and then votes for legislation that favors those businesses."

Madison nodded.

Ellie's desk phone rang. She hit the speaker button.

"Hello … "

"Ellie Nelson?" a woman said.

"Yes."

"Ellie, It's Renee Dumont, executive assistant to Governor Greg Wilson of Indiana. We met when you and your father attended the *Hoosier Hoedown Hop* last summer."

"Oh yes, Renee. I remember. How are you?"

"I'm fine, but how are you doing?"

"Okay, but still missing my dad a lot."

"So is Indiana. Your father's absence makes our job harder. Do you have a moment to speak with the Governor?"

"Of course."

"I'll connect you."

Ellie and Madison heard some clicks, then, "Ellie, it's Greg Wilson, how are you?"

"A little better this week, Governor."

"That's good to hear. I wish I could have attended the funeral, but I was at a Beijing trade conference that week."

"I understand."

"I also wish replacing your father was going better. I have a lot of wannabees begging to replace him for the interim. It's a real dog fight."

"I can imagine."

"Three key guys want the job, but all three would vote against USMed. I'm for it, like your father. If I chose one of the wannabees, the other two will throw hissy fits and cause political and legislative problems for the state. Which we don't need now. I can't seem to find the acceptable compromise person here to replace him."

"It must be difficult."

"It was until I realized something."

"What's that?"

"One person could replace him with little criticism."

"Who?"

"*You!*"

Ellie sputtered ... "*Me?*"

"Sure. You've worked closely with your father and others on legislation for years. You've helped him with USMed. You're an attorney with a lot of DC legislative healthcare experience. You know the ins and outs of Congress. And you know Indiana politics. Like your father, your legal residence is here in Shelbyville, where you visit regularly and practiced law for a while. You spend a lot of time each year. And, as the interim Senator from Indiana, many of us feel you'd honor your father by voting for USMed—his life's goal. And I know he'd love you to vote for him. What do you say?"

Her stomach was churning ... her pulse pounded in her ears.

"I say *whoa!* Governor. I'm very flattered, but I'm not the right person for this job."

"Your credentials suggest you are. And after this brief interim assignment, you could, if you like, decide to leave the Senate. Or choose to run for another term. Either way, it's no problem. What do you think?"

Ellie paused. "I'm very flattered. But I need to think about this, Governor. Can I tell you tomorrow?"

"Of course. Ellie, you'd do a great job for our state. You have the right stuff ... the right DC experience. The right name. Your dad was beloved. And you have the right talent."

"Thank you, sir."

"Speaking of talent, do you know mine?"

"Persuasion?"

"Crooner on a cruise ship."

"No way."

He cleared his throat, and sang ... *Back home again in Indiana ... oh how you long for your Indiana home ... "*

Ellie was still laughing after they agreed to talk tomorrow and hung up.

"Bing Crosby's singing love songs to you?" Madison said.

"The Governor Crooner himself is."

"He's got my vote!"

"He wants *me* to fill my father's spot as interim Senator."

"My God, Ellie—that's terrific! What an honor! But you've always told me you hated all the shenanigans and backstabbing in politics."

Ellie paused. "I do. But the Governor said something that made sense."

Madison waited.

"My dad would want me to take the interim spot. The Governor thinks I have enough legislative legal experience. And if I vote for USMed, I'd help achieve my father's lifelong USMed goal."

Madison nodded. "The Governor is right. But can you really put up with all the political crap?"

"Maybe for a few months. And then I'd get out."

"What if you learn to like it?"

"No damn way."

* * *

The next morning, Ellie's life changed.

She made her tough decision.

She rewarded herself with her rare two sinful fingers of Jameson's Irish Whiskey in her dark roast coffee. She gulped some down and felt the heat rush through her body like hot soup.

Last night, she'd analyzed the pros and cons of Governor Greg Wilson's interim Senator offer. And after a few hours of restless sleep, she woke up, made her decision, and went back to sleep.

She sipped more Jameson's, took a deep breath, grabbed her phone before she could change her mind, and dialed the Governor's office. Renee picked up.

"Good morning, Ellie."

"Good morning, Renee. Is Governor Wilson available?"

"Yes. I'll connect you now."

Two clicks later, the Governor said, "Ellie, good morning."

"Good morning, sir."

"Hope you slept well."

"I did—*after* I made my decision."

"Which is … ?"

"I accept your offer."

"Excellent decision. And I thank you on behalf of the citizens of Indiana and myself."

"You're welcome, Governor. But I should also mention that I don't anticipate running for the seat after the interim period."

He paused. "No problem. That's a whole different election. But if you do decide to run, or not run, let me know as soon as you know."

"I will. So what's next? Will the state legislature vet me? Will they dig into my wicked past and discover I pinched Stevie Slaton's cute butt in third grade?"

He laughed. "No. I simply submit your name."

"To whom?"

"To myself. Congratulations Senator Ellie Nelson!"

* * *

Madison worked in her hotel when her phone started ding-a-linging. She saw Ellie's name on Caller ID and picked up.

"You decide yet?" Madison said.

"Yep."

"And?"

"You're talking to Indiana's newest Senator."

Madison shot her arm in the air. "Congratulations, Ellie! Terrific! Your dad would be so proud, but ... "

"But what?"

"God save Indiana!"

"Smart ass!"

"So what's next?" Madison asked.

"Governor Wilson's office is organizing the swearing-in ceremony."

"Our agency can handle any PR and social media for that if needed."

"Thanks, Maddy, but I'm not even sure what's needed at this point."

"I am."

"What?"

"A celebration dinner. On me."

"Perfect."

TWENTY-TWO

The Guardian walked into his private meeting room where Donald Bennett and Archie Braun sat at a glass conference table reviewing their latest vote count.

"It's looking better," Bennett said. "We persuaded another Congressman to vote against USMed."

"How?"

"We promised him he wouldn't tell his wife about the other wife he's still legally married to. Or her spousal abuse claim against him."

The Guardian nodded approval. "We need his vote because Governor Wilson just named Ellie Nelson to fill her father's senate seat."

"Doesn't the state legislature have to confirm her?"

"No. The Governor can make the decision."

"Shit!" Donald Bennett said, cramming a fistful of cashews in his mouth. "She'll vote for USMed like her father. We have to stop her vote."

The Guardian nodded. "But not like we stopped her father. Too suspicious."

"So how?" Bennett said.

The Guardian paused. "She once told me she jogs in the early morning."

"Outside her apartment?" Archie asked.

"No. In Rock Creek Park."

"When?"

"Around 7 a.m."

Archie Braun smiled. "Some women who jog in DC parks get *kidnapped*. Some get raped. Some get killed. Remember Chandra Levy, that Congressman's girlfriend?"

"Lots of joggers-in-forests abductions," Bennett said.

Archie Braun nodded. "We grab her, hide her away until after the vote, then release her."

The Guardian shook his head. "Grab her, hide her—but *don't* release her."

Bennett nodded. "Kidnap victims often remain missing for years."

"Some are never found," the Guardian said.

TWENTY-THREE

"Who loses most if USMed becomes law?" Special Agent Stanford asked Madison and Detective McCall in a Hoover Building conference room.

McCall said, "Ellie says it's big-time pharma and healthcare industries. USMed would slash their profits by billions ... and their executive bonuses by millions.

"But everyday Americans would win," Madison said, "because we would pay only around 10% of what we now pay for prescriptions and hospital services. That's what people pay in over two hundred other industrialized countries."

"No wonder millions of Americans are getting their prescriptions from Canada, Mexico, and other countries," McCall said.

Madison nodded. "And no wonder more Americans are getting their surgeries done overseas, often by US-trained surgeons who charge only about 15% of what the same surgery costs here. A hip replacement in the states costs $40,000 to $50,000 ... compared to $10,000 in many European countries."

Stanford said. "What about babies born in hospitals?"

"Today, babies born in U.S. hospitals can cost from $25,000 to $40,000 thousand–versus around $2,000 thousand in Europe. With USMed babies born in hospitals could drop to around $2,000 dollars."

Stanford nodded as his phone rang. He checked the Caller ID. "This caller might help."

"Who is it?" McCall asked.

"Doctor Gorman at the military's Aberdeen Proving Ground."

"Hang on, Doctor, while we Zoom you in with Detective McCall, Madison, and me."

Doctor Elijah Gorman popped on screen. He was a tall fiftyish Black in a white coat with horn-rimmed glasses on a neck chain.

"Doctor, can you see us?"

"See you fine," Dr. Gorman said, adjusting his red bowtie. "We just got the final toxicology results for some USMed victims."

"Any surprises?"

"Shocking ones."

They waited.

"More victims died from the same nerve agent," Dr. Gorman said.

Madison felt her muscles tighten. She'd read how fast nerve agents killed.

"Which one?" Stanford said.

"A deadly form of VX called ... Nervochok. The Russians called it 'Sudden Death' for good reason. It's five times faster than VX. Kills in a couple minutes, as they've proven many times."

Dr. Gorman cleared his throat.

"First victim, Senator Nelson," Dr. Gorman said. "But oddly, we found no trace of a nerve agent on his clothes, or in his office. Yet it somehow got into his system."

"Who else died from Nervochok?" Madison asked.

"Senator Clete Ruskin," Dr. Gorman said.

"Again, CSI found no trace of Nervochok on his clothes or in his cabin," Stanford said.

"How can this be?" Madison asked.

―

Dr. Gorman shook his head. "The killers have developed an ingenious way to deliver Nervochok into the body without leaving any trace on their clothes."

No one spoke.

"Any other Nervochok victims?" Stanford said.

"Wendy Shuman, a researcher for Dr. Nelson. She collapsed into a chair in her office lobby and was dead four minutes later. We found Nervochok in her blood. But no trace on her clothing, or in the lobby, or her chair, or the Subway tuna she ate, or the taxi that dropped her off."

"Anyone else?" McCall asked.

Dr. Gorman said, "LaTisha Darnell, a young USMed aide-activist. She dropped dead on a DC Metro platform. Nervochok in her blood, but again no trace on her clothes or the Metro platform."

No one spoke.

"Also, Congressman Woodwillow. Nervochok in his blood. None in his clothes or office."

Madison heard the growing frustration in Dr. Gorman's voice.

Madison asked, "What's the most probable or likely way to deliver Nervochok to a victim?"

"Aerosol. Spray."

"Any hint of a spray?"

"No."

"Could someone drink Nervochok?" Madison asked.

"Yes. But no Nervochok was found in their stomachs."

"Can Nervochok be injected?" McCall said.

"Yes. But no injection marks were found on their bodies or scalps."

No one spoke.

Stanford said, "So this assassin has a terrifying new way to attack his victims … a way that leaves no trace of Nervochok on, or around, his victims."

Dr. Gorman nodded. "It's a mystery. But we *have* to solve it."

Before it kills more pro-USMed members of Congress, Madison hoped.

———

TWENTY-FOUR

ROCK CREEK PARK

Ellie tightened her Nikes, stretched her legs, and jogged off at her warm-up pace into DC's Rock Creek Park. The cool morning air felt so invigorating she'd sprint her last two hundred yards up Heartbreak Hill if she didn't wimp out.

She waved to a familiar jogger who waved back as he headed down another trail. She ran over a small rock bridge that led into a narrow pathway. Trees arched over the trail like a cathedral roof, cutting off most early morning light, making the pathway even darker in the morning fog.

"Looking strong, Ellie," a fellow jogger shouted, as he jogged past heading in the opposite direction.

"You too, Dirk."

She picked up her pace as she jogged up a small rise, huffing harder. She loved the purple and yellow flowers hugging the path border, and the scent of evergreen shrubs, and the birds tweeting their morning sing-along. And she loved jogging early in the morning, before DC heat hit her like a blast from a pizza oven.

She ran over the summit and started down the hill into thicker, darker forest. A hundred yards ahead she saw a large man jogging slowly toward her. She'd never seen him here before.

Behind her she heard a fast-paced jogger gaining on her. The slow jogger and the fast runner would reach her about the same time, so she jogged onto the shoulder path to give them both room to pass.

But then the guy in front locked his unsmiling eyes on her as he ran faster toward her.

Her lizard brain shouted danger. She slowed her pace, unzipped her belt kit and started to reach for the mace spray.

But the fast runner behind her gripped her arms.

The big jogger in front grabbed her shoulders.

She struggled but couldn't free herself.

As she started to yell, the guy behind held a wet cloth over her nose. Breathing hard, she inhaled something sweet in the cloth. Seconds later, she felt dizzy and disoriented.

They led her off the path into dense forest. Through the branches, she saw a white van with red cross on the door.

And then she saw nothing.

* * *

Madison worked in her Marriott room, considering some provocative concepts for USMed commercials. She planned to run USMed ads on NBC, CNN, FOX, ABC, CBS newscasts, then on local news channels, family shows, and movies. Plus ten fifteen-second clips on social media.

She stared at photos of sixteen young children aged three to nine.

Dead children. Their poor, uninsured parents couldn't afford the costly healthcare insurance, surgeries, or prescriptions that would have likely saved their lives. Sixteen young kids unlucky to be born to their parents … unlucky to be born in America. Because if they'd been born in any other industrialized country with *universal* healthcare, they would very likely still be living.

Madison remembered that last year over forty thousand Americans died because they couldn't afford American health insurance. Forty thousand.

She looked at a photo of an eighty-two-year-old woman, Delores. Her cancer had required years of extended hospital admissions. Her ongoing hospital bills grew so enormous she and her husband used all their savings, and even sold their house to pay off some deductibles. But her hospital bills still grew worse. They owed $270,000 and moved to a one-room flat in a slum. One week later, despairing and desperate, they sat on their sofa, swallowed full bottles of sleeping tablets, embraced each other, and died in each other's arms.

Madison felt their pain.

Elderly suicides due to medical debt were growing in America. *One in five* seniors declare bankruptcy due to high medical bills.

Bankruptcies due to healthcare-debt grew *200%* over the last fifteen years.

Madison's phone rang. Estelle, Ellie's assistant was calling, and breathing hard.

"Madison, have you heard from Ellie this morning?"

"Not yet."

"I'm worried about her."

"Why?"

"She was supposed to meet me two hours ago to go over some things in her father's office. But she didn't show up or call to cancel. I phoned her cell and apartment phone, but she's not answering. She always calls if she'll be late. It's not like Ellie. I'm worried."

Then so am I, Madison thought. "Ellie was also supposed to call me but hasn't. We're meeting later. Hang on, I'll phone her."

Madison dialed Ellie's number. It rang four times and bounced to voice mail. It was full. She tried her home phone, got no answer, and left a call-me message. She texted. No response.

She switched back to Estelle.

"Estelle, she's not answering my calls either. She usually goes jogging in the early morning. Do you know where?"

"Rock Creek Park."

"She might have fallen. Does she jog with her phone?"

"I believe so," Estelle said.

"I'll call Detective McCall. Maybe he can triangulate her phone location and send someone to search the area. If she calls you, let me know fast."

"I will," Estelle said, her voice shaky. "Please call me if you reach her."

"Okay." Madison phoned Detective McCall's cell.

McCall picked up.

"Ellie might be missing."

"Since when?"

"This morning, or maybe since last night. Estelle and I can't reach her. And she missed a meeting with Estelle this morning. Estelle says she probably went jogging early in Rock Creek Park. No word since then. We're concerned."

McCall paused. "You tried her cell?"

"No answer. Nor to my text."

McCall said. "The police normally wait twenty-four hours before they search for a missing person. But since she's a missing US Senator, Ellie gets more Federal Government attention *now!*"

"So, what next?"

"We'll scan Rock Creek Park for her phone. Now."

"I think she was abducted to prevent her vote!" Madison said.

"So do I."

TWENTY-FIVE

Madison's GPS map showed nearly two thousand acres in Rock Creek Park. Much of it heavily forested. A lot to cover. She wondered if Estelle knew the area where Ellie jogged. She called, but Estelle had no idea which area.

"Does Ellie ever jog with anyone?" Madison asked.

"Abby Sylvan. An attorney at Ellie's former law firm. Hang on, I've got Abby's number."

Estelle gave Madison the number.

Madison called Abby and explained Ellie was missing. Abby agreed to meet them at the Rock Creek Park location where Ellie and she usually started their jog.

Fifteen minutes later, Madison, Abby, Detective McCall, and six police officers met at the park path near Beach Road.

"We usually start down this path," Abby said, pointing to a narrow dirt path with lots of shoeprints, leaves and twigs. "We wear the same Nike model. Her prints will look like this."

Abby pushed her Nike into the damp soil and left a clear tread print.

Everyone studied it.

McCall spread out his officers on both sides of the path. They started tracking the path at a slow pace, hunting for any clue.

Madison checked behind the bushes and fallen branches. She saw a fallen tree trunk thick enough to hide several bodies but was too terrified to go look behind it. A policeman checked behind it and kept on walking. Madison exhaled.

A few yards farther she saw a woman's muddy Nike. *Why one shoe? Was it Ellie's?* No. Wrong tread.

Moments later, an officer held up part of a blue jogger belt and showed it to Abby.

Abby shook her head. "Ellie has a red belt."

"Does she carry protection?" McCall asked.

"Mace."

They continued searching.

Madison dialed Ellie again. No answer. She tried her landline phone. No answer. Ellie hadn't mentioned any appointments when they'd agreed to meet for lunch. *Where in hell is she?*

"What's this?" an officer said, a few feet off the path.

They hurried over to it and looked at a red plastic canister with bits of wet leaves stuck to it.

"That could be Ellie's Mace kit," Abby said.

McCall asked an officer to put the Mace kit into a paper evidence bag. "We'll check it for fingerprints."

"What about these fresh shoeprints," a tall young officer said. She pointed at the path.

Madison and Abby saw a cluster of fresh prints in the dirt ahead.

Abby pointed to one. "This Nike print could be Ellie's. Size is right."

McCall said, "Look—beside her print are several man-size prints. But *dress-shoe* prints. They approached her from the front.

"Who wears dress shoes to jog?" Abby said.

"Maybe he walked," Madison said.

"No, he ran," McCall said. "The distance between his shoeprints suggest a large man running toward her."

"And look," Madison said, "these other running prints stop right *behind* her."

"They attacked her from front and back," McCall said.

Madison agreed. "Where do her prints lead?"

They looked around and soon saw Ellie's and the two men's prints veering off the path.

"*This way!*" another policewoman said, pointing. "Their fresh footprints head down here in the mud."

"And farther down here too. The prints head toward Beach Drive," McCall said.

They tracked the footprints down to Beach Drive.

"From here, they drove away, or were picked up," McCall said. "Anybody see security cameras?"

Everyone looked. No cameras.

"Maybe those buildings across the street have cameras," a young female officer said.

"Probably. Check it out," McCall said.

"Is that a camera?" Madison said, pointing up at a small black device attached to the oak tree limb twenty feet above her head.

McCall looked up. "*Yep!*"

Madison prayed the camera showed Ellie and the men getting in a vehicle they could track.

But the camera looked old and she saw no green light indicating it was working.

"Let's go view CCTV videos for this street and area," McCall said.

✳ ✳ ✳

Ellie felt nauseated as she peeled open her eyes.

How long have I been unconscious? Did I trip and hit my head on a rock?

No. I was jogging ...

A big man jogged toward me ... another jogger came up fast behind me. They grabbed me, clamped a sweet-smelling cloth over my nose that made me dizzy. Now I'm in a windowless van.

She saw the same two men sitting beside her in the van. They wore medical white coats now. But she saw no medical equipment in the van.

She reached for her pocket and realized her wrists were flex cuffed. She felt for her phone. Gone. They'd taken it and her watch.

Why me?

Where are they taking me?

✳ ✳ ✳

Madison, Agent Stanford, Detective McCall, and Abby worked in an FBI video room. Their table was covered with a large map of Rock Creek Park, and several empty coffee cups.

They watched large screen monitors panning park pathways and streets in and around Rock Creek Park.

So far, no sign of Ellie.

"Check monitor four," McCall said.

Madison watched screen four. The video showed Rock Creek Park along Beach Drive. The camera zoomed in on a tall man helping a woman walk out of the trees toward a BMW parked along the street.

"Not her," Madison said. "Ellie's a lot thinner."

"Screen eight," McCall said.

All eyes swung to screen eight, where Madison saw a light-gray Ford minivan parked along the street. Seconds later, two men and a woman in a jogging suit emerged from the park. The men were on both sides of her, in dark jogging clothes.

"Not her. Ellie's taller," Madison said.

"Screen five," McCall said.

They watched the video flicker to life.

Madison saw a white Toyota van with a large Red Cross on the door parked alongside Beach Drive. The driver wore a black hoodie pulled up over his head. *Why pull a hoodie up on a hot, muggy morning?*

Then, two men and a woman in jogging clothes emerged from the forest and headed toward the white van. The men held her elbows as she wobbled toward the street. Her face was turned away from the camera, but her height and body shape matched Ellie's.

Then she faced the camera.

"That's *Ellie!*" Madison said.

"That's her blue jogging suit!" Abby said.

Ellie looked drugged. Her face was blank, her legs unsteady. She resisted being forced into the van, but the men lifted her in, jumped in, and the van sped off.

Madison checked the license plate. Mud covered most numbers.

"That red cross logo on the door is fake. Too skinny," Detective McCall said.

"This is kidnapping," Agent Stanford said.

"What now?" Madison asked.

"We try to track the van, Stanford said. "And also see if her abductors make some kind of demand."

"I doubt they will," Madison said. "They want one thing: to kill her vote for USMed."

Maybe by killing her …

* * *

Hours later, Madison's phone rang. She listened, then hung up.

"More bad news. Estelle said the Governor of Indiana just heard Ellie'd been abducted. He said that if she's not rescued in the next twenty-four hours, he's required to replace Ellie as interim Senator. And he doesn't like his three replacement choices."

"Why?"

"They oppose USMed."

Madison's hope sank. "So, what now?"

"We find her fast. Track the van leading away from the park," Stanford said.

"And find it before they hide Ellie and the van," McCall said.

Or worse, Madison thought.

TWENTY-SIX

Ellie's eyes felt glued shut. She opened her left eye and saw she was lying on the floor in a small dark room.

Is it day or night?

In the van, she remembered a man had placed the damp, sweet-smelling cloth over her nose again, and she fell unconscious. She knew ether smelled sweet. She also knew it could be deadly if administered incorrectly.

She looked around the room and saw shelves stacked with new packages of men's sweatsuits, boots, T-shirts, and towels. Nothing she could use to defend herself.

The door squeaked open.

A giant walked in.

He looked at least six-seven, two hundred sixty pounds, with thick eyebrows and a large forehead over light blue eyes. He placed a tray of food on a small table.

"Here's some nice food for you," he said in a soft, almost childlike voice. "They have nice cookies too. I like cookies very much."

"Thank you, but why am I here?"

"I don't know."

"Who knows?"

"Maybe my boss does."

"Who's your boss?"

"He didn't tell me his name."

"What's your name?"

"My name is MayMay. But my dad calls me NerdNerd! My parrot's name is Cecil, but we call him Ce-Ce. He's a boy bird. He's eight years old. He was born on a Thursday at 8:14 a.m., Eastern Standard time."

MayMay's gentle smile revealed some missing teeth. His speech revealed some kind of mental condition.

"What's your birthday?" he asked her.

Why does he want my birthday?

She told him the year and date.

"Tuesday," he said.

"What?"

"You were born on a Tuesday."

"You're right." She was amazed.

"What's your mom's birthday?"

She told him.

Two seconds later, "She was born on a Sunday."

My God, right again! He's a savant.

She was fascinated.

"Bye. See you later," MayMay said.

When he left and locked the door, she heard her abductors mumbling in the outer room. Clearly, they abducted her to prevent her vote for USMed.

But after the vote, what? It's obvious. Even though they wore semi disguises, she could probably identify them. They knew that. They would dispose of her. They had no other choice.

But by now, Estelle and Madison wondered why she'd missed their meetings. Estelle knew she went jogging many mornings. Maybe she and Madison checked her apartment, saw her Nikes missing, and called Detective McCall.

The police and the FBI would be looking for her. Should she sit tight and hope they were?

Or try to escape?

* * *

The Guardian walked into Donald Bennett's soundproof meeting chamber and saw Bennett and Archie awaiting him. Bennett's fingers, as usual, rested next to a half-empty bowl of cashews and a half-empty glass of whiskey.

The Guardian sat down. "Did we find our friend?"

Both men nodded.

"Where?"

"Like you said. Jogging in Rock Creek Park," Archie said.

"Who found her?"

"Me, B, and C," Archie said.

The Guardian nodded, checked something on his phone, then said, "Where'd you take her?"

"She's at our temporary location," Archie said, "to make sure no one tracked us. No one did. Next, we'll take her to the island. Later we'll take her to our storage room at *Heaven Scent Cigars* in the DC mall."

The Guardian nodded. "When this is all over, lose B and C."

Archie looked troubled. "Both guys?"

The Guardian nodded.

"But they're my—"

"—they're drunks who brag. Maybe to the wrong person. They can be linked to her and us. They'll cave to the cops."

Archie frowned, clearly frustrated at the direct order to eliminate two of his men, but nodded. He had a stable full of capable back-up guys.

"What about her?" Bennett asked.

"Keep her until after the USMed vote. Then disappear her."

"Any special way?" Archie looked eager to handle her.

Guardian thought a moment. "Yes."

"How?"

"I'll tell you later."

* * *

"That's the white van with Ellie!" Madison said as she sat with Stanford and McCall in the FBI conference room watching CCTV video of DC streets.

Madison watched the van leave Rock Creek Park and drive into central DC and change direction several times as though trying to lose anyone tailing them. She watched it cross the Potomac into the Maywood district.

A few miles farther, the van drove into a garage next to a dental clinic. They watched the garage front exit to see if any white vans drove out. None did.

"Is there a rear exit?" Agent Stanford said.

"Yes," McCall said.

They watched the rear exit and front exit on a split screen.

They fast-forwarded both screens to see if the white van drove out over the past hour or two. It did not.

"Does the garage connect inside to the dental clinic?" Madison said.

"No. I've parked here before," McCall said. "To reach the clinic, you have to walk out onto the streets in front or in back."

Stanford said. "So, they may still be in the garage."

"Possible," McCall said. "The garage manager just emailed us the inside garage video. Let's watch."

They fast-forwarded the videos.

Minutes later, they watched the white van with the Red Cross enter the garage and drive into a dark corner and park behind a concrete abutment with no CCTV camera coverage.

The van, the men, and Ellie disappeared behind the abutment.

"Where the hell'd they go?"

No one spoke.

"Quick—*recheck* videos of the exits to the front and rear streets," McCall said.

They checked all street exits video but didn't see Ellie or the men come out.

"They might be still in the garage," McCall said.

"Or they drove out in another car," Madison said.

TWENTY-SEVEN

"I'm so sorry, Beth," said Dr. Steven Handler.

Senator Beth Bradley closed her eyes, lowered her head, and took a deep breath. She felt like someone jabbed a red-hot poker into her stomach.

Or more precisely into her pancreas.

Beth whispered, "Doctor, does your diagnosis confirm both my Mayo Clinic and Sloan Kettering diagnoses?"

"Yes."

"Stage-Four?"

He nodded.

She swallowed a chalk-dry throat. "How long?" She'd read it could be a few months to several months.

"It's hard to say, Beth."

"Your best estimate?"

Doctor Handler paused, stared down at the floor.

"Six to nine months."

Beth felt hot tears fill her eyes. Eight months ago her upper stomach pain started. She lost appetite, lost weight, lost energy.

And with Dr. Handler's estimate, she lost hope.

At least she wouldn't leave any children behind. Or her husband, Roger, who died in a car accident six years ago. But she would leave many friends she dearly loved. And a job she dearly loved … as senior Senator from Wyoming.

Dr. Handler leaned closer to her. "Some new treatments might help slow the progression, Beth."

She nodded but felt shattered. She had so much she still wanted to do. Like pass USMed, and fair immigration laws, and very affordable college tuition rates for all.

"Doctor, please keep me breathing long enough to vote for USMed. I promised my constituents."

"We'll do our best, Beth."

She knew USMed could not save her life.

But voting for it, and passing it, could save the lives of millions of uninsured Americans.

TWENTY-EIGHT

The Guardian hung up his burner and considered what his informant just told him. Democratic Senator Beth Bradley, a long-time acquaintance of his, had Stage Four pancreatic cancer. Her life expectancy? Six to nine months.

Long enough to vote for USMed. Unfortunately.

Bradley was a highly successful advocate for USMed, and radical terrorist groups like Me Too and Black Lives Matter.

She'd already convinced several members of Congress to vote for USMed. She could persuade more. Some colleagues would likely pity her illness so much they'd vote for USMed. A final tribute to her. He had to prevent her persuasiveness and her vote. But how?

Minutes later, a solution bent his lips in a smile.

The Guardian called Donald Bennett and explained what he wanted.

* * *

An hour later, Donald Bennett's chauffer drove him to Kunming's Asian Foods on Park Street in Baltimore's Chinatown.

Bennett entered the store and smelled refreshing woody ginseng, anise, and other pleasing Asian spices that always made his mouth water. Maybe tonight he'd go to David Chu's China Bistro for cashew chicken. He nodded at the young woman manager, then walked down to the food shelves in back. He placed his left thumb on a scanner and the shelves opened, revealing a staircase. Bennett descended the stairs into the secret, LED-lit laboratory.

He was here to see Mr. Hunann Lee, whose fake passports, driver's licenses, and birth certificates had been declared authentic by custom agents, police, and document experts around the world for years.

"Mr. Bennett, right on time as always. Good to see you."

Bennett nodded, and noticed Lee's thin body with envy. The guy had muscles, perfect skin, and jet-black hair combed straight back in a ponytail held in place by a gold butterfly clamp.

"How may I assist you today?"

Bennett handed Mr. Lee a typed letter, some handwritten letters, and a fountain pen.

"We'd like this typed letter written with this fountain pen in the exact same handwriting you see on these other handwritten letters."

Mr. Lee scanned the letters and nodded.

"Are these handwriting samples enough for you?"

"More than enough," Mr. Lee said, smiling.

Bennett said, "Here's half our fee. The rest upon completion." He handed Lee an envelope with fifteen thousand dollars.

Lee thanked him and bowed. "You are most kind. When do you need the letter?"

"As soon as possible. Tomorrow evening latest."

"You shall have it tomorrow morning by 10 a.m."

✳ ✳ ✳

The mini spy camera he'd installed yesterday gave Archie Braun an excellent view inside Senator Beth Bradley's condo.

He watched her walk with a glass of red wine into her study. She sat in a black leather Eames chair, took a deep breath, and began reading *The Washington Post*.

She sipped more wine but didn't appear to detect the slightly metallic taste of the deep-sleep drug he'd put in her open wine bottle … the drug that put Michael Jackson to sleep for eternity.

She drank more propofol-laced wine and continued reading. She looked exhausted, thanks to her morning's painful radiation treatment.

Pain she deserves, Archie felt. Years ago, Senator Bradley, a women's rights radical, voted for the stupid law that permitted women to serve in limited combat positions. As a result, Archie wound up with a dyke bitch commanding officer who ranted and raved at him non-stop. The bitch demoted him for alleged insubordination, making his life miserable. Tonight, was payback for Senator Beth Bradley's stupid law resulting in his unjust demotion.

Minutes later, as expected, her head began to nod. Soon, the propofol took over and she slumped in the chair, unconscious, wheezing for air.

Using his bump key, Archie re-entered her condo, wearing gloves. He walked over and felt her pulse wind down … slow … then slower.

She was circling the drain…

Her pulse stopped.

He opened her letter written in her handwriting by the talented Mr. Lee and read it.

Dearest friends,

By now you all know the devastating news I received recently. My cancer is stage four … and quite painful. It will take my life within a few weeks or months. I saw my mother go through a year of increasingly painful surgery, *chemotherapy, radiation therapy, and other excruciating treatments. I saw her lose her faith due to overwhelming depression and disease, until she was no longer able to speak or recognize us. I saw her wither to seventy-eight pounds. I saw her lose hope. I do not want to see that happen to me, or have my friends see that happen to me. I want to leave while I can still think clearly and say good-bye to my dear family and friends.*

But there's good news. My decision will save hundreds of thousands of dollars in medical costs for my treatment ... savings that I hope will soon benefit some of the nearly seventy-five million Americans who can't afford adequate healthcare or none at all.

Our new USMed will finally bring full healthcare to ALL Americans.

Please understand why I do this ...
My love to you all,

Beth Bradley

He placed her suicide letter on the lamp table beside her chair. He wrapped her still warm fingers around the fountain pen that Mr. Lee used to write the letter and placed the pen next to the letter. He placed her fingers on the vial of propofol and placed it beside her glass of wine.

Then he removed his tiny spy cam from her bookcase, walked over to her body and stared at her a few moments.

"Men only in combat."

TWENTY-NINE

In her hotel room, Madison agonized over Ellie's abduction. How was she? Where was she? They had no idea. And no word from her abductors.

Madison's phone vibrated: Stanford calling.

"News on Ellie?" she asked.

"Nothing yet. Did you hear about Senator Beth Bradley?"

Madison's stomach muscles tightened when she heard Stanford's tone.

"No."

"Suicide."

Stunned, Madison collapsed in her chair. "My God, she was a leading promoter for USMed."

"I know. But her suicide letter says she was overwhelmed by her Stage-Four pancreatic cancer, her imminent physical pain, her treatment, her memory of her mother's slow agonizing death from the same cancer. The letter is clearly in her handwriting.

Her fingerprints are on the pen that wrote the letter, and a vial of propofol was beside the letter. Propofol was in the wine she drank. It killed her."

Madison couldn't speak.

"Her doctor said she had just months to live."

"Are you convinced it's suicide?" Madison asked.

Stanford paused several moments. "Everything points to suicide. But something's not right."

"What?"

"She had six to nine months to live. And her friends say she would have held on a few weeks to vote for USMed. *Then* maybe taken her life. USMed meant too damn much to her."

"I got that impression when we met. So the suicide letter might be a forgery?"

"That's the problem," Stanford said.

"Why?"

"Our three handwriting experts say they're 99.9% certain *Beth* wrote the note. It's her handwriting. No question about it."

Madison paused. "People will write what they're told to write when a gun's aimed at their head."

* * *

Thirty minutes later, Madison met Special Agent Stanford in an FBI audio-visual room.

"Still nothing on Ellie," he said, lowering his eyes.

Madison's hope sank. "Why didn't we find the white van in that garage sooner?"

"Because it was hidden *behind* the garage where there's no CCTV. Also, her abductors had stripped off the Red Cross and the stuck a *Mary Ann's Flowers* sign on the van door. We recognized the van by the mud on the license. Then we watched more garage videos of walkers and vehicles leaving the front and rear exits."

"And?"

"We didn't see her or the men *walking* from the garage. But we saw three vehicles she might have been driven out in. But we need you to look closely at the women in the videos."

"Show me."

Agent Stanford ran a video showing a Toyota SUV exiting the garage. Two men in front. In back, a large man sat beside a woman. The tinted windows made it hard to see her face, but she wore light-colored clothing, perhaps Ellie's light blue jogging suit. The SUV turned and Madison got a quick look at the woman's face.

"Wrong hair. Not Ellie."

"Maybe a wig?"

"Wrong nose, chin."

Agent Carras nodded and fast-forwarded to a green Ford SUV driving out. Again, two men in front, a man and woman in back.

Madison squinted at the woman's face in the shadows. Madison realized she looked a bit like Ellie, but something was not right.

"Can you rerun that?"

Carras reran it and the woman raised her hand into the sunlight.

"That woman's wearing a wedding ring." Not Ellie.

"Last possibility." Carras ran the video.

Madison saw a black Mercedes pull out of the garage exit and turn left. Two men in front, one man in back with the woman. The woman wore something blue, maybe Ellie's jogging suit. The car turned left and the sun lit up the woman's face.

Madison pointed. "That's Ellie!"

"How do—?"

"—her face! Haircut. Jogging watch."

Stanford zoomed in on a close-up of the license.

Madison saw dark mud over some numbers.

"Only clear letters are RS. The next to last number is an 8. That helps," Stanford said.

"Run the RS and 8 in those plate locations through the Motor Vehicles computer systems. Meanwhile let's try to track the Mercedes."

Madison and the others watched the black Mercedes drive down the street and turn onto Highway 193.

A mile later, using FBI drones, Stanford saw the Mercedes turning onto Highway 603, then taking rural back roads through forests for several minutes to the Potomac River near Bealls Island.

Madison grew worried as they parked on the riverbank. Why bring her to the river? How deep was it? Were ropes tied to concrete blocks in the trunk?

The men took Ellie out of the Mercedes as a motorboat docked at their shore. The motorboat took them all over to Bealls Island.

Madison watched them step ashore and disappear into the forest. The trees and mist were too dense to see through the branches. But the video caught something flicker through the trees. The glint of glass? A cabin window?

"A hideout," Agent Stanford said.

"Now what?" Madison said.

"Time for HRT."

"HRT?"

"Our FBI Hostage Rescue Team."

THIRTY

"Who died from Nervochok so far?" Detective McCall asked Dr. Browner.

"Senator Nelson, Senator Ruskin, and Senator Woodwillow. And we just learned that LaTisha Darnell on the Metro station platform. And Wendy Schumer, Senator Nelson's aide both had Nervochok in their blood."

McCall shook his head in amazement. He and Dr. Browner sat in the MedTech Labs, studying the victims' toxicology reports, trying to determine *how* Nervochok entered their bodies. So far no luck. If they knew how, they could warn potential victims.

McCall said, "Maybe a fellow Metro passenger sprayed LaTisha Darnell with Nervochok."

"Maybe. But the Metro CCTVs revealed no sprayer," Dr. Browner said. "No one got close enough to spray her."

A bearded technician hurried in and handed a folder to Dr. Browner. "Here's Darnell's final tox."

Dr. Browner scanned the pages inside, raised his eyes toward Detective McCall, and shook his head in frustration.

McCall watched a technician walk in and give Dr. Browner another folder. Browner scanned it. "Wendy Schuman's final tox report. She ate a Subway lunch, took a taxi back to her office building. In the lobby, she felt exhausted, sat in a lobby chair to rest, and was dead four minutes later. This tox report found Nervochok in her system."

"Any traces on anyone's clothing?"

"Absolutely none."

"So how the hell did Nervochok get into her system?" McCall said.

Dr. Browner shook his head. "By some ingenious new attack system that scares the bejesus out of me!" He rubbed his eyes and opened them wide as a tech handed him another folder.

He opened it, scanned the findings, and lowered his head.

"Ernest Woodwillow had Nervochok in his blood. But no trace on his suit or in his office."

No one spoke.

McCall said, "What about Congresswoman Anne Wilson who died when her laptop fell in her bathtub water and electrocuted her? Are we sure she wasn't attacked with Nervochok first? Maybe Nervochok incapacitated her so much she accidentally knocked her laptop into the bath."

"No Nervochok was found in her blood, bathwater, or clothes," Dr. Browner said.

"So now what?" McCall said.

"We need our nerve-agent weapons expert again," Dr. Browner said. "I'm checking back with Dr. Elijah Gorman." He grabbed the phone. "He specializes in weapon's research and development at the US Army Aberdeen Proving Grounds in Maryland."

THIRTY-ONE

In an unmarked Chevy van, Madison and Special Agent Stanford watched video of the FBI Hostage Rescue Team surrounding the large cabin on Bealls Island.

Madison noticed a cabin light was on.

Please be safe inside, Ellie ...

The FBI team inched closer to the cabin. Stanford told Madison the HRT wore full tactical gear, fire-retardant clothing and carried MP5/10 submachine guns, Sig Sauer 9 mm handguns and assorted weapons. This team had rescued hostages in war-torn Afghanistan, Iraq, and the USA. And now hopefully, on tiny, peaceful Bealls Island in the Potomac.

She watched one HRT team member peek in the cabin's small back window. He signaled the shade was down. Same with a side window. Three FBI men took positions at the back door. Four men inched toward the front door.

"Shock and awe time!" Stanford said to her.

She watched the video switch from the overhead drone view of the cabin to the HRT team leader's body-cam view of the front door.

On his silent three count, they burst through the door shouting, *"FBI!"* and tossing flash-bangs that blasted and blinded her view inside the cabin.

Seconds later, when smoke and vision cleared, Madison saw the main room looked empty. Team members searched two small rooms, bath and kitchen, shouting:

"Clear!"

"Clear!"

"Clear!"

"Clear!"

"No Ellie! No bad guys!" the team leader said.

He looked at the kitchen stove. Madison saw eggs and sausages in the frying pan. The leader touched the handle.

"Frying pan's warm. Stove's still turned on. They left when they knew we were coming."

"Someone tipped them off."

"Maybe CCTV cameras warned them?" Stanford said.

"We saw no cameras in the trees," the team leader said. "Someone warned them."

"Or someone followed us and told them," Stanford said.

Madison said, "So now what?"

"We track them leaving the island," Stanford said.

"What if they're still hiding on this island?" Madison said.

"If they're here, we'll find them. Two more HRT teams are combing the island now. It's only two thousand feet long."

She stared at the fast-flowing Potomac.

Did they take Ellie with them?

Or sink her to the bottom of the river?

＊　＊　＊

Madison, Detective McCall, and Agent Stanford watched the satellite view of Bealls Island, hoping to see the kidnappers and Ellie leave the island—and then track them.

Because Ellie was a US Senator, NSA gave them the last three hours of satellite surveillance video on Bealls Island. No one left the island in the first hour.

But forty-two minutes later, the same small fishing boat docked at the island. Moments later, the kidnappers and Ellie emerged from the cabin. She wobbled as though drugged. They walked her toward the boat, boarded, motored to the other shore, got back in the same black Mercedes that brought them, and drove off.

The satellite tracked the Mercedes through various forest roads until they entered US 270 heading back toward Washington. The satellite followed the Mercedes into the greater DC metro area where they pulled into a huge multi-level parking garage attached to a big new shopping mall, *The Avenues,* in central DC.

Minutes later Stanford, Madison and other FBI agents boarded an FBI chopper, flew to DC, and landed a mile from the garage. Thanks to the chopper's speed, they got to the garage just twenty-three minutes after the Mercedes did.

"Are we certain the Mercedes is still in the garage?" Stanford asked the FBI agent at the scene.

"Yes."

"Did it exit?"

"Not yet. But lots of cars are leaving and entering."

Madison wondered if this was another car-switch garage?

FBI Agents watched the exits in front and back for the Mercedes. The mall security guards also watched to see if the kidnappers and Ellie walked into the shopping mall. So far, no sightings. An FBI Hostage Rescue Team entered the garage and searched floor by floor.

Minutes later, they found the empty Mercedes parked in a dark corner. A broken overhead garage light and disabled CCTV camera failed to record where the kidnappers and Ellie headed when they left the Mercedes.

"They might have escaped in another car again," Stanford said.

"Or through the tunnel to the mall," Madison said.

THIRTY-TWO

Congresswoman Maria Elena Vasquez rode her favorite stallion, Amigo, down the scenic trails of her family's ranch a few miles north of Tucson. Her father, Pepe, the son of migrant workers, had saved every peso and dollar for thirty years and parlayed them into his successful horseback riding academy, *Rancho Maria Elena.*

Maria Elena loved escaping Washington's hot, muggy, crowded streets for Tucson's warm, dry open spaces. She loved watching the golden sun creep up over Mount Lemon and warm her skin and her soul. She loved being home.

She even loved being with her mouthy younger sister, Catalina, riding beside her.

"What a joy to ride with my favorite and awesome younger sister, Catalina."

"I'm your only sister. But you're right—I'm extremely awesome!"

Maria Elena laughed.

As a first-time Congresswoman, she felt honored to champion new legislative bills, particularly USMed. It would make life healthier for *all* her constituents, many of whom could never afford health insurance.

Fifty yards later, they rode onto a grassy path with stunning mountain views that always calmed her.

Her phone rang and she answered. Her Congressional aide, Todd, calling. He said, "USMed just picked up an unexpected vote from a House Republican."

"Great. We need it!" They chatted a bit more and hung up.

"So how's DC really?" Catalina said.

Marian Elena paused. "It's stimulating, and despite all the political games that waste taxpayer dollars, it's very interesting."

"Can it ever get more efficient?"

Maria Elena shrugged. "Only when Congress realizes something its predecessors learned and practiced."

"What?"

"That *compromise* is a win-win. Both sides win."

"*Compromise*? Dream on, older sister."

"Dreams can come true."

Maria Elena's phone rang again. She listened for the caller, but no one spoke.

"Who's bugging you now?"

"These mountains. Sometimes they block phone reception in this narrow pass. Oh … I forgot to ask Todd about a meeting."

She dialed Todd back but was bounced into voice mail. She left him a message, knowing he would handle it well.

Suddenly, some critter in the weeds spooked Amigo, causing him to jerk and fling her riding gloves to the ground. She got down, placed the gloves in the saddle pocket, and climbed back in the saddle.

"Maria, speaking of dreams come true, are you still seeing that ex Notre Dame football player, now hunky-lawyer?"

"Dinner with Brad next Friday."

"OMG! My sister's dating a hottie!"

Maria Elena laughed. Then stopped cold. Suddenly her lungs felt crushed. Her heart started pounding. She coughed hard, and her chest tightened even more.

She couldn't breathe air in ... or out. Couldn't stop her heart from slamming against her ribs. Couldn't stop her eyes from blurring. Couldn't stop her dizziness. She grabbed the saddle horn to keep from falling off.

What's wrong?

"I can't brea..." She slumped forward, slid off the saddle, and collapsed onto the path.

"*Maria?* What's the matter?"

Maria Elena lay face down in the dirt.

She couldn't breathe.

THIRTY-THREE

In *The Avenues* multi-level parking garage, FBI rescue teams had rechecked every inch of every level for some sign of Ellie. No luck.

Madison knew they were also checking each of the 207 stores in the mall.

Meanwhile, she, Agent Stanford, and Detective McCall returned to DC MedTech Labs and met with Dr. Browner. They hoped to determine *how* the deadly Nervochok toxin entered its victims.

"Dr. Gorman just arrived here from Aberdeen Proving Ground," Dr. Browner said.

The door opened, and Madison watched the large white-coated Black man enter smiling.

"Welcome again, Doctor Gorman," Dr. Browner said. "As you know, Special Agent Tim Stanford, Detective Mark McCall, and Madison Parker are also helping on this case."

"Good to see you folks again."

Dr. Browner said, "Doctor, we're dealing with victims of Nervochok. But we're still trying to figure out how they were attacked."

"Well normally, as you know, VX, Nervochok, Sarin, and other nerve gases are delivered in aerosol form," Dr. Gorman said, rubbing tired eyes.

Dr. Browner nodded. "But we found no evidence that aerosol or liquid was used with these victims."

"Still no trace on their clothes?"

"None."

Dr. Gorman's gray eyebrows rose in surprise. "You checked skin, face, nose, neck and hair?"

"Yes. No trace."

"You checked their drinks?"

"Two coffees, one water, and one scotch. No Nervochok."

"Injection marks?"

"None."

Clearly puzzled, Dr. Gorman scratched his brow.

Agent Stanford's phone rang. He picked up, listened, and hit the speaker button.

"We may have a new victim."

Everyone stared at him.

"On the speaker I have Officer Lopez near Tucson."

"Who's the victim?"

"A young Congresswoman. Maria Elena Vasquez," Officer Lopez said.

"What happened?" Browner asked.

"Her sister Catalina says she and Maria Elena were horseback riding on their father's ranch. Everything was fine. Her riding glove fell to the ground. She retrieved it and got back in her saddle. But a minute later, she slumped forward and fell to the trail. She gasped, had trouble breathing, and vomited. Her sister called 911 and a MedEvac chopper arrived in just four minutes. They flew her to a nearby hospital."

Madison sensed the Congresswoman's accident might somehow be connected to the USMed deaths.

"How is she?" Stanford said.

"Critical."

Dr. Gorman said, "Test her for nerve agent poisoning."

"We already are. We got Agent Stanford's Nervochok alert yesterday concerning Congress members."

"When do you expect tox results?"

"Within an hour."

"When you get them, please call us immediately."

Forty minutes later Officer Lopez called back with a military doctor, Dr. Santiago.

Dr. Santiago said, "With the help of nearby military scientists we tested her for nerve gas poisoning."

"And?"

"The test just found a minor amount of Nervochok in Maria Elena Vasquez's system. *Far* less than what you reported in your previous victims."

"Why so much less?"

"No idea."

"What's her status?" Stanford asked.

"Critical. But we started nerve-agent treatment immediately so we're optimistic she might make it."

"That's terrific," Madison said, delighted by rare piece of good news. "One last question: Is her sister Catalina with you now?"

"Yes."

"Please ask her whether Maria Elena was planning to vote for USMed?"

Officer Lopez asked Catalina.

Madison heard Catalina say, "Yes."

THIRTY-FOUR

Ellie remembered back in the cabin when the men forced her to swallow a liquid that made her groggy. Her vision blurred so she could barely see where they were taking her.

She also remembered leaving the cabin, getting in a small boat, and then in a big Mercedes. The Mercedes drove for a long time, during which she drifted off.

When she woke up minutes ago, they were back in DC and parking in a huge garage. They made her put on a blonde wig, and a Nationals jacket and baseball hat. The men also wore Nationals hats and jackets.

They led her through a dark narrow passageway that exited behind the parking garage. Then to the rear of what appeared to be a large shopping mall. They unlocked a small door marked *Private* and took her inside.

They climbed a stairwell several floors, maybe four or five, walked down another hallway to a steel door. The muscular man used a key, unlocked the door, and they led her inside to a small room.

The scent of cigars overpowered her. Through a small opening in another door, she glimpsed what looked like a cigar shop with boxes of cigars and bottles of wine on rows of shelves.

"Don't go anywhere," the muscular man said, grinning, as he locked her in.

* * *

Madison and Agent Stanford watched video of shoppers walking through a tunnel from the multi-story parking garage into *The Avenues* Mall. No one looked like Ellie.

Stanford said, "We have a problem."

"What?" Madison asked.

"The parking garage has rear exit stairs and passageways with no CCTV-cameras."

"So they could have walked out back."

"And probably did," he said. "Also, the mall itself has private back doors with locks and buzz-ins. But with no CCTV cameras."

"So, they could have entered back there and hidden her in one of the mall stores," Madison said.

"Yes."

"How many stores?"

"207."

* * *

"That advertising woman Madison is a problem," Donald Bennett said to Archie.

"Why?"

"Her new USMed TV commercials are almost ready to run on the networks."

"So?"

"My informant says even the rough-cut unfinished commercials are extremely persuasive. They'll motivate people to push their representatives to vote for USMed."

"I'll handle her," Archie said.

"Not her."

"So how—?"

"—handle the commercials. Call a guy named Waylon," Bennett said.

"Who's he?"

"A junior TV producer at Madison's agency, Turner Advertising. Waylon owes serious gambling money to the mob and serious child-support payments to ex-wives. Call him now."

Bennett gave Waylon's burner number to Archie. He dialed it as Bennett placed an earbud in his ear to listen in.

Waylon picked up and Archie explained who he was.

"Waylon, my friend tells me you think the rough-cut USMed TV commercials are good," Archie said.

"They're not good. They're frickin' *awesome!* They hook the viewers. Very persuasive."

Bennett feared they were too persuasive.

"When will the commercials start running?"

"In four days."

Another pause. "Where are the USMed commercials and related materials now?"

"In the final stage of production here at our agency studios."

"Anywhere else?"

"Copies in the Cloud."

Bennett sipped his coffee and nodded for Archie to continue.

"What if an industrial accident at the agency destroyed the rough-cut commercials?" Archie said.

Waylon paused. "Disaster! Our TV producers would go apeshit! They'd have to start over. Rebuild the commercials from scratch. Re-edit rough footage."

"Many days to make new versions?"

"*Several* days! Why? "You making this a request?"

Archie looked at Bennett who nodded.

"Yeah!" Archie said.

"Hang on … " Waylon paused for several seconds. "To do that I'd be taking a serious risk. I'd need more money. A lot more."

"How much?"

"Waylon paused. "Like, uh … twenty thousand."

Bennett nodded to Archie.

"You got it!" Archie said. "So if the videos and the Cloud backup copies are destroyed, they'd have to rebuild everything from scratch, right?"

"Right."

"That would set their TV schedules back a lot."

"Like two weeks maybe."

Bennett realized two weeks would be *after* the USMed vote.

"Okay. My associate will call you in a few minutes," Archie said. "He and his partner will handle the job. Just tell him how to gain entry, where the USMed commercials are located, the computer passwords, and for the Cloud stuff. Can you do all that?"

"Yeah. When?"

"Tonight."

"That's fast! I need half the money this afternoon."

Bennett nodded to Archie.

"You'll get it. The rest on completion."

"Deal."

They hung up.

Bennett looked at Archie. "Destroy those commercials!"

THIRTY-FIVE

E llie woke up on a hard floor, smelling wine and cigars.

I'm in a bar?

Then she remembered. She opened her eyes and saw the door to the cigar shop she'd glimpsed earlier. She was surrounded with hundreds of boxes of cigars and cases of wine stacked along the walls.

She saw a sign on the wall: *Heaven Scent Cigars.*

My abductors brought me here to stop me from voting. The Governor will have to replace me as interim Senator. Maybe he already has. Most likely my replacement will vote against USMed. Most likely my abductors know that.

And after the vote, what?

No way they'll release me.

She would remember their faces. Could identify them. But not their names. They called each other A and B and C.

She heard them in the next room, walking toward her door. Whispering.

Her door cracked open and she saw A, B, and C silhouetted in the door. Behind them she saw the dimmed yellow lights of the cigar shop.

The muscular man they called A, the boss, walked up to her and said, "Let's chat a bit over here." He gestured toward the nearby table.

She paused, unsure what they really wanted. Why would they need to chat with her?

The tall man, B, yanked her off the floor and over to the circular oak table, and pushed her into a chair. Even the heavy cigar aroma could not overpower B's manly fragrance, *Eau de Armpit.*

B closed the thick door to the cigar shop.

She heard a voice in the cigar shop and considered screaming *HELP!*— but A read her mind and aimed his silenced gun at her face.

"Don't even think of yellin'."

She said nothing.

"We want to know stuff."

She waited.

"What did the medical examiner say killed your father?"

"Why do you want to know?"

He pushed the gun hard into her cheek.

"I ask. You answer."

"The medical examiner said my father's cause of death was cardiac arrest. Heart attack."

Ellie would not tell them about the Nervochok. The less they knew what the police knew, the better.

"Was that all the doctor said?"

"That was enough."

"But what did he think caused your dad's heart attack?"

"He didn't know. He was really puzzled. Said these attacks just happen sometimes."

"And what about Senator Clete Ruskin?"

"I heard heart attack also caused his death. But he was old."

"And Ernest Woodwillow?"

"Even older. Eighty. I heard he had a stroke," she lied.

A paused, then looked at her like she was holding back information.

"That's all they said?"

"That's all I heard."

"I don't believe you. Do you believe her B?"

"She's lyin'."

"Do you believe her C?"

"No fuckin' way. Bitch is lyin'."

"So we gotta refresh your memory," A said.

He walked over to her and pushed up her sleeve. He opened a small hard case and took out a syringe filled with a clear liquid.

Grinning, C held her arm down flat against the table.

"If this is what you gave me earlier, I won't remember anything. I'll pass out."

"This is different stuff. This'll relax you so you *wanna* tell us the truth."

A chuckled as he injected her with what she prayed was only sodium pentothal, truth serum. She had to remain strong and not tell them about Nervochok.

But soon, despite wanting to remain strong, she felt the drug relaxing her. Within minutes, she was calm and serene. She remembered that some reporters knew about Nervochok. Maybe if she said some substance was found in the victims' blood, these men would stop using Nervochok to kill others. She wasn't sure what to tell them. She grew more confused.

A said, "Now tell us what else the scientists discovered."

She took a breath. "Well, one doctor found some ah … stuff in the blood."

"What stuff?"

She wasn't sure what to say, so she made it up. "I don't know. Maybe some kind of stuff like a poison, like maybe anti-freeze. Something that starts with M, Z, or maybe K, I can't remember. The doctors weren't sure what it was."

"M, Z or K?"

"I think that's what they said. But I'm not sure."

"How did this poison stuff get into their blood?"

She felt herself growing more drowsy and yawned. "That's their big problem. The doctors have no idea. They said it's a huge mystery."

A and B smiled knowingly at each other.

"They can't figure out how it got into them," she said. "They're really puzzled."

"Last question. Give us the names of your two best activists pushing Congress members to vote for USMed."

Ellie yawned again, pretended to think hard. "I can't remember well now ... "

"Remember *harder!*"

She wrote down the names of two people. One guy was in her third-grade class who became a Buddhist monk. The other was a sushi chef. Neither was a political lobbyist. She handed him the two names.

"These guys are your best?"

"That's what people say."

"Where are these guys campaigning now?"

"One's in Hawaii. The other's in Alaska."

The men looked disappointed by the distance.

She yawned twice, feeling groggy again.

They asked her something, but she didn't hear it.

Her eyes closed. *Did they give me truth serum?*
Or poison?

THIRTY-SIX

M adison felt guilt wash over her. *I pushed Ellie to consider the interim Senate seat. She wasn't that interested at first, then I pressed her hard to accept the offer, suggesting her father would want her to.*

If she's injured, or something terrible happens to her, I'll have to live with it. The guilt will be with me for life.

Madison sat with Agent Stanford in a small FBI conference room still awaiting news of Ellie.

None came.

The longer they waited, the more Madison feared for her best friend's life. Was Ellie suffering? Being tortured? In pain? Her chances of being rescued unharmed or escaping, or even staying alive, grew smaller with each hour.

Stanford's assistant opened the door. "Dr. Gorman is back."

The door opened and Dr. Gorman hurried in. Madison hoped he'd gained insights on how Nervochok attacked the victims.

"Anything new?" Stanford asked.

"One thing," Dr. Gorman said. "It appears all victims received nearly the exact same amount of Nervochok—except Maria Elena Vasquez in Tucson."

"Does that suggest injections or sprays?"

"Injections more than sprays."

"But," Madison said, "the autopsies revealed no injection marks on the bodies, or traces on their clothes. Including Maria Elena, right?

"Right," Dr. Gorman said.

"So maybe they ate or drank the same amounts," Madison said.

"Possible. But again, their stomach contents did not reveal any measurable trace of Nervochok," Gorman said.

Agent Stanford nodded. "Which leaves us where we started—searching for an ingenious attack system. *What* the hell delivers the same amount of Nervochok into their bodies?"

Madison nodded. "And how do we figure out that system?"

Dr. Gorman said, "Our people are going back over each physical location where they died. But this time we'll use our new high-tech sniffer-detectors from Fort Detrick. They're much more powerful. Maybe they'll detect a minute trace of Nervochok in the victims' rooms, or on their clothes."

"Should we also check what these victims were doing before they died?" Madison said.

"We did. Most were working on their files, attending meetings, texting, drafting memos and sending out correspondence. But maybe we missed something. We'll check again," Stanford said.

"*Someone* attacked them with Nervochok a few minutes before," Dr. Gorman said, "Or *something* happened to them a few minutes before they died."

"How can you be so sure it was a few minutes before?" Stanford said.

"Because Nervochok kills within minutes."

* * *

Madison, Dr. Gorman, and Special Agent Stanford walked into Ellie's father's office. They studied the spot where he collapsed.

Stanford's phone rang. He listened, hung up, and said, "We're still checking all shops in the mall for Ellie. We reviewed all parking garage video and found three men and a woman we think might be Ellie. The men and the woman wore Nationals jackets and baseball hats. It looks like she wore a blonde wig. Despite the wig and sunglasses, her face profile and body shape looked like Ellie. The video shows them leaving through a garage back door, but then they walked out of camera range. So, we don't know if they got in another car in back of the mall and drove away or entered the mall from one of its private rear doors. We're checking all possibilities."

Madison grew even more concerned for Ellie.

"Let's recheck Senator Nelson's office here," Dr. Gorman said.

They started searching specific areas for some device that might have delivered the Nervochok to him. Like an aerosol spray, a nasal spray, a cologne spray, an asthma inhaler. They found nothing.

"Did Dr. Browner check Senator Nelson's medications?"

"He takes no meds. Just a daily Centrum Silver multivitamin and an 81 mg aspirin."

"Was the multivitamin a capsule or solid?"

"No. A solid blue tablet Ellie told me," Madison said. "Why?"

"Capsules can be refilled with fatal stuff. Remember the Tylenol refilled capsule poisoning deaths?"

As they walked around the office, Madison realized everything was exactly as she and Ellie had last seen it days ago. Nothing was moved.

They walked over to his desk, opened the center drawer and looked in at the neat dividers. Pens and pencils in one slot, paper clips in another.

Madison noticed a small tape recorder in the corner.

Stanford pushed the Play button.

Madison heard Senator Nelson's soothing baritone leaving notes for himself. Things to do. People to meet. Normal political stuff. Nothing suspicious. She hoped Ellie would listen to her dad's calming voice when she needed to.

"We've rechecked everything here that could release Nervochok. I found nothing," Dr. Gorman said.

"So what's next?" Madison said.

"Senator Ruskin's cabin."

Twenty minutes later, they turned onto the gravel driveway of Senator Ruskin's forest cabin. They searched the office where he died. His whiskey, cigar, everything looked the same as before. They found no hint of how the Nervochok entered his body.

"Next is Congressman Earnest T. Woodwillow's Rayburn Building office," Dr. Gorman said.

＊　＊　＊

Ellie pressed her ear against the door's small crack, and heard the men whispering about how long they might hold her captive.

"So, after the USMed vote, what?" B said.

"We got options with her," A said.

"Like how we done them others?"

"No. Something special," A said.

"Like what?"

"The man will tell us."

"Why wait?" C said. "We got the concrete blocks. We got the ropes. We got the Potomac. Splish splash she's takin' a bath!"

"That ain't special."

Ellie pictured them cuffing her hands behind her back, tying a concrete block to her legs and tossing her in the river.

She felt her blood stop.

THIRTY-SEVEN

Madison, Stanford, and Dr. Elijah Gorman entered Ernest Woodwillow's Rayburn Building office. After several minutes of rechecking everything, they found no device that might have delivered Nervochok to Woodwillow.

From there they visited the Metro station where LaTisha Darnell collapsed and died. They checked video. They found nothing

Stanford's phone rang. He answered, hung up, and shook his head, and turned to Madison.

"Sorry, still no news on Ellie."

Madison's felt nauseated. "Where next?"

"Anne Wilson. The Congresswoman electrocuted in her bathtub," Stanford said.

The group entered Congresswoman Anne Wilson's luxurious condo in the Dupont Circle area.

Madison admired Wilson's signed lithographs by Dali and Picasso, an antique red Isfahan Persian carpet, a colorful Dale

Chihuly chandelier. Agent Stanford said Anne Wilson had inherited millions and gifted much to St. Jude Children's Hospital and other charities.

They walked into the bathroom where Wilson was electrocuted.

"What do they think happened?" Madison said.

Stanford said, "Anne came home from work, had a glass of wine. Decided to take a bath. Apparently placed her plugged-in laptop on a stool right next to the bathtub to listen to music, which her best friend said she often did. She got in the tub. Laptop probably beeped that a message arrived. We assume she reached over to get the message, lifted the laptop. But her fingers were wet or soapy—the laptop slipped from her hands into the water and electrocuted her."

"Did her wine contain Nervochok?" Dr. Gorman said.

"No," Stanford said. "And no other lethal toxins."

Dr. Gorman asked, "Did she have any history of serious depression or suicidal thoughts or attempts?"

"Absolutely not," Stanford said.

"Women don't commit suicide nude," Madison said.

Stanford nodded. "By all accounts, Anne was a very positive, happy, successful Congresswoman."

Dr. Gorman said, "Someone might have *tossed* her laptop into her bathwater."

"Possible," Stanford said. "But we examined it and the bathroom and condo for fingerprints. No prints on the laptop because soapy bathwater washed them off. Only her prints on the faucets."

"Anything else here indicate foul play?"

Stanford shook his head. "No. But we did find one male fingerprint."

"Where?"

"On the refrigerator."

"How do you know it's a male print?" Madison asked.

"Women have more acid on their fingers," Dr. Gorman said. "And tongues. Like my acid-tongued wife."

Madison and Stanford laughed.

———

"Whose male print?"

"Her fiancée's. He's been in Brussels. Flying back tonight."

"So the bottom line?" Madison asked.

"Ms. Wilson's death appears accidental," Gorman said.

Or a homicide, Madison thought, *if someone tossed the laptop in her bath water.*

* * *

Madison stared at Agent Stanford as he walked into the small conference room.

"Sorry Madison, still no news on Ellie." He looked as frustrated as she felt.

Madison's hope sank.

"Our people reviewed *The Avenues* mall and garage videos again. No sighting of Ellie. We've interviewed sales personnel in all shops. No one saw her. We're not even sure she's in the mall, or ever was."

"So, who else did not die by Nervochok?" Madison asked.

"Congressman Ethan Anderson," Stanford said. "He was robbed and shot in the underground garage of his apartment building. Video shows two armed masked men approach him in the garage. They asked him for his wallet. He gave it to them. They inspected his driver's license, like making sure it was Anderson."

"How is he?" Madison asked.

"Critical. Maybe 50-50 chance to survive."

"He planned to vote for USMed, right?"

"Right."

"Also Jesse Lee Howell died this morning while sculling on the Potomac. Blunt force trauma. A blow to his head.

"Bottom line," Stanford said, "Someone's still going to extreme lengths to kill USMed voters in *different* ways."

"But with the *same* goal," Madison said. "Kill the USMed bill by killing those who'll vote for it!"

THIRTY-EIGHT

Ellie saw only two ways to escape. Two doors. The front door led into the cigar store where her abductors were. The back door led to stairs that might take her back down to a door where the men brought her in from behind the mall. The back door was her only choice.

But both doors were locked. Always.

She sat surrounded by hundreds of boxes of cigars. She stood and searched for matches to light a lot of cigars, maybe set off a fire alarm. She found no matches, nor a fire alarm.

But searching whipped up a lot of dust. She sneezed and reached into her back pocket for a tissue. She felt it and felt something else. Something she'd forgotten was there.

Something that might help her now.

She had an idea. *Could this possibly work?*

Moments later, she heard someone walking toward her room.

Please not A, B, C again …

The front door unlocked, and she relaxed when she saw MayMay, her gentle savant babysitter, walk in. All six-foot-seven of him. MayMay was not like A, B, and C. He didn't even know their names. MayMay was kind and considerate, but he clearly had no idea why she was being held here.

MayMay brought her coffee and a cup for himself. He sat at the table and smiled at her.

"I got your coffee. And one for me. Plus cookies. I like cookies. Sometimes I eat too many. Do you eat too many cookies sometimes?"

"Sometimes, MayMay."

She remembered his phenomenal savant memory. Suddenly a plan formed in her mind. Should she try it? Is it too dangerous?

"Are they fresh cookies?"

"He looked on the package. "It says they're best before September 29, 2023."

"What day of the week will that be?" she asked to get him talking.

He blinked. "A Friday."

"You're amazing, MayMay!"

"I remember numbers and stuff. If you don't want your cookies, I'll eat them."

"Okay." She handed him her cookies. He scarfed them down, as tiny crumbs tumbled into his shirt pocket.

She finished her coffee fast.

"The coffee is really, really good, MayMay."

"Do you want some more coffee?"

"I'd love some more coffee. Very much. You make such great coffee."

"Thank you. I'll get you another cup. Maybe some banana raisin cookies, too. They're delicious."

"Okay, MayMay."

He stood, then used the blue key on his chain to unlock the front door. He relocked the door, stepped into the cigar store, then walked to get her coffee.

Quickly, she reached in her back pocket and took out a tiny baggie containing five Ambien tablets. She'd taken Ambien for sleepless nights after her father's death. She dropped all five Ambiens into MayMay's coffee and stirred the dissolving tablets with the tiny spoon.

A minute later, he returned with her coffee and some banana raisin cookies.

"Thank you, MayMay. You know I'm fascinated by your memory. Can you remember something you read in the newspaper like two days ago?"

"Yes." He sipped his coffee.

"Like what?"

"What I read."

"Even the stock numbers?"

"Uh-huh. I like to check the stocks."

She grabbed an old nearby newspaper and turned to the stock market. "What about AT&T stock two days ago?"

He paused, closed his eyes. "$29.99."

"Yes!"

"And General Motors?"

"$32.02." He sipped more coffee.

"That's right. Incredible."

"What about Martha Stewart?"

Another pause. "$6.54."

"You're amazing, MayMay!"

"I remember stuff. I don't know why."

He yawned wide, blinked, then drank more coffee. He shook his head a bit and yawned again. The five Ambiens were taking effect. Just one Ambien could knock her out in minutes.

"When are A, B, and C coming back to the shop?"

"Later, I think. But I can stay with you." Another big sigh, then he rubbed his eyes.

"Ellie asked, "What day was December 6, 1943?"

He paused, blinked, yawned. "A Monday."

"That's my good friend Victoria's birthday. You're amazing, MayMay!"

"Thank ... you."

She noticed his words slurring, eyelids drooping and head sagging. He was about to doze off. Another giant yawn.

She asked about a couple more dates and he answered them very slowly. Moments later his chin dipped to his chest. He placed his thick forearms on the table.

"My eyes are kinda tired. Maybe I'll rest them a little bit." He laid his head on his arms.

"Okay... "

He was fading, and seconds later drifted off.

She waited a few moments and nudged his huge arm. No reaction. His breathing grew heavy and deep. He was asleep. Had she given him too much Ambien? Her nurse friend told her it probably took ten or more tablets to maybe kill an adult, but she wasn't sure. And he was huge.

Slowly, she reached under his heavy arm to take the door key off the chain. She felt the chain, unclicked it, and slid off the orange key. Then she closed the keychain and eased his arm back down.

Suddenly, he stirred as though waking up.

She froze.

But he sighed and resumed deep breathing.

Ellie walked over and unlocked the back door. She saw no one in the dark hallway.

She walked out, shut the door, locked it, hoping she had the only key, and hurried down the hallway.

To her left, she heard men's voices hurrying in her direction from another hallway. Who were they? She hid behind two large vending machines.

The men hurried past the vending machines so fast she couldn't identify them. They continued down the hall and turned down another hallway.

When she heard no one, she left the vending machines, ran down the hall to a stairwell. She rushed down the stairs to the bottom floor and looked for the door that led outside, the one the men brought her through.

She couldn't find it.

She rushed down another hall to a door marked *MALL*. She opened it and found herself in a mall hallway beside a closed Payless Shoe store and a vacant storefront.

The door behind her clicked shut and locked itself.

Where are the mall exits? She had no idea.

She turned the corner and saw a mall EXIT-ENTRANCE sign at the very far end of the hall.

She also saw a tall man, maybe B, hurry in the ENTRANCE.

He looked in her direction.

Does he see me?

THIRTY-NINE

Madison watched Agent Stanford answer his phone and listen. His face froze.

"You're sure?" Stanford said. He hung up in obvious frustration.

"Ellie?" Madison asked, terrified.

He nodded.

"What?"

"The Governor of Indiana is required to replace her as Interim Senator."

Madison felt saddened, then upset, then relieved that Ellie only lost her appointment, not her life.

"Why?"

"Her prolonged disappearance, their inability to contact her, documents she hadn't signed, and the uncertainty of when she'll return. He's required to name a replacement now."

"Did he name someone?"

"Yes."

"Who?"

"A long-time state legislator, Cyrus Mackey."

"Is he against USMed?"

"Yes. But Mackey was the only person the state legislature and the Governor could agree upon. The Governor had to maintain peace with the legislature. He had to name him."

"But Mackey is another torpedo that can help sink USMed," Madison said.

* * *

Archie, Barney and Cheech—A, B and C—entered the mall and took the escalator up to the third level.

They entered *Heaven Scent Cigars,* a store owned by a shell company secretly owned by Don Bennett. The store manager, Leo, didn't know of the shell company, and didn't care what they stored in his back room as long as they didn't steal cigars and wine.

"Everything okay in the back room, Leo?" Archie asked, loving the tobacco aroma.

"Quiet, like always."

Archie nodded, then he, Barney and Cheech walked toward the back room. Archie inserted his key, opened the door, and froze.

He couldn't believe it.

Ellie Nelson was gone! And MayMay was asleep, his head on the table, snoring like a winded buffalo.

"What the fuck?" Archie hissed, enraged.

He rushed over and shook MayMay's thick shoulder. The giant stirred but didn't wake up. Archie shook him harder and slapped his face. Nothing. He slapped it again.

MayMay's eyes peeled open.

"Where's the woman?"

"MayMay looked around the room. "She is not here."

"I can see that idiot! How'd she get out?"

MayMay looked dazed. "I do not know." He looked down at his key chain.

"My orange key is gone!"

Archie ran to the back door and tried to open it.

"She locked it from the outside!"

He hurried into the cigar shop and got another orange key. He ran back, opened the door, and stared into the empty hallway.

"When did she leave?"

"MayMay blinked. "After I brought her coffee."

"When did you bring her coffee?"

He looked at his watch. "Five minutes and thirty-four seconds ago."

"Is that your coffee?"

"Yes."

"She drugged you, you fuckin' moron! If you weren't the boss's fuckin' relative, I'd shoot your ass!"

Archie smashed his fist into MayMay's face, causing his nose to bleed.

MayMay began to cry and buried his face in his hands.

Archie turned to B and C. "She's only got a few minutes head start. She's gotta still be in the fuckin' mall! Go find her."

The two men raced out the back door.

* * *

Madison, Agent Stanford, and Estelle met in Senator Nelson's former office.

Estelle looked concerned as she hung up her phone. "Another pro-USMed voter might flip to vote against USMed."

"Who?" Madison asked.

"Senator Bolton from Idaho wants Federal money for a new highway to his friend's gambling resort near Lewiston. If he gets enough votes for the highway, he'll vote for USMed. If he doesn't get enough votes, he'll vote against USMed. Word is, he can't get enough votes. So, we'll lose his USMed vote."

Madison was troubled by how easily Congress horse-traded votes, sometimes sacrificing badly needed national health programs for local pork projects like a gambling casino.

"Meanwhile," Estelle said, "you probably know the Indiana Governor had to name an anti-USMed interim Senator to replace Ellie because she may well be unavailable. And he can't prove she'll be present to vote. So, her replacement, Cyrus Mackey, is another lost vote."

Madison nodded in frustration. "What about *undecided* Senators?"

"Best guess—three, maybe four."

"Any more potential flip floppers?"

"Two."

"Who's most likely to flip and vote *for* USMed?" Madison asked.

"Gray from Kansas."

"What will it take for him to vote for USMed?"

"He wants a Federally-funded bridge in his district. The bridge is needed. But again, he doesn't have enough members to support it."

"So our bottom line?"

"USMed's not looking good for passage in the Senate right now. And the vote's coming up soon."

"We need something very persuasive very soon to encourage USMed votes," Stanford said.

"Our final USMed advertising campaign will start soon. Hopefully it'll persuade Americans to tell their legislators to vote for USMed," Madison said.

"That should help," Stanford said.

"If it doesn't, USMed may be stillborn."

* * *

In Manhattan, behind Turner Advertising, Kurt Schick and Jack Miller stepped from their Toyota Sienna van into the night blackness on 56th Street. They checked for security guards in the shadows, saw none.

They hurried to the agency's rear entrance where Waylon, their Turner Agency contact, told them to enter the agency.

Using Waylon's duplicate key, Schick unlocked the door and he and Miller stepped inside.

"The guard is making his rounds in the client-services departments for another twenty-one minutes," Schick said. "We gotta be gone by then."

Miller nodded.

Schick looked at the agency floor plan Waylon gave him.

They climbed the stairs to the seventh floor, opened the door, and stepped into the agency's television production department.

"The stuff we need is in the Video A-1 Department down this hall to the right."

They walked down to Video A-1 and used another key to enter the *Commercials & Social Media Office*. Both men began searching drawers and file cabinets for USMed-labeled materials. Soon, they'd filled a large leather satchel with USMed thumb drives, USBs, discs, even some color newspaper ads.

Behind him, Schick heard something. He turned as a side door squeaked open. He saw a forty-something cleaning woman push her sweeper into the room. She saw Schick at the computer and her eyes shot wide open.

"Are you allowed in here?" she asked.

"Of course," Schick said. "I'm finishing up a job for a TV producer."

"Which one?"

"Ray."

"I don't know any Ray in TV production. No one told me you'd be here now. Management always tells me."

"Ray's a new freelance guy."

Behind the woman, the door opened. Silently, Miller stepped into the room. Schick nodded for Miller to handle the woman.

Miller karate-chopped the side of her neck. She slumped unconscious, but he caught her and laid her on the floor. He flex-cuffed her hands and ankles, and duct-taped her mouth.

Then Schick sat at a computer and searched for more USMed materials, and all backup commercials. He deleted everything he found.

Using the password Waylon gave him, he accessed the Cloud and began deleting all USMed commercials and related social media programs stored there.

Seventeen minutes later, they left the agency, placed the satchels filled with USMed materials in their van, and drove off toward Newark.

An hour later, they were buying drinks for the gang at a trendy new beer bar.

Ale Mary's.

*   *   *

Ellie saw B and then C enter the mall hallway and turn in her direction. Had they seen her? She wasn't sure.

She hid in a locked restroom stall for a while. Five minutes later, she left the restroom and hurried down an empty hallway, looking for a pay phone. She quickly realized the mall didn't seem to have any. Do they still exist in malls?

She looked around. She saw a blind man tapping his walking cane at the far end of the hall. Two teenagers hurrying down another hallway, heading the other way. An old man dozing on a bench beside a bubbling water fountain.

"There she is! THERE!"

Ellie looked up and saw C, the short skinny man, on the second level, leaning over the railing, pointing down at her.

She turned and ran in the opposite direction, looking for a store where she could get help or hide. It was late. Most stores were closed, two open ones were empty with no sales personnel in sight. It looked like a ghost mall.

She saw C and B coming down the two escalators, one man on each side, pointing at her, planning to trap her between them.

She turned left and sprinted back down a side hallway. She saw more empty shops. No customers. No salespeople. If she went in a store, B and C would see her. She started to panic.

She turned a corner and ran.

Then luck. She saw a *Maintenance* door slightly ajar. She ducked inside the small janitor's closet, shut the door, praying they didn't see her enter. Seconds later, she heard the men run past the door.

"Check all stores on both sides!" A yelled. "She's gotta be in one. I got this side!"

Ellie slumped down and listened to her heart slam into her throat. She felt the doorknob for some kind of lock mechanism but felt none. She pulled the light string. The bulb was burned out.

Any second, they'd yank open the door.

FORTY

Madison was in the FBI office when her phone rang: Christine, her assistant, calling from their Turner Advertising.

Christine didn't call with minor concerns.

"Hi Christine, what's up?"

"Two men broke into our agency last night. They entered the audio-visual department and destroyed all our USMed TV commercials. *And* all our USMed social media materials."

Madison's heart stopped. She gripped the heavy table so hard it scraped the floor. She couldn't speak. Destroyed USMed commercials. A disaster. Millions of dollars of work destroyed at a time when USMed most needed their commercials on television reaching Americans. She took a deep breath, closed her eyes, and told herself to relax. It didn't work.

"We're supposed to ship the commercials to the networks and cable *tomorrow!*" she said.

"We were ready to ship," Christine said.

"How'd they break in?"

"A back door on 57th."

"Forced entry?"

"No. The police say they likely had a key. When they got inside, they punched in the correct security code. They had inside help."

Madison swallowed the pain of betrayal. "Did our CCTV cameras tape them?"

"Yeah, but they wore hoodies, sunglasses, and full beards. They knew exactly where the USMed materials were. They grabbed all the USB software, flash drives, and thumb drive copies. Then one guy worked on one of our computers for a while."

"Doing what?"

"Deleting our USMed materials."

Madison's heart sank. "Please tell me we still have our copies in the Cloud?"

Christine paused too long.

"Sorry, Madison. The guy knew the Cloud password. He entered and wiped out all our Cloud USMed backup work."

Madison grew enraged.

"And there's more bad news."

"What?"

"Mary Alice walked into the editing room with her sweeper and saw them. One guy knocked her unconscious, gagged her, and tied her up."

"Oh my God—is she—?"

"—she'll be fine. But the doctor told her to stay home for a day or two."

Madison exhaled. "Make sure Mary Alice stays home as long as she wants. Pick up all her medical expenses. Help her any way she needs."

* * *

Still hiding in the small, smelly janitor's closet, Ellie heard her abductors searching nearby stores for her.

"Clear!" they yelled, as they moved from store to store.

Moments ago, she'd found the door's inside bolt-lock at the very top of the door, and manually locked it. She hoped the door required an outside key to release the bolt-lock.

After a few minutes, men mumbled past her janitor door.

"She's gotta come outta one of them stores when they close up," B said.

Footsteps walked close to her door and stopped. Someone rattled her doorknob.

"It's locked," C said. "But I seen it open when I come by early today. How's come it's locked now?"

"Janitor locked it, dumbass!"

Someone rattled the doorknob again.

Can they pop it open?

"She musta run down to the end of this hall. Then she run down the side hall and maybe found a way out to the parking lot."

"You two go check the parking lot," A said. "I'll hang around these stores. See if she comes outta one."

Her heart pounded as she heard two men run off.

She wasn't going anywhere. She'd stay here until the janitor came.

FORTY-ONE

Madison phoned Christine in the Manhattan office.

"How's Mary Alice doing?"

"She's fine," Christine said. "The doctor checked her. Just a sore neck bruise where the thief hit her. And of course, the shock of being attacked."

"I can imagine. Thank God she's' fine. I'll call her later. Did you find any backup copies of the USMed commercials?"

"No. The cabinets where the producer stored backups were also empty. He swears he put backups there. The thieves knew all the places to look."

Madison felt sick. "Who betrayed the agency?"

"No idea yet. But we'll find the person."

"We've got no USMed commercials to run … and they're scheduled to start running in four days. We'll have to cancel our early media schedule. Pay last-minute cancellation penalties. Please connect me to Sophie."

"Hang on."

The phone line clicked a few times and then rang. Sophie Greenberg was Kevin's brilliant Associate Creative Director. Sophie and her teams of copywriters and art directors created award-winning, sometimes humorous, sometimes outrageous, sometimes provocative, but always persuasive advertising for their clients' products.

"Madison—you calling about the disaster?"

"Yes."

"I'll nail the son-of-a-bitch traitor!"

"Please do, Sophie, but first search for anyone who might have made USMed commercial copies."

"I have. No one made final copies yet. We were still fine-tuning the final versions."

"Okay. So start reproducing the commercials."

"I already started."

"Good. How long to remake the commercials from scratch."

"Best case—maybe six days and nights!"

"We've got three days and three nights. Grab all the help you need to get the best commercials ready to run. Use freelance. Pay double-time, Sophie. Whatever! USMed needs this campaign *now!*"

"I'm on it."

They hung up.

Madison leaned back in her chair. It was moments like this when she wished Kevin was here. He always found shortcuts to re-edit and remake commercials quickly.

She phoned him.

He didn't pick up. Still shooting commercials in the Belgium's Ardennes forest. And his voice message box was jammed full.

* * *

In the *Heaven Scent Cigar Shop* back room, Archie Braun phoned Donald Bennett.

"She escaped," Archie said.

"*WHAT?*" Bennett shouted. "*How the fuck—*"

"—she drugged MayMay, stole his key, went down the back stairs into the mall. We thought we cornered her in a hallway but couldn't find her in any stores."

"Did you check all the connecting halls?"

"She wasn't in 'em. Not in the shops neither."

"Did you lean on the salespeople?"

"Leaned hard. Showed our fake cop IDs. The salespeople swear they didn't see Ellie. I believe 'em."

Bennett took a deep breath. "What's our police contact say?"

"She ain't called the cops or showed up at her apartment yet."

"So, she's still hiding in the mall. *Find her!*"

"We're checking. But there's 207 stores. We're even checking women's restrooms."

"Check the men's too."

* * *

In the janitor's closet, Ellie watched the light fade under the door like a slow dimmer. Night had fallen, and moments later the mall turned off its interior hall lights.

Her abductors had taken her phone and watch, but she guessed it was around 10 p.m., maybe mall closing time.

Were the men lurking in the empty halls? Waiting for her to emerge from a shop? If she stepped out on the hall's empty white floor, she'd be as visible as black ink.

She heard heavy shoes clicking along the hallway, coming her way. Was he a janitor?

The janitor would have a phone.

The man walked slower and paused, as though he was looking in a nearby shop window ... or looking for someone.

The footsteps lingered near her door. She held her breath and grabbed her only protection off the floor: a rusty paint scraper.

He rattled her door handle. Not a janitor. He'd know how to unlock it.

She froze.

He rattled it harder.

She held her breath.

Then the footsteps moved on, and she drained the air from her lungs.

She would stay in the locked room. In the morning the janitor would likely show up early, followed by store clerks and salespeople, mall-walkers, early customers. People who could help her. That's when she'd escape.

Suddenly, she heard the same footsteps coming back.

Back toward her door.

FORTY-TWO

Representative Arlene Taylor realized she forgot to wear something to her town hall meeting.

Fire-retardant clothing.

Her Kansas City constituents were ready to burn her at the stake over health care.

They blamed her for relatives who died because they couldn't afford costly life-saving surgical procedures.

They blamed her for monthly prescriptions that cost more than their monthly wages.

They blamed her because one in seven Americans was in debt due to high healthcare costs.

They blamed her for forcing many elderly folks into bankruptcy due to outrageous hospital and prescription costs.

They blamed her because *seven million* Americans lost their health insurance coverage during President Trump's first two years.

They blamed her that 46,000 Americans died last year primarily because they couldn't afford health insurance.

And the blame game went on.

Finally, Arlene took the mic and said, "Is anyone here pleased with America's present healthcare systems? If so, please stand up?"

Slowly, one well-dressed man stood. "I'm a pharmaceutical salesman ..."

"And a thief!" someone shouted.

The crowd booed the salesman back down into his seat.

An attractive, middle-aged Latina woman stood up. "Today's healthcare is a mess ... an overpriced, complex failure for millions of Americans. Let's face it, we don't have months to decipher thousands of changing healthcare plans offering thousands of different options with extremely complicated rules ... and high out-of-pocket costs ... and outrageous drug and hospital prices that cost you four times higher than the rest of the world pays for them. Our government has allowed this to happen and it's a shameful failure."

The crowd cheered the woman loudly.

Congresswoman Taylor couldn't dispute that the angry woman made sense.

After the meeting, Arlene reviewed and rethought everything she'd just heard as she taxied to the Kansas City airport. She thought about how privileged she was to be covered by the Congress's comprehensive, excellent health insurance: The Federal Employees Health Benefits Program. It included a slew of big benefits, lifetime benefits, even after leaving office.

In the airport, waiting to fly back to DC, she made a big decision. She grabbed her phone and Zoomed a meeting with her Congressional staff. She waited until they were all on screen and said ...

"Everyone sitting down?"

"Why?" someone shouted.

"Because I've changed my mind."

"How?"

"I'm voting *for* USMed!"

Their faces froze so long, she thought the Zoom had locked up. Then, three of the five smiled in disbelief or maybe even happiness. Three people applauded.

Hours later, after flying back to DC, she pulled into her garage in residential Washington.

She entered her house, tossed her keys on the kitchen counter, and headed for her study. She realized she'd left her desk drawer open. She never did that.

First time for everything.

Behind her, a floorboard squeaked.

She froze.

Turning, she saw a muscular ski-masked man walking toward her. He pointed a handgun at her.

She held out the wallet for him. "Here take it!"

"Later."

He shot her in the forehead.

She collapsed onto her thick sheepskin Flokati rug.

* * *

Archie Braun felt terrible about Congresswoman Taylor's dark-red blood soaking her Flokati. He loved sheepskin rugs. Had some in his condo. But this one would be forever stained blood red. How sad.

He searched for his Beretta 9 mm shell casing in the three-inch fur but couldn't find it there or in the large patterned Moroccan rug beside it.

Screw it! This gun will be at the bottom of the East River in minutes.

He emptied more drawers, tossed papers and clothes on the floor, pocketed some pricey jewelry, cash, and credit cards from her wallet.

Just another robbery gone bad.

FORTY-THREE

At 8 a.m. in her hotel room, Madison again phoned Kevin in Europe. The phone rang, but he didn't pick up.

She missed him. Missed their time together, missed their mommy-daddy-baby-Mia playtime. Being together, even for a few minutes, always rekindled their relaxed, easy love for each other. She didn't like being away from him or Mia for long periods like this. And Kevin didn't like being away from them. But their jobs required it. Too often.

But good news was coming soon.

In three months, her agency would open an in-house nursery and day-care center for all employees' toddlers. Employees would see much more of their kids, and Kevin and she would see much more of Mia. In addition, employees would have the option of working from home via the internet three days a week.

Meanwhile, Kevin was producing car commercials in Brussels six hours ahead of Manhattan. Or maybe he was still filming them in the Ardennes where he said he was out of cell tower range. Or maybe he was visiting the World War II Ardennes American Cemetery where his grandfather was buried.

She called again and tried to leave him a voice message about the destroyed USMed commercials, but his message box was still full. And her text messages were not answered. She grew more frustrated, because Kevin always seemed to find a way to remake commercials faster than anyone she knew.

But not in a forest four thousand miles away.

He's unreachable.

Like Ellie.

Where is she? Is she in pain?

She already lost her appointment as interim US Senator.

Has she also lost her life?

* * *

A loud metallic screech in the hall jolted Ellie awake. Someone opening a store entrance. She was still trapped in the dark, cramped, stinking closet with a wet mop and a bucket.

She sat up, rubbed her eyes, and noticed faint natural light seeping under the door. Morning had arrived.

Did A, B, and C arrive?

Were they waiting for her to emerge from a store? Were they guarding mall hallways and exits? She had to assume so.

She heard footsteps, men voices mumbling. Maybe shopkeepers heading to open their stores?

Or maybe A, B and C ...

The light under the doorsill brightened. The mall's daytime lights were turned on and she heard other men walking down the hall, sounding like regular guys.

Now or never, she told herself.

She grabbed her paint scraper weapon just in case, unlocked the door, opened it an inch, and peeked out. She saw no one looking at her, just a few store personnel way down at the far end of the hall, hurrying away toward their shops.

She opened the door a bit wider and looked the other direction. Empty.

She stepped out into the hall and hurried down to a nearby restroom, relieved herself, splashed water on her face, and raked fingers through her hair and came out with cobwebs and a dead spider.

She was sure A, B, and C or their thugs were guarding the exits.

She had to call the police, but they'd taken her phone.

She hurried into a nearby Nordstrom. Saw no one. Then finally, she saw a young blonde clerk setting up a new lipstick display in the cosmetics area.

Ellie hurried over to her.

"Please help me. I just escaped from some men chasing me!"

The shocked young woman stared at the area behind Ellie.

"I have to call 911, but they stole my phone. May I use yours a second?"

She paused. "Sure." She handed it to her.

Ellie ducked down and dialed 911. The phone clicked but didn't ring for some damn reason. She quickly dialed Madison's phone. Madison didn't pick up, probably because she didn't recognize the Caller ID.

In a store mirror, Ellie saw a tall man who looked like B walking down the mall hallway behind her. He wore a dark Nationals jacket.

Like the jacket I'm wearing! A dead giveaway. She forgot she was still wearing it, yanked off the jacket, and dropped it in the wastebasket. The clerk stared at it, puzzled.

B was walking toward the Nordstrom entrance.

Ellie ducked down below the counter.

"You all right?" the salesgirl asked.

"Did the tall man in the dark Nationals jacket like the one I just threw away walk by your store?"

The salesgirl looked. "Yes. He's on the escalator heading up to Level Two."

Ellie exhaled and stood up. "Can I please try the call again?"

"Sure."

Ellie dialed, prayed Madison answered, and listened to the rings.

"Hello?"

"Maddy ... it's *Ellie!*"

"Ellie? Where are you?"

"In *The Avenues* mall in the CityCenter area. I hid here overnight. I'm in the Nordstrom makeup department by MAC lipsticks display."

"I'll be there in ten minutes."

FORTY-FOUR

Her heart pounding, Madison jumped from a taxi, rushed into *The Avenues* mall, and hurried toward the Nordstrom store. She entered the store and asked a greeter where the MAC lipstick display was. The woman told her and pointed.

She rushed down two long aisles, turned left, and saw several lipstick and makeup counters. Which one?

Then she saw a young blonde saleswoman, badged Nora, standing behind a MAC lipstick display. But no Ellie. Nora stared at her and Madison hurried over to her.

"Are you Madis—"

"Yes."

Nora nodded toward a dressing room behind her.

Madison thanked her, hurried over to the dressing room door and knocked. "Ellie?"

The door clicked open, and Ellie threw herself into Madison's arms. Madison hugged her trembling friend until they both calmed down.

"Let's get the hell out of here," Ellie said.

"No! Wait!" Madison said, "Detective McCall's sending police to this Nordstrom counter any second! They should be parking outside now."

* * *

"What do you mean you can't find her?" The Guardian shouted into his phone at Donald Bennett.

"She escaped out the back door of the cigar shop and down a long hallway."

"Who the hell guarded her?"

"Your cousin's kid, MayMay."

"MayMay couldn't guard a fucking plant! Where was Archie and his two guys?"

"Busy handling other targets."

The Guardian felt his face flush crimson.

"Why didn't they grab her downstairs?"

"Couldn't find her. Maybe she called someone."

"How? You took her phone."

"Musta borrowed one."

The Guardian fumed at the damage Ellie Nelson could do. She might even be reinstated as Interim Senator. If that happened, they'd again have to offset her USMed vote.

"Is she back home yet?"

"Archie says no. But she's bound to turn up there eventually. We'll grab her there," Bennett said.

"Don't even try. They're guarding her too close."

"So how do we handle her?"

The Guardian closed his eyes. "I'll handle her."

* * *

"I smell like the janitor's mop," Ellie said as she, Madison, and Agent Stanford entered Ellie's apartment.

"Your hair looks like one," Madison said, smiling.

"Shower time!" Ellie said, hurrying to her bathroom.

After showering, Ellie walked into the kitchen where Madison had whipped up Ellie's favorite breakfast of pancakes and strong coffee. She scarfed them down in a minute.

"I feel reincarnated," Ellie said.

Madison smiled, but knew Ellie was still recovering from her terrifying abduction and being held captive. Her left eyebrow looked bruised and Madison wondered if her abductor hit her.

Special Agent Stanford hung up his phone. "Ellie, your FBI bodyguard, Gabriel Allen, will be here any minute. He spent two years on the Presidential security detail, so he knows how to protect people. He'll be assigned to you full time from now on."

"Even when I jog?"

"Yep. Don't try to outrun him. Gabriel's a marathoner. He'll be with you until the USMed vote, and after, if necessary."

"Thank you," she said.

Madison hoped Gabriel eased Ellie's paranoia about her abductors. Ellie told her she feared the men would come after her again.

"Tell me about your abductors," Stanford said.

"Thugs. They enjoyed making threats, taunting. I just hope they don't take it out on poor MayMay, my savant babysitter. I put him to sleep with Ambien so I could escape."

"What's MayMay's last name?"

"I don't know."

"Did you hear the other men's names?"

"No. They only called themselves A, B, and C."

"We'll try to find MayMay and talk to him," Stanford said.

Madison said, "Meanwhile you should tell Governor Wilson you escaped."

"But you said he's already named my replacement."

"Yes, but now *you*—his *first* choice—are free! So you should let him know," Madison said.

"What are the governor's options?" Ellie said.

"No idea," Stanford said.

"Only one way to find out," Madison said.

Ellie nodded, reached for her iPhone and remembered her abductors took it. She grabbed her apartment landline phone and called the Governor's direct office number, which she'd written on the phone-pad a few days ago.

The phone rang several times before it was picked up.

"Governor Wilson's Office ... "

"Renee, this is Ellie Nel—"

"—*Ellie!* My God—are you okay? We've been worr—"

"—I'm fine. I just escaped."

"That's terrific! Let me connect you to the Governor. He just walked in his office."

Ellie heard some clicks, then ... "Ellie, how are you?" Governor Wilson asked, obviously concerned.

"Free at last! And I'm fine, Governor. But clearly my abductors did not approve of me as your interim Senator."

"I'll approve their life sentences!"

"Please do." She smiled.

"But your absence forced me to name a replacement Interim Senator. A man I'm frankly not comfortable with."

"I'll understand if you have to stick with him."

"I'd rather not."

"Why?"

"He's against USMed and other key legislation our state needs. But he was a political compromise."

"So what now?" she asked.

"I'm not sure. These are different circumstances, Ellie. We've never had this two-interim Senators situation before. Do I have to retain Mackey to preserve peace in the legislature ... or can I reinstate you—my first choice?"

"Who knows?"

"My attorneys and legislative advisors, I assume. And maybe the state legislature has a say. We're swimming in unchartered legal water."

"With sharks, I noticed."

"Me too. Please be careful, Ellie."

"I will. But, as you know, I'd be honored to replace my father for the interim and vote for USMed."

"I'm sure he'd be honored, too. As would I. I'll call you as soon as I know more. Do we have your phone number?"

"My abductors took my phone. This is my landline phone at home."

"Okay."

"She gave him the number and they hung up."

"How'd it go?" Madison asked.

"He says it's a unique situation. He'll check things out, but I sensed he'll have to stick with Cyrus Mackey as interim Senator."

"And Cyrus will eliminate your USMed vote."

Ellie nodded.

FORTY-FIVE

"*H*ow?" Madison asked Stanford.

"How what?"

"How the hell does Nervochok enter its victims and not leave a trace on their clothes?"

Agent Stanford shook his head. "No idea. And our weapons-tech people and nerve-agent scientists are also baffled."

"Our techs too," Detective McCall said.

They had to learn precisely how the victims were attacked—so they could warn potential Congress victims to be on guard.

"Maybe Dr. Gorman learned something," Stanford said. "We've scheduled him to Zoom now."

Stanford punched numbers on his iPad ... the screen darkened, then the familiar face of Dr. Gorman wearing his red bowtie popped onto the screen.

"Doctor, can you see us?" Stanford asked.

"Perfectly. And Ellie, I'm greatly relieved to see you back with us!"

"Thank you, Doctor."

Stanford said, "Doctor, we're still trying to learn the killer's Nervochok attack method."

"We are too," Gorman said. "Our question is—how the hell could Nervochok attack all these people in all these diverse locations without leaving any trace of Nervochok on what they were wearing?"

"Any thoughts?" Stanford said.

Dr. Gorman shook his head. "Our current thinking is that someone entered the victim's space earlier, deposited a Nervochok *device*, and left. Then, when the victims entered the rooms, the attacker somehow knew, and remotely activated the device to release the Nervochok."

"What kind of device?" Ellie asked.

"Hard to know. But one that precisely delivered the nerve agent into their respiratory system."

"What about spraying it *on* the skin as they walked by the attacker?" Madison asked.

"Maybe. Enough Nervochok on the skin can seep through to the bloodstream and kill. But again, your medical examiners found no trace on the victims' skin. Is that correct?"

"Correct," Stanford said.

Dr. Gorman said, "So again, we're dealing with some ingenious new delivery system. A new kind of attack. I'm meeting with our weapons experts here at Fort Detrick to look at possibilities."

"What can we do?" Madison said.

"I'd suggest your techs again search each location, this time for a much smaller device. Pencil eraser size. Nose dropper size. Flash drive size. Mouth spray. Perfume spray. Eye drops. Look at all sprays.

"We just did. Found nothing."

"Did you check the surfaces of the papers they were working on? Memos, file pages?" Stanford said.

"Yes. We checked some pages," Dr. Gorman said. "Nervochok can be infused into paper. If the victims hold the paper long enough, or if their fingers are moist enough, the nerve agent is absorbed through the skin into their blood stream."

"Find anything like that?" Stanford said.

"No. No trace of nerve agent on the papers they were working with. No trace on their fingertips."

* * *

"The new *USMed HealthLine* program sounds fabulous," Ellie said to Madison.

"Just what the doctor ordered."

"How will it work?"

"You can contact *USMed HealthLine* via phone, Zoom, Skype, text, or email to ask health questions of a medical doctor, medical assistant, or nurse. The medical expert will listen, diagnose, advise, and if needed, prescribe treatment and have your medications delivered to your home. Focus groups have raved about how quickly they got good medical advice, correct diagnoses, and fast delivery of medications. They also raved that USMed's *HealthLine* costs—next to nothing, and in some cases *nothing!*"

Ellie's apartment phone rang. She picked up.

"Hi Ellie, it's Renee in Governor Wilson's office. Can you talk to him now?"

"Of course."

"Hang on. I'll connect you."

Ellie was certain the Governor was forced to retain his anti-USMed Cyrus Mackey as interim Senator after the *Indianapolis Star* suggested that Mackey might be a better qualified interim Senator because of his vast state legislative experience.

She heard more clicks and buzzes, and then Governor Wilson was on the line.

"Ellie ... ?"

"Yes, Governor."

"I've met with my legal and political advisors. They're all delighted you're okay and doing well."

"Thank you."

"Many want you as our Senator, but many want to retain Cyrus Mackey."

"Must be very difficult decision."

"It's easy."

"Why?"

"I get to decide. Congratulations, Senator Ellie Nelson. Again."

FORTY-SIX

"*Lucky bitch!*" Donald Bennett shouted after learning Ellie was safe at home with Madison Parker, Special Agent Stanford, and Detective McCall.

He also learned that Madison's agency was somehow quickly reproducing the USMed TV commercials that Archie's thugs destroyed. The new ads would be ready soon—maybe even running on TV late tomorrow, persuading Americans to push their legislators to vote for USMed.

"What's Ellie doing?" Bennett asked Archie.

"In her apartment working with McCall and FBI Agent Stanford."

"You're positive MayMay didn't mention your names to her?"

"Positive. MayMay don't know our names. We only called each other A, B, and C."

Bennett's phone dinged. He checked a text message. *"Fuck!"*

"Now what?"

"The Governor of Indiana just reappointed Ellie Nelson as the interim Senator from Indiana."

"What we gonna do?" Archie said.

Donald Bennett paused, rubbed his eyes, tossed a fistful of cashews in his mouth. "We handle her another way."

"Says who?"

"The Guardian. He'll handle this."

* * *

The Guardian stepped from his limo and walked toward the large white Victorian home near the American University. The 1871 mansion had four floors, ornate windows, bright green trim, a second-floor terrace, and a third-floor widow's walk balcony.

The old house was a widow-maker.

He placed his thumb on the door scanner and heard it click open.

He entered and headed down the hall, then into an elevator that lowered him into a large gleaming white subterranean laboratory. He walked past stainless-steel cabinets with biohazard logos and saw several white-masked scientists jackknifed over lab tables, wearing gloves as they worked on devices.

Dimitri, the lead scientist, hurried over and greeted him, as he usually did.

"Are they ready?" the Guardian asked.

Dimitri smiled. "Very, very soon. They're working as quickly as possible. The work is most delicate."

"Not as delicate as our USMed vote count. You must fill my order by tomorrow noon latest. Can you?"

Dimitri stared at his worktables where his five scientists worked on the Guardian's order.

"We're making excellent progress. So yes, I believe we can."

"*I believe* is not good enough," The Guardian said, drilling his dark eyes into Dimitri's ice blue eyes.

"They *must* be ready by noon. No exceptions. If they're not ready, bad things happen."

"Bad things?" Dimitri stepped back.

"ICE bad things. Immigration agents might discover your technicians, and you, are here illegally. They're searching hard for illegals these days. They might even deport your group back to those delightful Siberian winters."

Dimitri blinked, obviously remembering his years freezing in the gulag near Novosibirsk.

"I shall personally deliver your order to you before 10 a.m.!"

"Most excellent, Dimitri!"

The Guardian walked out.

Dimitri rushed over to his fellow scientists.

* * *

Estelle Tompkins loved tidying up Senator Jonathon Nelson's former office. It flooded her with great memories. Of their many enjoyable years working together, their stimulating conversations and meetings, their fun gossiping about weird Congress members. He'd often included her suggestions on legislation and gave her the credit publicly.

She took his Montblanc pen, a gift from the Shelbyville Indiana Lions Club, and placed it in the center drawer beside his USMed phone, a free phone gift from the USMed Promo Group. But an unused phone now.

She called the USMed Promo Group's director to let him know the Senator Nelson's free phone was now available for someone else. The director picked up on the second ring.

"Des Arrington."

"Des, this is Estelle, Senator Nelson's former executive aide."

"Oh yes, Estelle. How are you getting along?"

"Well, better now ... but I really miss the Senator."

"Don't we all. Especially, here at USMed Promo Group. He was our leader, our inspiration."

"He inspired us too. I was Jonathon's executive aide for sixteen years. Such a wonderful, honest man. By the way, I just found Jonathon's USMed phone in his desk. I thought I should send it back to you for someone to use."

"Good idea."

Estelle paused, amazed she hadn't thought of something. "Oh wait! I just remembered. Ellie's phone was stolen by her abductors. She needs a phone and I'm sure she'd love it. Like a memento."

"Terrific idea, Estelle. Just give it to her. We'll make a note here."

"Thank you, Mr. Arrington."

"My pleasure. By the way, Estelle, if you're ever looking for a new position, please let us know. We need someone with your skills."

"Thank you, Mr. Arrington. But for this interim term, I'll be working for Ellie."

FORTY-SEVEN

Madison and Detective McCall followed Special Agent Stanford into an FBI laboratory. A technician had something to show them.

In the lab, Stanford saw his technician, Tomas, holding a straightened paperclip with a bullet casing hanging on the tip.

"We found this shell casing in the bloodstained rug in Congresswoman Arlene Taylor's apartment."

"Any fingerprint match?" McCall asked.

"No. But we got a shell casing match."

"Matched to—?"

"—the bullet that shot Congressman Ethan Anderson in his apartment garage."

"Same gun?" Stanford said.

"Same gun."

"Whose gun?" Madison asked.

"No idea," McCall said.

Stanford said, "So the gun that shot Congressman Anderson, a USMed voter, in his garage also shot and killed Congresswoman Arlene Taylor in her home, just hours after she switched sides to become a USMed voter?"

"That's right."

"Where's the gun?" McCall asked.

"Still looking for it."

"To be used for more shootings maybe."

McCall nodded.

Special Agent Kate Carras hurried into the FBI lab. Madison hoped Kate had discovered *how* the Nervochok attacker attacks.

"Anything new?" Stanford asked her.

"A little," Kate said. "Our newest super-sniffer detector retested the clothes Senator Nelson, and some other victims, wore when they died."

Madison waited.

"And we found a microscopic trace of Nervochok on Senator Nelson's shirt."

"What about Senator Ruskin?" Stanford asked.

"A trace on his sleeve."

"Wendy Shuman?"

"Trace on her blouse."

"Ernest Woodwillow?"

"Trace on his shirt. And LaTisha Darnell had a trace on her blazer lapel."

Madison nodded. "But the elderly lady on the platform said Darnell was standing all alone when she collapsed."

"True," Stanford said. "But maybe she unknowingly sprayed herself a minute earlier."

Kate shook her head. "We checked all victims personal sprayers. No Nervochok."

"So someone sprayed her earlier," Stanford said.

"Not much earlier," Madison said, "The doctors say Nervochok kills within a couple of minutes."

"What about a delayed-action Nervochok?" Stanford said.

"We asked Dr. Gorman. He doesn't know of any delayed-action Nervochok," Kate said.

But someone might have developed one, Madison thought.

* * *

Ellie unbuckled her seat belt after her Delta flight landed at Indianapolis International Airport. She was back home for her swearing-in ceremony. As a special tribute to her father, she'd be sworn in at the Shelby County Courthouse, instead of the State Capitol.

Madison sat beside her.

On Ellie's other side sat her new FBI bodyguard, Gabriel Allen. Early-thirties, six-three, brown hair, powerful build, and eyes as green as Heineken bottles. She was relieved to have his protection.

As they walked off the aircraft, Madison whispered to Ellie, "Your bodyguard is a hunk!"

"But can he type?" Ellie asked.

"Who gives a shit?"

"Not me!" Ellie said, laughing.

Ellie glimpsed a group of passengers a few rows behind her arguing over the upcoming season's Indiana University-Purdue basketball game. Behind them, she saw a man who sort of resembled A, the muscular man who abducted her. But this man wore tinted glasses, a mustache, and his hair was lighter ... or maybe bright lighting made it look lighter.

With Gabriel beside them, Ellie and Madison exited the airport. Ellie looked around but didn't see the muscular guy anywhere.

Ellie, Madison, and Gabriel got into their waiting Suburban and were driven off toward Shelbyville.

* * *

Archie Braun stepped outside the Indianapolis Airport, took off his tinted glasses, and got into the gray Toyota Corolla waiting for him. The driver, a big bald guy named Vlady, followed the Suburban, staying several cars behind his target.

"As you requested," Vlady said, handing Archie a Beretta m9.

Archie had been given a green light to handle Ellie if the right opportunity presented itself. Like in her swearing-in crowds. If he saw the right moment, he'd handle her.

* * *

As Ellie, Gabriel, and Madison drove through Shelbyville, Ellie smiled as she looked out at the original Major Hospital where her dad, Jonathon Nelson, MD, practiced medicine for many years before running for Senate. She had many fond memories of visiting him in his clinic office and their comfortable family home in town. Familiar faces, familiar places. Like always, it felt great to be back home in … *Sweet Home Indiana.*

Minutes later, they pulled into the parking lot next to the Shelby County Courthouse, an impressive, gray stone three-story building. Rows of vans, cars, pickups, and media vehicles surrounded the building.

"Look—you're a star!" Madison said, laughing.

"I'm lucky. I got born to the right dad!"

"But you escaped the bad guys—"

"I had no choice."

"Look! The media biggies are here!" Madison said, pointing.

Ellie was shocked to see the vans from CNN, FOX, NBC, CBS, *The Indianapolis Star, The Shelbyville News,* and some radio stations. She waved to her award-winning journalist pal, Judy Sprengelmeyer, who waved back.

Getting out of their car, she heard police sirens racing toward them. Three black Suburban SUVs roared up to the entrance and parked. The Suburban doors opened and Governor Greg Wilson, his bodyguards, and Renee stepped out.

Ellie walked over and greeted them.

The Governor smiled. "So, Ellie, is it *good to be back home again in Indiana?"*

"No, Governor. It's *great.* And humbling!"

"Then let's go celebrate this great and humbling occasion!"

They entered the courthouse together.

Ellie saw cameras flashing selfies, hands clapping fast as hummingbird wings, iPhone cameras clicking away. People squeezed into the stuffed courtroom lined with the media and locals. Ellie smiled at many long-time friends and former neighbors.

After brief opening remarks by the Governor, he turned it over to the Honorable Judge Louis Kuhn. The Judge smiled at her. His thick glasses turned his eyes into golf balls.

"Let's begin, folks," Judge Kuhn said. "Ellie, please place your right hand on this bible and repeat after me."

The room hushed quiet as a library. Cameras moved in close to her. As he read, she repeated his words …

"I, Eleanor Anne Nelson, solemnly swear that I will support and defend the constitution of the United States against all enemies foreign and domestic … that I will bear true faith and allegiance to the same; that I take this obligation without any mental hesitation or purpose of evasion; and that I will faithfully discharge the duties of this office on which I am about to enter … so help me God."

People applauded. Outside they applauded and cheered as they watched on two large screen televisions.

Judge Kuhn shook her hand, followed by Governor Wilson, Mayor Krebs, and city dignitaries. Neighbors and friends surrounded her with best wishes.

Madison hugged her. "Your dad's applauding this."

"Or wondering what his daughter got herself into," Ellie said.

They headed outside where Madison and she had arranged a tent party for her constituents. She heard a small trio already playing an Indiana classic, *On the Banks of the Wabash,* followed by one of Ellie's all-time favorites—a famous Hoagy Carmichael melody, *Stardust,* written in a Bloomington restaurant-bar."

The ex-cruise ship crooner himself, Governor Wilson, took the microphone and started singing *"Sometimes I wonder how I spend the lonely night … "*

"So's your wife!" someone shouted.

Everyone laughed.

Ellie did too, but then thought of *her* many lonely nights after the love of her life, Liam, died in an IED explosion in Afghanistan. So many lonely nights, so many nightmares.

As she chatted with neighbors, she noticed her new guard, Gabriel, scrutinizing everyone who came close to her, especially the men. None looked like the men who'd abducted her, or the muscular man she'd noticed on her arrival flight.

Then, oddly, at that moment she glimpsed a man with a similar muscular build and height of A far back in the crowd. But wearing different clothes than the guy she saw on the Delta flight.

This muscular guy wore a red *Indiana University* sweatshirt and baseball cap. Then he disappeared in the crowd. Was this another paranoid moment? Would she suspect every man that height and shape?

She noticed that Gabriel was tall and muscular and attractive. She remembered Lawrence Kasdan's terrific film, *The Bodyguard,* in which the main character and her bodyguard developed a romantic relationship.

No way that would happen with Gabriel and her. Hunky Gabriel was probably married or chased around DC by gangs of beauty contest winners.

After the party, Ellie, Madison, and Gabriel climbed back in the black Suburban and were driven back to Indianapolis International Airport. They checked in and headed to the departure gate.

She looked around at her fellow Hoosiers waiting to board. She had immersed herself in their major needs: jobs, healthcare, industry, farming, smarter immigration laws, and equal treatment of women in the workplace. It was a lot to do. And she was eager to do it.

The loudspeaker called her flight. She noticed Gabriel checking the men around her. None looked like her abductors.

As they lined up to board the aircraft, she thought she saw the same muscular man she'd seen at her swearing in, and on their earlier Delta flight. But he was walking away, passing her gate. Again, his build seemed similar to her muscular abductor A, but he was wearing different clothes.

He walked away, toward Baggage Claim and the exits. He wasn't even boarding this plane.

She breathed out.

Stop being so damned paranoid.

* * *

Archie Braun watched Ellie stare briefly at him despite his blond hairpiece and new sunglasses. No way she could recognize him. Still, he'd play it safe.

He continued walking toward the Airport Exit, then ducked into a men's room. He entered a stall, took a blue windbreaker from his carryon and put it on, donned darker sunglasses, and a blue Indianapolis Indians baseball cap.

He came back to the gate, boarded her flight, and walked down the crowded aisle unnoticed by Ellie, who was busy talking to Madison.

He sat a few rows behind her.

FORTY-EIGHT

At Turner Advertising, Mary Alice Grayson rubbed her sore neck where the thief karate-chopped her the other night in the agency's video center. The bruise felt a little better today, and it felt good to be back to work since Madison had just promoted her to manager of cleaning services.

She locked her desk, gathered her purse, and smiled at shy Sam, the cute night security guard, hovering near her department as usual.

"You leaving early?" Sam asked.

"All done. And I don't want to miss my subway train."

"If you can wait fifteen minutes, I'll drive you to your train."

"Thanks, Sam, but if I leave now I might even catch the early train. Saves me twenty-three minutes."

"Next time maybe." He smiled.

"Sounds good." Mary Alice noticed Sam had been extra protective of her since the guy knocked her unconscious. She liked Sam. And he seemed to like her.

But it took a karate chop to my neck to finally get more of cute Sam's attention.

Outside she walked toward her subway station a few blocks away.

* * *

In the dark shadows near Turner Advertising, Jack Miller and Kurt Schick watched Mary Alice Grayson walk outside. Schick worried about her. She had stared at his face too long in the TV Studio and could ID him.

She was the only person who saw him on the computer destroying the USMed commercials. No way he'd let her testify to that.

Schick and Miller began following her.

Silently, they closed the distance to her. Soon they would drag her into an alley ahead.

Then Schick heard footsteps coming up fast behind him.

Schick turned and saw a large security guard hurrying toward them. *What the hell?*

The guard pulled something out of his pocket—a weapon—maybe a handgun or stun gun?

The guard shouted, "Stop where you are!"

Schick saw the dark alley right beside them.

"Fuck this guy!" he said. "Take the alley. Run!"

Mary Alice heard someone shout behind her, then turned around as the two men darted into the alley and ran for their lives.

Sam ran up to Mary Alice, explained that she'd left her neck pain medication on her desk, and handed her the prescription container.

"Oh geez ... thanks, Sam."

"Those two guys acted like they were going to rob you."

"Or worse," she said. "I remember the shorter guy hacked into the computer in our TV studio just before his pal knocked me out the other night."

Sam stared at her a moment, then down the alley where they disappeared.

"Mary Alice, I'll call the police. They're already looking for those two guys."

"Please do."

"Then I think it's safer if I drive you home. My car is across the street. Billy will cover for me at the agency."

She smiled. "Thank you, Sam."

FORTY-NINE

Madison watched Ellie prioritize her Senate legislation. She'd stacked file folders on her desk, on two card tables, and along the floor. Despite the stacks, Ellie always knew exactly where to find the subject she wanted in the stacks, often quicker than online. In college, Ellie could digest mountains of information a couple of hours before an exam and ace it. Madison wasn't so gifted.

Madison's phone rang: Kevin calling from Europe.

"Where are you?" she said, comforted and relieved to finally hear his voice.

"Brussels. Sorry about not calling sooner, but we were filming in the Ardennes forest. No cell tower near us."

"I figured that."

"But there's good news," he said.

"You found the Nazi stolen gold in the Ardennes?"

"Even better. We've found a way remake most of the USMed TV commercials and promotional materials destroyed by those agency thieves."

Madison shot her arm in the air. "But I thought the Cloud USMed copies were also destroyed."

"They were. But not the backup copies I stored in my special *Dropbox* folder a few days ago. So we're finishing another set of backup commercials as we speak."

"Incredible! When will the commercials reach the media?"

"Seven hours ahead of our scheduled time slots. So we avoid media cancellations or late penalties."

"Terrific, Kevin!"

"We got lucky. But were the police lucky enough to arrest the two bastards that destroyed our ads?"

"Not yet. They had inside help."

"Any idea who our traitor is?"

"No. But police are interviewing everyone in the audio-visual department who had access to the commercials."

"Good. How's everything else?" he asked.

"Ellie's back."

"I heard! That's great news! Is she okay?"

"Okay enough to be sworn in as interim Senator from Indiana earlier today."

"Great! Congratulate her for me."

"Will do. When are you back home?"

"In three days. Promise."

"Little Mia misses you. Your mommy misses you. And your beautiful wife misses you most."

"I'm awfully missable."

"Let's family-Zoom later. I'll set it up," she said.

Madison hung up and realized she had to rush to another social media meeting. She turned to Ellie.

"I'm off to a USMed briefing. See you later. Maybe we can work on more marketing ideas later."

"Sounds good. I'll be working here," Ellie said.

"You okay to be alone?"

"Alone? What's Hunky Gabriel in the other room? Chopped liver?"

Madison smiled. She was delighted that Ellie didn't consider Hunky Gabriel chopped liver. More like caviar, she hoped.

* * *

Minutes later, someone knocked on Ellie's door.

She checked through the peephole and saw Estelle holding a cardboard box.

Ellie opened the door. "More of dad's stuff?"

"Yep. His office files, mementoes, knickknacks." She walked in and placed the box on a nearby table.

"Thanks, Estelle."

"Thought you might like to go through these. I'm sure he'd want you to have some."

"Like what?"

"His daily agenda. It tells you what he was working on last, and who he was working with. Plus his address book. And his overall strategic plan for USMed. He spent the most time on that."

"Then so will I."

"But I left his office photos on the walls. Family shots, some of him with Obama and George Bush, Reagan and even John Kennedy. I figured you might want to keep them there."

"You're right. Do you have his contact lists ... the people he contacted most often?"

"Yes. Here are the people he phoned most. And his USMed phone. It's yours now. Donated to you by the USMed-Promo Group."

"That really helps. My abductors took my phone."

"You ready to move into his office?" Estelle asked.

"In a couple days."

"I'll help you move," Estelle said. "Just give me a list of his furniture to keep in the office."

"His furniture is fine as is, Estelle. I'm only here a few months."

FIFTY

Madison asked the taxi driver to hurry so she could make her USMed social media meeting in fifteen minutes. She worried she was not spending enough time with those campaigns, or for that matter with her other agency clients, mainly because of her concern for Ellie and the mushrooming USMed workload.

Ellie seemed nearly recovered from her horrific abduction. And she was safer thanks to her FBI bodyguard Gabriel watching over her like a papa bear. He was always close by.

The closer the better, Madison thought. Something about the way they looked at each other suggested a relaxed, growing mutual attraction. Madison hoped their attraction heated up as Ellie's chaotic life cooled down.

Madison remembered Ellie's serious past relationship. Three years ago she'd lost the love of her life, a JAG lawyer, Lieutenant Liam Collins, to an Afghanistan roadside IED. Liam's death crushed her, and she fell into a months-long depression that worried Madison and Ellie's dad. Slowly, Ellie grew out of it, and dated a few times. Nice guys. Nothing serious. It was time for *serious*.

She phoned Ellie.

"Ellie, this USMed media meeting might take longer than I thought. I'll call you later."

"Okay. I'll be here working on all this legislative stuff."

"And don't forget—you've got hunky Gabriel Allen just outside the door to protect you. Who knows—he might even take you to lunch."

Ellie smiled. "You're Matchmaker Maddy now?"

"If not me, who?"

"Thanks, mom," Ellie said.

* * *

Matchmaker Maddy! Ellie smiled.

Maybe she's right. Maybe I've been afraid of a serious relationship for too long. And maybe I can't handle another devastating loss like Liam. And maybe I can't handle nightmares with his exploding body parts splattering me.

On the other hand, I should start dating again.

She'd had a few dates with two attorneys she'd worked with. Pleasant, smart guys, but lacking Liam's easy charm and sense of humor.

She watched Gabriel walk by in the hall. He turned and smiled at her. His smile could melt a polar ice cap. He watched over her, scrutinizing anyone who came near her with his emerald eyes.

Maybe Maddy was right ... he is seriously dreamy!

Her phone rang.

"Hi Estelle, what's up?"

"I found more of your father's USMed notes. Would you like them?"

"Absolutely."

"I'll email them. And send a thumb drive of his contacts address book."

"Thanks, Estelle."

They hung up.

Someone knocked on the door. It opened and Gabriel looked in. "Ellie, would you like me to pick up lunch from Nate's Deli down the street?"

She realized she was hungry and had nothing fresh in the fridge thanks to her abduction.

"That sounds terrific. I'd love Nate's Chicken Caesar sandwich."

"Hail Caesar!" he said, smiling his smile, as he headed out.

Ten minutes later, Gabriel opened the door, and placed her chicken Caesar sandwich on the corner of her desk.

"Thanks, Gabriel."

"Any time."

As he started to walk away, she gestured toward her desk.

"*Mi desk es tu desk,*" she said. "Please chow down here if you like."

"I like."

He smiled, sat at the desk, and they began eating.

"So Gabriel, are you stationed here in DC?"

"FBI Headquarters."

"How long have you been a Special Agent?"

"Four years now."

"Are you from DC?"

"Michigan. But I graduated here in DC at American University. Then from Michigan Law School."

"We're Midwest neighbors. I graduated from Indiana Law School. So here we are, two Midwest lawyers having a fabulous Nate's Deli lunch in DC. Shouldn't we be chasing ambulances?"

"Absolutely. But I'd rather be chasing bad guys. Especially yours. You were lucky to escape them."

"Damn lucky," she said.

"I feel lucky, too," he said.

"Why?"

"Because I'm dining with Indiana's first woman Senator!"

She smiled. "Speaking of lucky, who's the lucky lady?" she said, pointing at the gold ring on his ring finger.

"My daddy."

She laughed.

"Dad left me the ring when he passed away. Two weeks ago, I slipped it on just to see how it looked. Couldn't get it off. That afternoon, playing football, I sprained the finger. It's still too swollen to pull the ring off."

"Sorry about your finger." *Delighted you're single.*

"So, Ellie, do you feel safe back home?"

"Much safer. Thanks to you and your fellow agents. But every now and then I see a man who reminds me of one of my abductors. The short, muscular man they called A."

Gabriel locked eyes on hers.

"*When* did you see this A guy?"

"As we got off the plane in Indianapolis. The guy was behind us. But he looked different."

Gabriel looked concerned. "Please mention anyone who looks even remotely similar or suspicious to you."

"Okay. But I'm Little Miss Paranoid these days."

"A little paranoia helps. Describe the guy to me and we can try to get video of him in the plane's passenger-cabin."

She gave him a general description. "I'm probably mistaken."

"Still, airport security CCTV might capture his face. Give us a better view. Maybe even a face-recognition name."

She nodded.

"There was another man, my babysitter, who sat with me in the cigar store's back room. A nice large man, and a savant. His name was MayMay."

"Spelled like the month?"

"I assume so."

"We've already interviewed the store manager of the *Heaven Scent Cigar Shoppe.* The back room is rented online to a firm in the Bahamas. The manager doesn't know who. He didn't even know you were in the back room."

"I never saw the manager."

"We'll check out MayMay. Maybe he knows the man called A's name."

"Go easy on MayMay. He's innocent in all this. He's a big, gentle, and sensitive guy."

"Like me?"

"You minus seventy pounds," Ellie said, laughing. It was good to laugh again. Gabriel did that to her. Made her laugh. And he did seem like a big, gentle, sensitive guy.

Except for one thing.

The Sig Sauer bulging under his coat.

FIFTY-ONE

Madison sat in her hotel room reviewing a possible new USMed television commercial script for Luxturna, a new drug that could change some children lives forever.

The commercial opens and we see a toddler, a blonde girl running her small fingers over her doll's face. She fingers the hair, fingers the lips, and fingers the eyes, because she can't see them.

Madison read the announcer's words aloud ...

"This is Zoey. She's four. A few months ago, she started losing her sight due to a rare genetic eye disease, IRD. It will blind her for life. Then came a miracle: a new gene therapy, Luxturna. It could *prevent* her blindness. But her poor uninsured single mom couldn't afford the Luxturna treatment price. *$850,000!*

After months of price negotiating, the price was reduced a few hundred thousand dollars. But still far too expensive for Zoey's mom. The day before they finally made Luxturna more affordable, Zoey went blind. The Luxturna cure cost would have been covered by USMed. And Zoey could have *seen* the rest of her life.

"There are *four million young American children* who have no health insurance. And no hope of getting the treatments that would cure their diseases. Many will suffer. Many will die. Please ask your representatives to pass USMed. As someone said, the life you save might be your own."

Madison's phone rang. Christine calling from the agency. "What's up Christine?"

"Another fake news USMed story online. It says the USMed Committee of Ten can terminate patients with no hope of recovery, or if the patient's treatment is too expensive to continue."

"That's a total lie!" Madison said. "There is no USMed Committee of Ten."

"I know. But the YouTube video says there is. People will believe it! Watch this video."

Madison saw a very sick older woman with jaundiced skin lying in a hospital critical care bed.

The announcer says: "This is Angela. She is 82 years old with cancer. Her doctor says she could live for maybe four more years, but her treatment costs $196,000 per month. These ten MDs, the USMed's Committee of Ten, will decide to continue—or stop—Angela's treatment."

The council leader says: "Those who favor terminating Angela's treatment, raise your hands."

Seven hands go up.

Angela's daughters hear the death sentence vote and weep hysterically.

The announcer says: "USMed. Where a Termination Committee decides whether you live or die."

"That's bullshit!" Madison felt enraged. "There is no USMed Termination Treatment Committee! It's a total lie! Get YouTube to remove it!"

"We will. But thousands have already seen it."

FIFTY-TWO

Madison, Ellie, and Agent Tim Stanford worked in FBI Headquarters. Madison hoped Ellie recalled more about the three men who abducted her, and who their boss was.

"They only referred to themselves as "A" … "B" … and "C," Ellie said. "One time C, the small skinny guy, started to call A something like "Arr," but quickly caught himself."

"Any physical marks?"

"B had an eagle tattoo above his left wrist."

"What sizes are the men?"

"A … is maybe five-nine and very muscular. He's the boss. Gave lots of orders. B is maybe six-two, two hundred pounds. C is five-six, skinny, and hunched over."

"Hair?"

"A … has short, buzz-cut brown hair. B, light brown hair. C, long greasy blond hair."

Stanford took notes. "What about the big MayMay guy?"

"Maybe six-seven, two hundred sixty pounds. A savant. Soft-spoken and timid."

Agent Stanford said, "We're trying to track him down."

"Probably only one six-seven savant named MayMay in the country," Madison said.

Ellie nodded, "I assumed MayMay was his nickname."

Madison said, "Maybe short for Maynard, Mayer, Major, Mayfield, Mayhew, or whatever."

Stanford nodded. "We'll run names close to MayMay and see if a name pops up."

Madison had an idea. "At MayMay's huge size, maybe he ordered XXL clothes online. Maybe from Amazon. Maybe Fed Exed, UPS, USPS delivered them to his local address."

"Don't we need a warrant to request his address?" Ellie asked.

"Ellie, this relates to your abduction, a US Senator," Stanford said. "An exception should apply. And we don't need to know *what* was delivered, just his *address*. I know a judge who might issue the warrant fast."

He grabbed his phone and called. Then he pushed the speaker button.

"Your Honor, it's Tim Stanford."

"Tim, what's up?"

Stanford explained what they needed, then hung up.

Four minutes later, Stanford's phone rang, he answered, held up his phone to show the others the judge's approved warrant.

"Let's hope his name is close to MayMay," Madison said. "And he lives in the DC area."

* * *

The Guardian walked into a meeting room in Georgetown where he saw Donald Bennett cramming cashews into his mouth. Crumbs tumbled onto his gray three-thousand-dollar Savile Row suit. The guy was a slob. He was also a brilliant businessman.

"Where's Ellie Nelson now?" The Guardian asked.

"Her apartment," Bennett said. "She's got an FBI bodyguard. Cops are asking mall workers if they saw three guys with her. So far no one has."

"Where's Archie?"

"Watching her apartment."

"What'd she tell the police?"

"Only that the three men called each other A, B, and C. But she never got their names."

The Guardian nodded. "And the cigar shop manager?"

"He never checked the back room. Never does. Knows nothing. Figured we stored more files there, like usual. Didn't know she was even back there."

"What about MayMay? Hard to miss him. Did anyone in the mall identify him?"

"So far no one has. He always came in the back way."

"I'm worried," the Guardian said.

"Why?"

"MayMay remembers everything. The cops may question him."

"They won't find him," Bennett said.

"Why not?"

"Our guys drove him and his mother down to Florida yesterday near Fort Myers. We'll hold them there until things cool down," Bennett said.

The Guardian nodded. "If the Feds find him and he starts talking to the wrong people, cool MayMay down all the way."

"MayMay? *All* the way?"

"Yeah."

"But he's your nephew," Bennett said.

"So what?"

* * *

Madison sipped her third coffee, hoping it would jumpstart her brain. It jumpstarted her nerves instead. She, Ellie, McCall, and

Agent Stanford were still working in the FBI conference room.

Madison's phone rang: Howard, her agency media director, calling.

Howard had once worked for the FBI, tracking felons. The judge warranted Howard to the search for deliveries to someone named MayMay. A limited time search. Maybe Howard had found Amazon deliveries to someone named MayMay at a local address.

She put Howard on speakerphone.

"Any luck with MayMay?" she asked.

"Only one hit."

"Who?"

"Mai Mai, a twelve-year-old Vietnamese girl. We figured MayMay is a nickname so we're still searching Mayor, Major, Maynard, Marian, or whatever. Should have results soon."

They hung up.

Stanford said, "Our FBI team is also searching for large *savants* in the DC area. Checking for savant support groups."

His phone rang: Caller ID said Agent Kate Carras. He punched the speakerphone.

"What's up, Kate?"

"I got a savant with the *family* name Mayo, M A Y O."

"They have a son?"

"Yes."

"Physical description?"

"Six-six or more, over two hundred sixty pounds, light brown hair, the neighbor says."

It's him! Madison thought.

"I'm at his address now."

"You think it's him?"

"I'm *sure* it's him!"

"Why?"

"I'm looking through his door window at his photo on a table. He looks exactly like the huge guy Ellie described."

"Where is he?"

"No idea. Yesterday, the neighbor lady saw two men hurry him and his mom with suitcases into a black SUV."

"What's the son's name?"

"Charles Mayo. His mother's name is Mary Margaret Mayo. But the neighbor says everyone calls the son *MayMay!*"

Madison's hope soared.

"Terrific! Check the airports?" Stanford said.

"They didn't board at Reagan, Dulles, or Baltimore airports."

"Check trains, Uber, Lyft, Greyhound, hotel chains, and Airbnb."

"We are. No luck so far."

"Find him! MayMay might know A, B, and C's names. He might even know the name of their boss ... the bastard behind all these murders."

FIFTY-THREE

INDIANAPOLIS

Back in Indianapolis, Ellie looked out at the faces assembled before her in the packed Indiana Statehouse. As their new Interim Senator, she'd been asked to address the State legislators.

She felt humbled by her new responsibilities. And embarrassed that most attendees in front of her probably knew more about her state's needs than she did. But she was a quick study. She had absorbed mountains of research on the state's goals and would commit herself to achieving them.

As she looked out at the sea of smiling faces, she couldn't help but wonder if A, B, and C were lurking among them, wearing disguises. At first glance, she saw no similar-looking men, but still, it was possible. The event was open to the public.

She was relieved to have Gabriel her bodyguard standing nearby, checking anyone who walked near her. They'd grown close in a short time. She liked learning more about him. She liked having him around. Let's be honest—she liked *him*. But after the USMed vote, she wouldn't require his protection and he'd be reassigned.

She waved to Madison sitting with Ellie's high school friends from Shelbyville.

The clerk smacked the gavel on the podium. The crowd hushed.

The State Speaker, Ms. Georgia Moore, delivered some flattering and humorous stories about Senator-Doctor Jonathon Nelson, and then introduced Ellie.

They applauded warmly as Ellie walked to the podium. She delivered her brief remarks and the audience applauded enthusiastically in all the right spots, suggesting they liked her goals. She felt encouraged. Maybe she could do this job after all. She finished to strong applause.

Several signs read *"Like Father Like Daughter."* Ellie prayed she could live up to her father's high standards.

As she walked toward Gabriel, she saw the Governor and several state dignitaries gathering nearby.

Then incredibly ... behind them ... she glimpsed *B?*

Maybe. But this man had black hair and a beard. Still, the tilt of his head and shoulders, and his tall body shape strongly suggested B.

He was surrounded by people, fifty feet behind the Governor and his bodyguards.

A State Representative asked her a question. She turned and answered him, but when she looked back, the B lookalike had disappeared.

She signaled to Gabriel. He read her concern and hurried over.

"What's wrong?"

"Maybe I saw B."

"Where?"

She pointed. Gabriel spun around, spoke into his wrist device, and unsnapped his shoulder holster.

Ellie said, "He was standing in the thick crowd behind the Governor a few seconds ago. But when I looked back, he'd disappeared."

Gabriel said, "You *think* maybe it was B?"

"Same tall body shape. But this man had black hair, not brown, and a beard. Still, something about his shape, his head, and the way he locked eyes on me. He saw me studying him and turned away."

Gabriel spoke into his wrist radio, "Check the crowd for a man who looks like our suspect B. Over six feet, two hundred pounds, black hair and beard."

Gabriel led her behind a wall. "Ellie, based on your possible sighting, you should avoid the reception outside."

"Why?"

"The reception area is surrounded by too many tall buildings with lots of windows. Sniper perches. We should fly you back to DC *now*. Say you have an important meeting later today. Can a couple of your people stay and handle the reception?"

Ellie wanted to stay and talk with friends, but understood Gabriel's concern.

"Okay. My aide, Norman, can handle the reception and any questions."

Quickly Gabriel and two other agents led her through the rear corridors of the statehouse.

Outside she didn't see the man who looked like B. They hurried her into the waiting Suburban and sped off. Thirty minutes later, they arrived at the airport. She boarded the small jet, thankful it was an FBI aircraft.

She looked out the window and relaxed ...

... until she saw a tall B-shaped mechanic walk toward their aircraft.

FIFTY-FOUR

Feeling like a lottery winner, sixty-two-year-old Lucinda Jefferson sat in her Rayburn Building office, sipping delicious Dunkin Doughnuts coffee. So much tastier than the watery coffee her parents could afford.

She'd been elected as Mississippi's first Black Congresswoman because her constituents loved The Gospel According to Lucinda. Namely, that USMed would cover *all* Americans: Black, white, yellow, or pokadotted.

Mississippians voted her into office by a large margin despite her opponent's massive television advertising campaign.

As a former Army nurse with decades of treating Gulf War soldiers and Mississippians, Lucinda grew up aware of her state's painfully higher death rates for Blacks, and the highest Black infant mortality rate in the nation: 71% higher for Blacks than for whites' infant deaths. The reason was simple. Many Black parents could not afford insurance. As a result, many sick Black babies didn't get the medical treatment they needed and paid with their lives.

Her phone rang: a fellow Congressman and friend, Lenny Dumont from Georgia.

"You called earlier, Lucinda?"

"Yeah Lenny, I heard the big pharma and healthcare gazillionaires are planning to dump fat donations into your campaign election bucket."

"Hey, I need fat donations to be reelected. You know how the system works!" Lenny said.

"Not anymore."

"Says who?"

"Me. What if some independent Super-PACs matched or beat your big Pharma and healthcare donations, but didn't tell you how to vote?"

"You're dreaming, Lucinda."

"I'll prove I'm not today."

"When?"

"Noon in the cafeteria."

"No bullshit?"

"No BS!" Imagine Lenny, voting how *you* and your constituents want you to vote. *Not* how your special interest donors tell you to vote."

Lenny paused. "You paying for lunch?"

Lucinda smiled, remembering his sweet tooth. "And desert."

"Deal."

They hung up.

Lucinda phone rang. Her sister, Irene. They chatted about their family reunion and hung up.

Lucinda sipped her coffee. Her phone rang again, and she picked up. The caller wasn't there, so she phoned another Congressman and confirmed their finance meeting at 11 a.m.

She drank more coffee and continued reading finance documents.

* * *

Minutes later Lucinda's staff assistant, Harold Smithers, walked into her office.

"Lucinda, don't forget your first meeti—"

Harold froze.

He dropped to the floor where Lucinda Mae lay unconscious. He tried to get her pulse, but couldn't, and began CPR. He grabbed his phone and called the building's medical emergency group.

They arrived within two minutes.

They tried reviving Lucinda.

Six minutes later they turned off their equipment and shook their heads.

Howard collapsed in a chair and wept.

* * *

The Guardian grabbed his burner and called Archie.

"Vote count?"

"We're up two in the House," Archie said.

"Based on?"

"Congresswoman Lucinda Jefferson just suffered a fatal heart attack in her office."

As planned, the Guardian thought.

"We also persuaded a fence-sitter to vote against USMed."

"How?"

"Got his kid admitted to a top Ivy League college with four-year tuition paid."

The Guardian approved. "Still, we need more votes."

"Why?"

"Last minute flip-floppers."

"I'm already working on a couple more votes on our list," Archie said.

"Work faster. And handle one more problem," the Guardian said.

"What?"

"Madison, the advertising woman."

"She don't vote."

"Her commercials persuade Congress members to vote."

"But we destroyed all them USMed commercials in the agency."

"Word is her agency is remaking them. Use leverage on her," the Guardian said.

"Her husband?"

"I think he's still in Europe," the Guardian said.

"Who else?"

"They have a two-year-old daughter."

FIFTY-FIVE

Madison watched Stanford's vibrating phone skid across the polished table like a hockey puck. He grabbed it and hit the speaker button.

"Detective McCall, what's up?" Stanford said.

"Congresswoman Lucinda Jefferson just passed away."

Madison's eyes blurred out of focus. She couldn't believe it. She'd met Lucinda and planned to maybe use her in a USMed commercial.

Minutes later, Madison, McCall, and Stanford rushed into the Rayburn Office Building and hurried down the long hallway to the yellow crime scene tape blocking off Lucinda Jefferson's office. Her aides and staff members mulled about in the hall, many dabbing their eyes.

Stanford, Madison and McCall entered her office. Madison saw white tape marking where Lucinda Mae collapsed on the floor beside her chair.

McCall introduced them to Lucinda's distraught aide. "Harold was the last person to see her alive."

Madison noticed Harold's red, wet eyes. He looked devastated.

"Were you here when she arrived this morning?" Stanford asked.

"Yes," Harold said. "Like always. We said hello. Then, I brought her coffee, her work folders, and today's agenda. She started working on her files."

"Where were you then?"

"Sitting at my desk, right outside her door."

"Was her door shut?"

"Yes. She likes it shut when she's working."

"Visitors?"

"None."

"You're positive no one came into her office during that time."

"Positive. They'd have to pass by me."

Madison looked at the documents on her desk. Most were healthcare studies. Also, a photo of Lucinda with her husband, children, and parents.

"How was her health?" Detective McCall said.

"Good. A little hypertension but controlled."

"Any enemies?" Stanford asked.

"If you're in Congress, you have enemies."

"*Serious* enemies?"

Harold Smith paused. "A couple of racist candidates she beat in her Mississippi primary." He paused and seemed to remember something. "Also, a Nazi white supremacist wacko who threatened to kill her."

Stanford stared hard at Harold. "Who?"

"A guy who changed his name legally to ... Swas Tika. But ... four weeks ago he—"

"—he what?" McCall asked.

"Escaped from the Mississippi State Pen."

★ ★ ★

Three hours later, as Madison expected, the tox report reconfirmed that Congresswoman Lucinda Jefferson died from Nervochok poisoning.

But *how* was she attacked? Harold saw no one enter her office. Did *Harold* kill her? He had no police record and had worked with her for seven years. And Harold was a former Jesuit seminary student. But then so was Stalin.

And Madison knew Harold's tears were real.

Stanford said, "The hallway video confirmed what Harold said. No one entered Lucinda's office during the time she would have been attacked. Only eight people walked down the hall past her office during that time. But Harold did go to the restroom for maybe sixty seconds."

Madison said. "Not enough time for someone to enter her office, Nervochok her, then somehow run down to the CCTV center at the far corner of the basement and edit himself out of the hallway video?"

"Agreed," Stanford said. "So how was she attacked?"

No one answered.

FIFTY-SIX

Stanford's phone rang.

Madison saw caller ID: Agent Kate Carras.

Stanford punched speaker button. "What's up, Kate?"

"I'm back at MayMay's house in DC. The next-door neighbor lady just got a phone call from his mom. She's with MayMay."

"Where are they?"

"In Florida near Fort Myers. She says two men took them and drove them down there. Then locked them in a small house. The two men are guarding them, but she found a throwaway phone in a closet and called. She's terrified."

"Do you have her location?"

"Getting it soon."

"Why were she and MayMay driven to Florida?"

"The men told them it was for their own safety. Which is bullshit. These thugs obviously work with A, B, and C, who paid MayMay to babysit Ellie. MayMay remembers everything. He may have overheard some names. These guys don't want MayMay talking to the FBI. Hang on … "

"What?"

"We just pinpointed Mrs. Mayo's location."

"Where?"

"Buckingham, Florida. Ten miles east of Fort Myers. The phone's at 14174 Oak Mill Drive."

"Be careful—these guys are armed."

"So's our Hostage Rescue Team."

"Good luck. Fly Mrs. Mayo and MayMay back to DC—ASAP. We'll have an agency jet at Fort Myers Airport waiting for them within thirty minutes."

Fifty minutes later, the conference room phone rang and Agent Stanford hit the speaker button.

Agent Bobby Reeves said, "We've got Mrs. Mayo and MayMay! They're still a bit shaken up, but fine."

"Good work, Bobby. Are their abductors coughing up names?"

"Just blood. They died in the shoot-out with our HRT team. We got nothing from them."

Stanford's hope for names sank. "Where are MayMay and Mrs. Mayo now?"

"Ten minutes from Fort Myers airport. The FBI jet is here waiting for them. Should have MayMay in DC in about two and a half hours."

* * *

At Fort Myers International Airport, FBI Agent Reeves and his fellow agent, Olivia Sanchez, watched Mrs. Mayo and MayMay roll their suitcases across the tarmac toward their waiting FBI jet.

Reeves hoped MayMay's phenomenal memory recalled something that could help Agent Stanford's investigation.

As Reeves checked the tarmac, he noticed a yellow-vested baggage handler driving a baggage cart slowly toward the FBI aircraft.

What's he delivering? The only approved luggage were the two suitcases Mrs. Mayo and MayMay were now rolling toward the jet. All other approved cargo was already on board.

Reeves spoke into his sleeve mic.

"Olivia, did you get an order to load additional luggage on MayMay's flight?"

"No. Just the two suitcases they're rolling."

"Then we have a baggage handler approaching the wrong plane. Or maybe a bad actor."

"Where?"

"Behind you at four o'clock."

"I see him," Olivia said. She walked toward the handler approaching the FBI aircraft.

As Olivia got close to his baggage cart, she flashed her badge and ordered the guy to stop the cart.

The guy stopped. Then he looked around as though checking if anyone else was watching him.

Reeves sensed the guy was checking for eyewitnesses. Seeing none, the guy reached in his jacket for something.

Reeves realized that Olivia couldn't see him reaching.

Reeves could, and sprinted toward the baggage handler shouting, *"HANDS UP!"*

The guy saw Reeves running toward him, but his hand dug deeper in his coat.

"Olivia—he's got a gun!"

The guy drew and fired at MayMay who was climbing the stairs to the aircraft. MayMay dropped onto the stairs.

The guy then aimed at Olivia.

Too late.

Olivia's shots ripped into his yellow vest.

Reeves's shots tore into his face and neck.

Blood red splotches spread fast.

The guy collapsed onto the tarmac, trembled a few seconds, then went stone still.

Another FBI agent hustled MayMay, who had only tripped on the stairs, and Mrs. Mayo inside the aircraft and shut the door.

Reeves sprinted over to Olivia and the baggage cart guy.

"You okay?" Reeves asked her.

"Yeah. But that's not." She pointed at the large wrapped package in the baggage carrier's cart.

Olivia had demolitions experience and a missing finger to prove it. She delicately opened the package and studied what was inside.

"Back away everyone! Now!" she said.

Reeves and the others backed up and gave her more room as she began disabling the explosive device inside. Ninety seconds later, she turned to him.

"Ten minutes after takeoff, this package would have blasted a six-foot hole in the aircraft."

Reeves exhaled slowly. He turned to the EM medical team attending to the bleeding baggage carrier. They shook their heads and pronounced him dead.

He called Agent Stanford, updated him, and hung up.

Seconds later, Reeves heard the jet engines whine.

He turned and watched MayMay's FBI jet roar down the runway and soar into a cobalt blue sky.

When he no longer saw the jet, he took a deep breath and relaxed.

FIFTY-SEVEN

"This is outrageous!" Madison said to Ellie as they worked on USMed marketing ideas in Ellie's apartment.

"What?"

"An uninsured low-income woman near Carlstown, New Mexico, had the flu. She went to the only hospital or medical care facility in her rural area. She couldn't afford health insurance, but they gave her a dose of antiviral meds. Minutes later, as she walked out of the ER, they handed her a bill. She recovered from the flu but not from her bill!"

"How much?"

"$6,000."

"For one dose of meds? You're joking!" Ellie said.

"True story. I saw the bill."

Ellie couldn't speak.

"The woman couldn't pay. Her friends warned her that the hospital would garnish her waitress wages or sue her."

"What happened?" Ellie asked.

"The hospital garnished her wages *and* sued her. But after months of haggling, the hospital graciously cut her bill to just $3,000. She still couldn't pay it. Turns out the same hospital sued several thousand low-income and poor patients in her area. People who couldn't afford any insurance."

"That story makes me furious," Ellie said.

"So will this story on YouTube," Madison said. "It says USMed will *assign* a doctor to you that you *have* to use. If you insist on keeping your former doctor, you're required to pay *triple* the cost!"

"Complete lies!" Ellie said. "USMed lets you choose any doctor you want."

"I know, but the story's online—spreading the lie! People will believe it," Madison said.

"Who wrote it?"

"No name. "Fake news liars disappear like-"

"-hit—and-run drivers!" Ellie said.

Her phone rang and she punched the speaker button.

"Agent Stanford. Any luck?"

"Yes. MayMay and his mom will land in DC in twenty minutes. Ellie, it would help if you talked to MayMay. I hear he likes you. See what he remembers about A, B, and C, and maybe the boss who hired them. Can you meet us here in the same FBI conference room in thirty minutes?"

"We're on the way."

✳ ✳ ✳

Forty minutes later, Ellie and Madison hurried into the FBI Conference Room. Ellie saw Agent Stanford sitting at the table with MayMay and an older woman with short brown hair and light-blue eyes, obviously his mother, but a foot shorter and a hundred fifty pounds lighter.

Stanford introduced everyone.

MayMay smiled at Ellie, who smiled back.

Ellie was certain MayMay didn't know the real reason he was hired to babysit her at the *Heaven Scent* Cigar backroom. The men, A, B, and C, had obviously lied to him … probably called her a babysitting job."

"How are you, MayMay?" Ellie said.

"I'm fine. I ate a yummy oatmeal-raisin cookie over there." He pointed at a coffee table. "Now there are eleven cookies left. Do you want one?"

"No. But they look good. Can I ask a few questions?"

"Okay."

"Were the men who drove you and your mom to Florida the same men who asked you to sit with me in the cigar store?"

"Oh no. The men who drove us to Florida are different men. The Florida men were meaner. They wouldn't buy any cookies. Also, they wouldn't let me watch *SpongeBob SquarePants* at ten-thirty. They said the TV didn't work. But it did. It made me very sad."

"I understand. Why did A, B, and C ask you to sit with me at the cigar store?" Ellie asked.

"They told me some bad guys were chasing you. They paid me two hundred dollars to protect you. But I didn't see any bad guys chasing you. Now, I think A, B, and C are the bad guys. They weren't nice to me like you were."

"And you were nice to me, MayMay. Did you hear the real names of A, B, and C?"

"No. But once I saw A's real name when he bought me three juicy cheeseburgers. When he took out his wallet, I saw part of his real name on his driver's license."

Madison and Agent Stanford leaned forward.

"What was his real name?" Ellie asked.

"Archie."

"What was his last name?"

MayMay shrugged. "I couldn't see his last name. It was too far away."

"Did he pay with a credit card?"

"No. Cash from his wallet."

"Who told Archie to hire you?"

"I don't know."

Ellie turned to Mrs. Mayo. "Mrs. Mayo, do you have any idea who might have asked Archie to hire MayMay?"

"Sorry. I have absolutely no idea."

"MayMay, let's look at some video near the cigar store. It shows men walking in and out of the store. Maybe you can see the man called A or Archie. Or B and C."

"Okay."

Stanford ran the video. MayMay leaned close to the screen, blinking at the parade of customers walking in and out of the cigar store.

Minutes later, MayMay sat up and pointed. "That's Archie!"

"Yes," Ellie agreed.

MayMay said, "He likes cheeseburgers, too. Look—there's B and C, too. B likes chicken. C only eats peanut butter with mayonnaise on it."

Madison said, "Archie is A?"

MayMay nodded.

Madison noticed how well A, B and C hid their faces from the camera, making it difficult to see facial features. It was impossible to get a good facial shot.

Mrs. Mayo coughed, raised her hand, and said, "I just thought of something. MayMay is a very talented graphic artist. He can sketch anything or anyone he's met. It's like he has photographic memory of faces he's seen."

"Great," Stanford said. "MayMay, will you sketch what A, B, and C looked like?"

"Okay. But my art materials are at home."

"We'll take you there now."

Mrs. Mayo said, "I just thought of something else. I wonder if *this* Archie might possibly be the same Archie who used to do odd jobs for a company run by a former high-school classmate of mine many years ago. I also worked there a while."

"Who was your classmate?" Ellie asked.

"He's a big shot now in the drug industry."

"What's his name?"

"Donald Bennett."

FIFTY-EIGHT

After meeting with MayMay, Agent Stanford called Donald Bennett's office.

Stanford explained who he was, and that they'd like to meet with him as soon as possible.

"Just a moment," his secretary said, "I'll check."

Madison remembered that Donald Bennett was a pharmaceutical CEO, a drug industry heavy breather. He was also a heavy eater. *National Enquirer* wrote that he'd porked up to 311 pounds. He'd been a highly successful CEO at three major pharmaceutical companies thanks to his fail-safe business strategy: reduce staff, reduce benefits, reduce overhead, and reduce executives who disagreed with him. He called it "Thinning the Herd." Worked every time.

Today, he was the silver-haired CEO of Paragon Pharmaceuticals, a highly profitable global drug company.

As such, Madison assumed he'd fight hard to protect those highly profitable drug company profits. Which meant he'd also fight hard to protect America's present thousands of helter-skelter healthcare systems against anything that would organize healthcare into an integrated industry that would reduce their high prices and excessive profits.

Like USMed.

USMed was a game changer. If it became law, his prescription prices would drop like a runaway elevator.

Which meant Donald Bennett would want to replace Ellie's *pro*-USMed vote with an *anti*-USMed vote. To do that, how far would he go? Would he kidnap her? Was he possibly involved with the Nervochok deaths?

Donald Bennett's secretary came back on the line. "Mr. Bennett will meet you at his office now."

*   *   *

Agent Stanford, Ellie, and Madison drove to the world headquarters of Paragon Pharmaceuticals, a major manufacturer of popular medications, including a growing choice of over-prescribed opioid-based painkillers and several over-the-counter drugs. The fifteen-story gray granite structure jutted into DC's blue sky. Sunlight glinted off the large glass windows tinted dark blue.

An impressive building, Madison thought. Built with Paragon's impressive profits.

They stepped into the reception area. Large, colorful paintings of Middle-Ages chemists' shops and famous historical scientists decorated the walls.

As they walked toward the receptionist, they were met by a tall, skinny, black-haired, thirty-something man with a pencil thin mustache and two emerald earrings. His herky-jerky walk reminded Madison of a rooster.

He introduced himself as Cyril, Bennett's personal assistant. He flashed gleaming white veneers and handed them visitor's badges.

"Just follow me," Cyril said, ushering them onto the Bennett's private elevator. "Mr. Bennett awaits you. If you need anything, please just ask me."

His affected accent sounded Downton Abbey-esque.

"Thank you," Stanford said.

They stepped off the elevator into a smaller, but equally lavish lobby. Madison noticed Impressionist originals and signed Miros on the walls. Obviously bought with more Paragon's profits.

Which infuriated Madison.

As they walked into a small conference room, Donald Bennett strolled in from his adjoining office.

"Welcome to Paragon," he said, smiling and shaking hands with them.

Madison was surprised how swiftly he moved his massive weight on tiny, gleaming wingtip shoes. His chubby hands were impeccably manicured.

They sat around a gleaming mahogany table.

"Mr. Bennett," Stanford said, "we learned from a former employee that a man named Archie once did odd jobs for your company."

"Archie?" He paused, seemed to search his memory. "I don't seem to recall any Archie. That's an uncommon name. But it doesn't ring a bell. Why are you interested in this man?"

"A man named Archie is involved in a case we're working on. A case that involves the abduction of Senator Ellie Nelson."

Bennett stared at Ellie.

"Do you think an Archie was involved in that?"

"We know he was."

"Well, sorry about your abduction, but I don't recall any Archie. But then I meet so many people."

"Do you remember someone named MayMay?"

He blinked and seemed to search his memory again. "That name seems to ring a bell."

"His mother worked for you many years ago, and she said you might know anyone who hired MayMay in the past."

"I recall hearing of MayMay years ago, but I, never personally hired him. My people might have. As I seem to recall he's a highly gifted savant, but quite shy when interacting with people."

Stanford nodded. "Do you recall any of your people recently hiring MayMay to watch the Senator this week?"

"No. But years ago I vaguely remember suggesting certain people might consider him for *easy* tasks … years ago. You know, dog walking, gardening, sweeping. Jobs that didn't overwhelm his limited interpersonal capabilities."

"So you have no idea who recently hired MayMay to watch Ellie?"

He shook his head. "Sorry. No idea."

"Could you or Cyril provide me with a list of your people you suggested might hire him in the past?"

"Of course." He punched a button on his phone console. "Cyril …"

Cyril swept into the room.

"Cyril, please give Special Agent Stanford a list of our people we might have suggested in the past to consider a man called MayMay for simple freelance jobs."

"Straightaway, Mr. Bennett." Cyril swirled away like he was on *Dancing with the Stars.*

"May I inquire as to what happened to poor MayMay? Is he okay?" Bennett said.

"Yes."

"Good."

Madison noticed that Stanford paused, as though not wanting to tell Bennett too much. Stanford turned to Ellie and nodded for her to tell her story.

"MayMay sat in a locked room with me. Three other men had placed me in the room against my will. I put Ambien in MayMay's coffee. When he fell asleep, I took his key, unlocked the back door and escaped."

"Good Lord! But I would think MayMay's not capable of guarding someone."

"The three other men were quite capable. They called themselves A, B, and C."

"No names?"

"We're working on those," Stanford said. "As you may know, Ellie is the interim Senator from Indiana, replacing her father."

"Yes. Congratulations, Senator. I read that your previous law firm considers you an excellent attorney."

"Thank you."

"You're welcome. I assume you'll vote for the USMed bill your dad worked so hard for."

"I will. But as a pharmaceutical and healthcare leader, I wondered how you feel about USMed?"

Bennett paused, his hand creeping toward his half empty bowl of cashews. "Well, it may surprise you to hear it from me, but there are certain aspects of USMed that I like."

Madison was surprised and wondered what aspects.

"Like what?"

He paused a moment. "Its simplicity. The ease of dealing with just *one* national healthcare structure. One organization coast to coast, should be a hell of a lot easier than working with thousands of competing managed-healthcare systems constantly changing their plans and coverage and thousands of hospital chains. So many healthcare entities are not always logistically easy for us to deal with."

He reached over, crammed cashews into his mouth, and chewed them. Crumbs fell from his lip to his double chins, then onto his shirt. He reminded her of Jabba the Hut.

"On the other hand, I'm very concerned about the catastrophic impact USMed would have on our drug prices. Our profits will disappear. As a result, our research and development of new life-saving drugs will shrink away."

So will the multi-million-dollar bonuses for pharma CEOs like you, Madison thought.

Cyril appeared at the door holding some papers. "Here are the names you requested. Plus, their work addresses, phone numbers and email addresses."

"Excellent. Thank you, Cyril."

Bennett ran his eyes over the names.

"I hope this helps." Bennett handed Agent Stanford the lists.

"Thank you. If you remember anything, just call me. And I'm sure we'll have further questions." Stanford handed Bennett his card.

"Cyril and I will be available."

In the car, driving back to Ellie's apartment,

Madison said, "Did you see Bennett's eyes shift left—a sign of deception—when he answered certain questions."

"When?" Ellie said.

"Like when he said he'd never personally hired MayMay, and when he said he liked certain aspects of USMed."

"I didn't believe him either," Ellie said.

"Nor did I," Stanford said. "Bennett has billions of drug profits riding on today's present drug and healthcare systems. USMed will terminate his huge profits. Bottom line: he has a tsunami-sized motive to terminate USMed first."

"You think he knows who hired MayMay?" Madison asked.

"Very possibly. I'll bet Archie's name does not show up on the list Cyril gave us."

Ellie scanned the list and nodded. "No Archie on the list!"

"Now, what?" Madison asked.

"We check these names for anyone connected to Archie or MayMay."

FIFTY-NINE

In the FBI conference room, Special Agent Kate Carras coordinated the FBI team phoning Cyril's long list of Paragon people who might have hired MayMay in the past. To help speed things up, Madison and Ellie also made calls.

Madison interviewed six people so far. All seemed truthful that they did not hire a MayMay or know any Archies who maybe suggested they hire MayMay.

She sensed Cyril stuffed useless names on the list to waste their time.

Madison checked her list, then called a Jessica Greenlee, a retired shipping clerk from a Paragon Pharmaceutical subsidiary. Madison asked Greenlee if she ever hired MayMay.

"No."

"Do you know any Archies?"

She paused. "Not personally, but years ago, my fellow worker, Dora, used a freelance guy named Archie over in our distribution security a few times."

Madison grew excited. "What did he look like?"

"Never saw him. He was never inside the office. Dora saw him outside loading trucks. She said he was muscular and had a big tattoo on his arm."

"What kind of tattoo?"

Greene paused. "Hang on, I'll ask Dora."

She put Madison on hold and came back on a minute later.

"Dora says Archie's tattoo was five Aces. All spades. On his left bicep."

"Did she recall Archie's last name?"

"No. He only worked there a couple weeks. They never kept records on pick up day labor."

"Okay thanks, Ms. Greenlee. If Dora remembers anything else about him, please let me know."

"Will do."

Madison turned to Stanford and Ellie and explained what she'd just learned.

Stanford said, "This sounds like the Archie we're looking for."

Madison nodded. "Ellie, did you see his five-aces tattoo?"

"No. He wore long-sleeved shirts all the time."

"Maybe MayMay saw the tattoo." Madison said.

"Let's find out."

Ellie called Mrs. Mayo's house.

MayMay answered.

"Hi MayMay. It's Ellie."

"Hi Ellie … "

"MayMay, did you see a tattoo on Archie's left arm?"

Pause. "Yes."

"What was it?"

"Five aces. All spades."

"Which arm?"

"Left bicep. The five aces had a red flower wrapped around them. A rose."

Ellie raised her arm and high-fived Madison.

"When did you see his tattoo?"

"When we ate lunch at the restaurant. Archie always rolled up his sleeves when he ate."

"This helps a lot. You also said you learned Archie's name when he bought you the cheeseburgers."

"Yes. Three deluxe cheeseburgers in pretzel buns. They were very good."

"How did you see his name?"

"Part of his driver's license."

"Just his first name. Archie?"

"Yes. But now I remember now his last name started with what looked like a *B* ... maybe *Br*."

"Br ... ?"

"Yes. That's all I could see."

"And Archie didn't mention the other two men's names? The names of B and C?"

"No. But C's big belt buckle had two initials—CJ."

"That helps."

"Do you remember anything else?" Ellie asked.

"We ate our cheeseburgers at 1:32 p.m. Sixteen people were in the restaurant. There were two security cameras outside."

"Were they working?"

"Their green lights were on."

"Do you remember the name of the restaurant?"

"Benjamin T. Burgers. 3718 19th Street." He remembered the restaurant's phone number and gave it to them.

"That's excellent, MayMay," Ellie said. "We'll get Benjamin T. Burgers' security videos. Maybe get a better face pictures of Archie, B and C."

"Oh ... I remember something else," MayMay said. "B talked to his girlfriend, Tanya, on the phone." He said, "I gotta work late! So, you gotta buy your own ah ... f-word ... crack."

"But Archie was the boss, right?" Ellie said.

"Uh-huh."

"But once Archie said, "I gotta tell my boss.""

"So Archie has a boss."

"Sounds like it."

"Did he mention the boss's name?"

"No."

"If you remember anything else MayMay, call me."

"I remember something."

"What?"

"Archie hates tomatoes."

SIXTY

In his office, the Guardian's burner phone rang: Bennett calling again.

We just spoke fifteen minutes ago.

The Guardian answered. "Now what?"

"The FBI traced MayMay to *me!*" Bennett sounded panicked. "Special Agent Stanford, Senator Ellie Nelson, and the ad woman, Madison, were just here asking questions."

"About what?"

"Whether anyone here at Paragon asked MayMay to do odd jobs."

"Like what?"

"Like guarding Ellie. I said no one here did. She said three men abducted her."

"She know their names?"

"No. As I told them to, they called themselves A, B, and C."

The Guardian eased air from his lungs.

———

Bennett said, "But I sensed they might know one name."

"Whose?"

"Probably Archie's. Maybe B or C accidentally called him Archie."

"So what are the FBI and cops doing now?"

"They asked me for a list of people we've suggested might have given MayMay simple freelance work in the past."

"And?"

"We gave them a very old, very long list of names. The cops will call and ask them if they hired MayMay. None did."

"Tell me Archie's name is not on that list."

"It's not."

* * *

In the FBI conference room, Ellie sipped coffee as she reviewed CCTV video of the mall hallways. She was still looking for a better view of Archie's face to give the police. Beside her sat Madison and Special Agent Stanford.

Ellie saw no one who resembled Archie.

They then switched to video of men visiting Paragon Headquarters. They wanted to see if Archie met with someone there, specifically CEO Donald Bennett, or maybe Cyril. They watched the main entrance, the parking lot entrance, and two small side entrances that required keys or buzz-ins. So far no visitors resembled Archie.

Ellie checked a small rear entrance door as a man in gray work clothes entered. Not him. Next two men dressed as painters pulled a paint wagon, pushed a door button, and spoke into a call box. The door buzzed open, and they entered.

Minutes later Ellie snapped to full attention. She watched a well-built man stroll toward the door. The right muscular body type, right height, but with a mustache, sunglasses, and a baseball hat. His face was in the shadows. Very hard to see.

But something was very familiar. Then she knew.

"Please replay that man walking to the door," Ellie said.

"Why?"

"His feet."

"What?"

"He walks like Archie ... left foot points at ten o'clock, right foot points at two o'clock."

"Freeze frame!" Agent Stanford said.

The picture froze.

"Close up of face, please."

The camera zoomed in on the face at a bad profile angle.

"That could be him," Ellie said, "if we could erase the mustache, glasses, and hat."

"We sort of can," Stanford said.

The technician tapped in some commands, outlined the hat, glasses, mustache. Then slowly the man's hat, glasses, and mustache pixilated into tiny flakes that floated away, revealing a computer-filled-in face.

Ellie said, "That looks a lot like Archie. Like maybe an eighty percent match."

"That's a high percent," Stanford said.

"His walk is a hundred percent Archie," Ellie said.

"So why is Archie, Ellie's abductor, and a felon, entering Paragon Pharmaceuticals wearing glasses and a mustache?" Madison said.

"Hiding his face to go inside and get his marching orders," Stanford said.

"From whom?" Ellie said.

"Donald Bennett maybe," Madison said.

SIXTY-ONE

After speaking at a pharmaceutical symposium, Donald Bennett walked into his office and stopped in his tracks when he saw Agent Stanford, Ellie, and Madison seated in his outer office.

Madison noticed he looked stunned, then concerned.

"To what do I owe the pleasure of yet another visit?" He flashed his CEO smile and ushered them into his office where he plopped down hard in his chair, whooshing air from the cushion.

"We identified a man of interest," Stanford said.

"Who?"

"A man named Archie. Ellie believes he's one of the men who abducted her."

"That's good news! Where'd you see him?"

"Entering this building."

"*What?*" Bennett sat up straight, looking very concerned.

"He came in a back entrance of your building last Thursday at 11:46 a.m. I recognized his duck-like walk and his face."

"What was he doing here?"

"We thought you might tell us."

"*Me?* I have no idea. Who'd he visit?"

"We don't know. But the hall video shows him heading toward your Building Maintenance Department."

"That direction suggests trade jobs. Maybe someone here used him for freelance work. We hire freelancers on occasion."

Bennett picked up his phone, called his Building Trades Department, and pushed the speaker button.

"Bill, Don Bennett here. I'm here with some FBI people."

"FBI?"

"Yes. Did your people hire a freelance man named Archie about a week ago?"

Long pause. "What's Archie's last name?"

"We don't know."

"Lemme check. Most of our freelance hires are IT people, computer networkers, phone techs, heating and cooling guys."

Madison heard Bill turning pages, then typing on his keyboard.

Moments later. "I've got no record of hiring a man named Archie for any freelance work."

"You're positive?"

"Yep. But let me check for Archies who applied for a *full-time* job."

Madison heard tapping on a keyboard, then heard a file cabinet open and Bill fingering through his files.

"Maybe something here," Bill said. "About five weeks ago a guy named *John Archer* came in looking for possible tech work. We told him we didn't have any open recs in his IT specialty at that time."

"What'd he look like?" Agent Stanford asked.

"Six-one. Forty-five."

"Did he leave his phone number and address?"

"No. He said he'd check back later. But according to this file he never did."

Ellie leaned forward and said, "Did he have a muscular build?"

Bill paused. "Normal build with a big beer belly."

Madison wondered if Bill was making up the description because he *knew* a muscular guy named Archie sometimes worked for Bennett.

Bill's other phone started ringing. "Gotta grab this customer call, Mr. Bennett."

"Thanks Bill," Bennett said.

They hung up.

"We'd like to talk to Bill and his people later," Stanford said. "They might remember something more."

"Sure," Bennett said, looking a bit relieved, but still nervous.

* * *

As soon as Stanford, Ellie, and Madison left his office, Donald Bennett grabbed his burner and called the Guardian.

"The FBI came back!"

"*Again?*" the Guardian said.

"Three minutes ago. They got CCTV video of Archie entering my building through a tradesman's back door."

"But you told him to wear disguises at your place."

"He did. But Ellie still identified him."

"How?"

"Because he walks like a fucking duck!"

The Guardian cursed, then went silent for several seconds. "Archie knows too much."

"He knows *everything!*"

"If they push him hard, he'll reveal everything."

"Archie won't crack."

"Everyone cracks."

"Not if I hide him in Mexico with a new ID and money," Bennett said.

"They'll track him anywhere. They'll tap calls to family back here. His mother. Two sisters. They'll trace him, grab him, extradite him back here. They'll squeeze him until he rats us out to cut a deal."

"I'll give him enough money to stay on the run."

"They'll still catch him."

Bennett knew the Guardian wouldn't change his mind.

"Where is he now?" The Guardian asked.

"In DC."

The Guardian paused. "Bring him in for a new assignment."

"What assignment?"

"His last."

SIXTY-TWO

Donald Bennett phoned Luca Rizzo, his fixer. The Guardian insisted Bennett use Rizzo, a wet-work specialist.

"Watcha need?" Rizzo said.

"Cleanup on aisle one."

"When?"

"Tonight."

Rizzo paused. "Same-day cleanups on aisle one cost double."

"Done."

"Send name, address, specifics to our draft folder."

"It's all there now."

* * *

Luca Rizzo sipped his second Puni Italian malt whiskey in the *Goal Line Bar* on 7th Street in a DC restaurant area.

Luca was pissed off. The bar was so noisy, he could barely hear his favorite soap, *Days of Our Lives*, streaming on his phone. He loved

Days, especially the star, sexy Chloe Lane. He'd go introduce himself to her someday soon. Women loved his dark eyes and wavy hair almost as much as his kinky talents in the sack.

Time to work, he realized, as the man a few barstools over slapped money on the bar and walked out.

Luca turned off *Days,* placed cash on his tab, and followed the guy outside.

On the street, Luca watched him walk toward his luxury condo in the nearby loft district. Luca was relieved the guy didn't hire a teenage hooker near the bar, like Bennett said the man often did. A hooker would complicate things.

Luca scanned the street. No witnesses. No cop cars. No bright streetlights. The alley he'd checked out earlier was just a hundred yards ahead. A dark alley. Luca liked working in dark places.

He reminded himself that this guy was a muscular ex-Marine.

But what this guy doesn't know is that I was an All-State junior college linebacker, six-two, 235 pounds, karate black belt, and oh yeah, I'm packing a Beretta 9-millimeter.

Luca watched the guy pause, light a cigar, puff thick white smoke into the black night, and continue walking. An ambulance sped past, flasher glowing, siren blaring, heading toward Dupont Circle, a central, trendy area with some excellent restaurants Luca liked. Like *Mama Santa's. Maybe I'll chow down there after this cleanup.*

As they approached the alley, Luca closed the distance between him and his prey. The guy was still on his phone, yakking loud, oblivious to Luca inching closer.

A few feet from the alley, the guy hung up, and Luca stuck his Beretta into his backbone.

"Turn into the alley!" he said.

"What the fu—? You know who I am?"

"Yeah. A guy with a Beretta on your spine!"

Luca pushed him into the alley, shoved the gun in harder.

"Stand beside the garbage dumpster."

The guy stood beside it. But his fingers started creeping inside his coat.

"Freeze your fuckin' hands!"

"Just getting my wallet out for you. Cash and cards."

"*FREEZE* your fuckin' hands!"

"You've picked the wrong man."

"Why?" Luca said.

"Cuz I can disarm you in seconds."

Luca almost laughed. "My Beretta'll disarm you in a nanosecond—*Archie!*"

Archie spun around, startled his mugger knew his name. He looked into the Beretta's suppressor.

"Who the fuck are you?"

"A hired hand."

"Who sent you?"

"Your friend."

"Who?"

"The fat one."

Archie seemed to recognize he meant Bennett.

"Why?"

"He says you screwed up bad."

"How?"

"I don't know. And guess what?"

"What?"

"I don't give a fuck!"

"Tell him I'll do better next time."

"This is the next time."

Luca shot Archie between the eyes.

Archie dropped like a sack of hammers, slamming his head against the cast iron dumpster.

Seconds later, Luca heard a motorcycle turn into the alley. He stepped in front of Luca. The Harley driver looked down and saw Archie's shoes sticking out.

"Everything okay with your pal?" The biker asked.

"Shitfaced again. Girlfriend dumped him. Poor guy."

The biker laughed.

Luca laughed with him, then shot him in the temple. *Sorry pal. Wrong place, wrong time. Nothing personal.*

Luca dragged the biker's body beside Archie's and pulled them both out of view behind the dumpster. Then he rolled the big Harley down to the far end of the alley and left it.

He phoned Bennett.

"What?"

"Aisle one is cleaned up."

* * *

"If we squeeze Archie, he'll contact his boss," Agent Stanford said to Madison and Ellie in the FBI conference room.

"Donald Bennett?" Madison said.

"Probably," Stanford said. His phone rang and he pushed the speaker button.

"What's up, Detective."

McCall said, "Newsflash."

Good news maybe? Madison wondered.

"We just located an Archie whose last name starts with Br. Last name: *Braun*."

"Is he talking?"

"Not anymore."

"Why?"

"He's dead. A 9-mm slug between his eyes."

Madison caught her breath.

"Who shot him?" Stanford asked.

"No idea."

"Where'd it happen?"

"An alley near his condo. Also found the body of a biker with him. Looks like the biker interrupted Archie's killer. The two bodies were found by a homeless guy."

"Did you get Archie's phone?"

"No. A homeless guy in the alley didn't have it. And it wasn't in the dumpster. Archie's phone is gone."

"Shooter took it. Or maybe Archie left it at his condo. We should do a search before someone else grabs it there."

Madison feared the shooter probably had the phone.

"We're heading to his condo now," Stanford said. "Let's meet there."

McCall gave them the address.

* * *

"Archie had excellent taste!" Madison was impressed as she, Stanford, and McCall looked around Archie Braun's chichi condo loft near Dupont Circle.

Madison was surprised that a man who yanked out fingernails and shot bullets into kneecaps for a living would surround himself with such serene paintings. She saw Matisse lithographs all coordinated with an eye-pleasing blend of contemporary and antique furniture, nestled on Persian carpets. The bedrooms were also furnished in calming hues and large white sheepskin rugs.

His bookshelves were stuffed with military books: Gulf War, Iraq War, World War II, Korea, Vietnam, Afghanistan, gun catalogs, CSI books, and true-crime mysteries. One wall displayed antique pistols.

His desk drawers were wide open, contents tossed on floors. Cabinets opened, dishes removed, cushions tossed, refrigerator and freezer doors hung open, dripping water on the floor.

"Someone got here first," Stanford said. "Took his computer."

"And everything else that might tell us who Archie reported to," Madison said.

Stanford's phone rang. He picked up, listened, and hung up.

"The police just found Archie's phone stuffed in an old tennis shoe in the dumpster. Homeless guy probably hid it there when he heard cops coming."

"Any callers we know?" Madison said.

"Not so far. Looks like ninety percent of his outgoing calls went to six burners."

"What about his incoming calls?" Stanford asked.

"Mostly from burners. A few from escort services."

"One number must be to Archie's boss?"

"Two other numbers may belong to B and C."

"Can you determine who his burner calls went to?" Madison asked McCall.

"Difficult. Depends on stuff like firewalls. And time."

Time we don't have, Madison thought.

SIXTY-THREE

Ellie and Madison saw Desmond Arrington, the Director of USMed Charities Group, waving at them as he hurried toward them down a long hallway in the Russell Building.

"Congratulations, again, Ellie," he said, with his usual smile.

"Why?"

"You're the only person in history who's been named Senator, then un-named, then re-named Senator twice in the same week."

Ellie and Madison laughed.

"So can I vote twice?" Ellie said.

"Ask Trump!"

They laughed.

"How are you doing, Madison?"

"Learning that politics is crazier than advertising."

He laughed. "By the way, some good news. I just learned Congressman Griffin, who's been undecided, is going to vote for USMed!"

"That's fantastic," Ellie said.

"Yeah. But I'm running late. See you guys later."

He hurried down the hall.

Ellie's aide handed her a document. "I just got the latest annual figure on what America spends per person on healthcare. Guess how much America spends per person?"

"A lot?" Madison said.

"$13,212 per person. All other industrialized countries spend only $3,000. Hell, General Motors spends more on healthcare than on steel!"

"Why? Why do we Americans spend so much more for our health?" Madison asked.

"Because our government doesn't negotiate low prices for us. For healthcare, and prescription drugs, and hospital services like all other industrialized countries do. So *we're* stuck paying the high prices."

Madison nodded. "I just read about an uninsured woman who got *minor* treatment in an Emergency Room. An hour later, as she left, they handed her a bill for $69,000!"

Ellie said, "If you're *un*insured like her, a hospital can charge you what they want. One *insured* man's hernia operation cost $5000. But an *uninsured* man had the exact same hernia surgery by the same surgeon the same day, and the same hospital billed the uninsured man $116,000. He'll be dead before he pays it off ... or dead trying to."

"All is fair in love, war, and medical billing," Madison said.

SIXTY-FOUR

In a seedy part of Baltimore, Donald Bennett entered what looked like its seediest bar. *The Last Gulp.*

He smelled stale beer, greasy fried food, five-buck aftershave, and maybe damp Depends. Large screen TVs showed the new Oriole rookie, Drew Manning, stealing home to win the game.

Customers roared and high-fived each other.

Bennett saw fat guys on barstools flashing butt cleavage, curvy women flaunting boobs, Harley types sporting muscle tattoos, and a bruised-face guy looking like Mike Tyson's punching bag.

No one here would recognize Bennett. The reason he chose *The Last Gulp.*

He sat in small corner booth on cracked, fake-leather cushions with ugly, yellow-stained foam spewing out like vomit. His two-thousand-dollar Ferragamo alligator loafers stuck to something on the floor.

A large pie-faced waitress strolled over and tossed a greasy menu on the table.

"You eatin'?"

Is today's special E.Coli? he considered asking.

"Gentleman Jack, if you got it."

"We got it."

She waddled off toward the long mahogany bar that ran the length of the saloon and moments later brought his Jack Daniels.

The bar door squeaked open and the man he was here to meet walked in.

Congressman Steve Campbell scanned the customers, then walked toward him.

"Welcome back to the wrong side of the tracks, Steve."

"I remember. Took me twenty years to escape to the right side."

Bennett knew it did. "But you could enjoy it a lot more if your present debts weren't crushing you and your family, right?"

Campbell paused, then nodded, and signaled the waitress to bring him what Bennett was drinking.

"I can help you, Steve."

"How?"

"For starters, we'll pay off all your debts."

Campbell blinked in surprise but said nothing.

"Your mortgage. Your past family doctor bills. Your kids' birth bills. Their private school tuition. Your wife's $168,000 hysterectomy surgeries and complications, healthcare costs incurred before you were elected to Congress. Even her parents' old hospital co-pay bills. We'll pay it all off, Steve."

Campbell's eyes widened in disbelief. "Are you serious?"

"Serious as cancer. We'll wipe your debts clean. This fast!" Bennett snapped his fingers.

Campbell stared at Bennett's fingers. He seemed to realize Bennett meant it.

The waitress brought Campbell's whiskey. He chugged half down.

"What would you want me to do?"

"Protect America."

"How?"

"By protecting America's present healthcare system."

"How exactly?"

"By voting against USMed."

Steve Campbell blinked again, "As you know, I've planned to vote *for* USMed mostly because my constituents tell me they can't pay or afford their medical bills."

"But our present system works."

"Only for those who can afford it. Like everyone in Congress. But not for the seventy-five million Americans who can't buy any insurance or have lousy coverage. US citizens spend *far* more on health insurance—yet we rank *last* in health, life expectancy, and infant mortality of all major countries. You've seen the research."

"Fake research," Bennett said.

"Rock-solid research. Several independent studies prove it."

"Focus, Steve. My offer removes all your debt. *All!*"

Campbell said nothing.

"Besides, our poll shows that the USMed bill will not pass the Senate. You'll waste your vote."

Bennett watched Campbell look around the dingy bar, obviously remembering his childhood poverty, his father's abandonment, his mother's despair, his sister's addiction struggles, his own hunger and anger as a young child on the painful side of the tracks.

"If I agreed, when do I get this money?"

"Immediately."

Campbell said nothing.

"One other thing," Bennett said. "Two months ago, Steve, you mentioned you're considering leaving Congress for the private sector."

"I am."

"Then I have even better news."

Campbell waited.

"After you vote *against* USMed ... and after your present term is up, you could announce your intention to leave Congress. Say you're looking for a working environment that lets you spend more time with family."

"That happens to be true."

"Good. Because after you leave Congress, we'll place you in a top executive position at Barker Thomas Greene. Your annual salary would double your Congressional salary, plus you'd get annual and spot bonuses."

Steve blinked, then gulped his drink and scanned the people sitting around them. "Obviously your offer is tempting. But I have to think about it and talk it over with my wife."

Bennett grew concerned. He thought Steve would snap up the big money. "You can't tell her that this offer is contingent on voting against USMed."

"I won't tell her."

"When can you give me an answer?"

"Very soon."

Bennett nodded. "I need to know tomorrow. We've got three other candidates who'd jump at this Barker Thomas Greene position."

"You'll have my decision tomorrow morning."

SIXTY-FIVE

"CNN reports the House just picked up another vote against USMed," Madison said to Ellie in Ellie's home office.

"Who?"

"They didn't say. And the House may start voting on USMed late tomorrow!"

Ellie's phone rang and she punched the speaker button.

"Hi Estelle. What's up?"

"Bad news, Ellie. My grapevine says Congressman Steve Campbell has just flipped—he'll now vote *against* USMed. Somebody got to him."

"Any idea who, Estelle?"

"My source says probably big money pharma and healthcare lobbyists."

"What a surprise," Madison said.

"Yeah. My source plays bridge with Campbell's wife. She said Steve may leave Congress after this term and take a big job in business."

"Where?" Ellie asked.

"A top executive position in Barker Thomas Greene."

Ellie nodded. "Baker Thomas Green is a huge and highly successful law firm. They handle a ton of pharmaceutical, healthcare, and hospital litigation. They also have a stable of high-octane, schmooze-talking lobbyists who hand out big campaign donations."

Madison said. "Does Baker Thomas Green have major healthcare-related clients?"

"Many. One of the biggest is Paragon Pharmaceuticals, headed by our good friend, Donald Bennett."

"Another surprise!" Madison said, once again amazed at how easily special interest corporate money bought Congress members' votes.

"So back to the vote count," Ellie said. "Bottom line, USMed is behind by maybe three or four votes in the House. In the Senate, we're probably two behind."

"With little time to catch up." Madison said.

"When will your television commercials start running?" Ellie asked.

"They started running three hours ago on the major networks, cable, YouTube. With clips on Facebook and Instagram."

"Great! That should help," Ellie said. "I saw the reel earlier. Your commercials are great!"

"Thanks," Madison said, "But let's pray they *work* great. And aren't too little too late."

* * *

Special Agent Stanford and Detective McCall continued searching Archie Braun's condo for anything linking Archie to his boss ... the boss who ordered Archie to abduct Ellie.

So far, they found no names.

Whoever ransacked his condo knew what to take. Gone were his computer, flash drives, USB drives, even decades-old floppy disks.

Gone were his burner phones and iPad. Gone were his office cabinet files. Gone was his trash from garbage cans. *Not* gone were his war and porn videos.

McCall said, "Did we get any names off his burner phone found in the dumpster shoe?"

"Not yet. His encryption is too strong," Stanford said.

"Does this condo have a landline phone?"

"No. He stopped using it six years ago," Stanford said.

"Still," McCall said, "I'll check his landline records back then. Get the caller names."

"Makes sense." Stanford walked into the living room and recognized a very expensive sofa, a three-cushion leather Le Corbusier like his wealthy aunt had. As a kid, he'd found a ten-dollar bill in between the cushions. His aunt let him keep the money.

Why not try again?

Stanford walked over and raked his fingers between Archie's seat cushions, searching for anything that might help. He raked out a woman's silver teardrop earring and a crumpled sticky note with written words.

"What's the note say?" McCall asked.

"Vodka, cigars, steak, wine, ice cream."

"All the important food groups," McCall said.

Stanford smiled and walked over to an expensive white leather Eames chair and ottoman, facing the 80-inch TV screen. Obviously, Archie's TV throne. He stuck his fingers down beside the chair cushion and pulled out a small nail clipper and another crumpled sticky note. He unfolded it and read aloud:

"Archie. Job well done."

The note had a printed phone number.

"Mack, I've got something here."

"What?"

"A "job-well-done" note. The handwriting looks like handwriting I've seen recently."

"Where?"

"I can't recall. But there's a phone number on the note."

"Dial it," McCall said.

Stanford punched in the numbers. It rang once and was picked up.

"This is Cyril. To whom am I speaking?"

Stunned and delighted, Stanford paused. "Special Agent Tim Stanford."

Long pause, deep breath. "Oh … I didn't know you had this number."

"I didn't either until we found it on a crumpled sticky note."

"Where?"

"In Archie Braun's lounge chair."

Cyril sputtered like he'd swallowed acid, then cleared his throat, but said nothing.

"Is Donald Bennett there?"

Pause. "Actually, he's out of the office in meetings."

"Please contact him now. Tell him it's urgent we speak to him *today.*"

Cyril paused. "Of course."

They hung up.

"I just remembered where I saw this large back slanting, big-loop handwriting," McCall said.

"Where?"

"In Donald Bennett's office."

SIXTY-SIX

Madison, Stanford, and McCall entered Paragon Pharmaceuticals and hurried toward Bennett's office.

"Did my list of names help you?" Cyril said in the reception area.

"It helped us eliminate all those names."

"Excellent. So, no one here hired MayMay."

"Actually, the crumpled note in my pocket suggests someone here might have hired him."

Cyril seemed shocked.

Madison saw Bennett's office door was closed.

"He's talking to London. Shouldn't be long. I'm required to ask what you'd like to talk to Mr. Bennett about."

"Just continuing our investigation," Stanford said.

Bennett's office door opened, and his giant pear-shaped body filled the doorway.

"Please, come in," Bennett said.

Cyril ushered them in Bennett's sprawling office, and they sat in the same chairs as before. Bennett plopped into his chair. Cyril perched on his chair near the door with his knees tucked up high like a Notre Dame gargoyle.

Stanford took out the crumpled yellow note.

"We found this note in Archie's condo chair."

Bennett stared at it.

"Archie—a job well done," Stanford read.

Bennett's eyes narrowed on the note.

"We saw this phone number on the note and called it. It's the number for your office."

"Why yes, of course. This number is printed on all my personal yellow notepads like this. I write hundreds of these thank-you notes."

"*Many* hundreds!" Cyril chirped in.

Bennett studied the note. "But part of this note, the part that says *From the Desk of Donald Bennett,* is missing for some reason. Maybe the note was ripped off fast."

"Maybe. But the notepad paper is identical to yours, right?" Stanford said.

"Right."

Madison noticed something else that looked identical. The handwriting on a paper on Bennett's desk had the same backward slant, and same large lower loops as the note.

"And this looks like your handwriting," Stanford said.

Bennett studied the slanted writing and slowly nodded. "It appears to be."

"So you knew this man Archie."

"Apparently so," Donald Bennett said, blinking rapidly. "But I have no idea of what he might have done for us. Again, I write so many thank-you notes, don't I Cyril?"

"Hundreds and hundreds."

"Perhaps he worked in your corporate security," Stanford said.

"No," Cyril said too quickly. "Earlier, I rechecked with our security people to see if an Archie, or Archer, or Archibald ever worked in the security division. None did."

"What about you, Cyril?" Bennett said. "Did you deal directly with an Archie?"

"Oh, heavens no. I'd remember for sure."

Madison watched Cyril's eyes flitter back and forth.

"And do you remember hiring him, Mr. Bennett?"

He shook his head. "Definitely not."

"Yet Archie had your personal thank-you note in your handwriting."

Bennett nodded and shrugged. "Well, it seems clear I wrote him this thank-you note. But for what I have no idea. Probably one our managers asked me to write it. Again, I write so many thank-yous. You understand, Agent, I'm a people-person CEO. Give credit to people where credit's due. They appreciate it. Cyril, why don't you recheck and ask if any one of our fifty-four managers and assistant managers used Archie for a freelance job and asked *me* to send this thank-you note to him."

"I'm on it!" Cyril dashed away like an escapee.

Stanford opened an envelope, took out some 8 x 11 color photos.

"We'd like you to look at some pictures of the man named Archie," Stanford said, sliding the photos over.

Slowly, Bennett took the photos.

"Despite his condition, does he look familiar to you?"

Bennett blinked rapidly as he stared at the very bloody headshots of the very dead Archie. His bloody left eye hung partly out the socket, inches away from a gaping forehead bullet hole that had bled onto his face and neck.

Bennett blinked twice, his chins quivered, then he turned his head away from the gory photo.

Madison wondered if he was shocked more by the bloody injuries or by recognizing his dead employee.

"Sorry, Detective, but I don't recall this most unfortunate man."

Bennett's flushed face suggested otherwise, Madison thought.

"Well, I'll ask you to recheck your people. See if someone here hired him. Let me know who here gave Archie this note. He abducted Senator Ellie Nelson. A major felony."

Bennett nodded. "But surely you don't think my company would have anything to do with that?"

"We know *Archie* had everything to do with that," Stanford said. "And someone here asked you to write Archie a thank you note on your personal notepad paper ... a paper found in Archie's condo."

"But the note must have been written years ago. Got stuck down in the chair cushion like you say."

"Our lab technicians can determine how long ago the ink was written on the paper."

Bennett blinked and eyes seemed to go out of focus. "Should I involve my attorneys?"

"Probably not necessary at this time."

Madison thought it probably was necessary, but obviously Stanford didn't want him lawyering up yet.

"We'll be in touch," Stanford said, standing. "Try to find out who Archie did work for here. Because you wrote him this thank-you note for some reason."

"So it seems," Bennett said.

The group left, got back into Agent Stanford's car, and drove off to FBI Headquarters.

"Did you see his face when he saw Archie's bloody face?" McCall said.

"Like he lost his best hitman," Madison said.

McCall nodded.

"Maybe Bennett's phone records and online communications will establish a link between Archie and Bennett," Madison said.

"We're already working on that warrant," Detective McCall said.

SIXTY-SEVEN

A whiff of warm pasta lured Madison and Ellie into Tosca, a popular restaurant on F Street.

Madison liked the ultra-modern décor, the eye-catching wall art, the white linen tablecloths, and the white-coated waiters zigzagging through tables like NFL running backs. But mostly she liked the mouth-watering aromas of Italian cooking.

She wanted to get Ellie away from the painful memories of her abduction and her father's passing and enjoy a relaxed meal.

Ellie asked, "You hungry?"

"Starving," Madison said. "What are you having?"

"Lasagna," Ellie said.

"What kind?"

"Any kind."

They were ushered to a corner table with a big window facing the street.

Their waiter came and they ordered.

Ellie looked around the nearly full restaurant, then looked out the window, finally looking relaxed and smiling. She had a lot of catch-up smiling to do.

But then her smile collapsed like shattered glass.

She stared at something outside.

"What's wrong?" Madison said.

Pause. "B might be across the street. He was looking at me."

"Where?"

"Near that Walgreen's. He was aiming a long-lens camera at me from a black van. He just drove away."

Madison looked across the street but saw no black van. She wondered if the long-lens camera was a weapon.

"Maybe you're just more aware of men looking at you."

"I have to be."

Madison nodded.

"I'm also a tad more paranoid these days."

"Understandable. But let me know if he comes back."

"I will."

"Maybe we should change tables," Madison said. She looked around and saw all tables were already taken and most customers were eating.

Minutes later, the smiling waiter appeared with Ellie and Madison's veggie lasagnas, salads, and glasses of Pinot Grigio. The first bite made Madison purr. Soon they were laughing about weird college friends like Silvia who collected navel jewelry, and zoology Professor Mason who opened a python petting farm in Tallahassee.

Tosca's food, they agreed, was even better than the reviewers said.

Madison looked around. Most diners looked like lobbyists, government people, and suppliers. Nearby a couple held hands.

"Look at that romantic couple," Madison said.

"Speaking of romantic couples," Ellie said, "how's your cute romantic husband, Kevin?"

"Just back from shooting commercials in France and Belgium. He reproduced all the USMed commercials in record time."

"Great! Did they arrest the men who destroyed them?"

"No. But they've identified them."

"Two career criminals?" Ellie asked.

Madison nodded. "Speaking of criminals, my research revealed this story about an ex-husband, a felon convicted of beating and choking his attorney wife. Her doctor treated her with counseling and Valium. But when she later applied for health insurance, she was rejected."

"Why?"

"Because her ex-husband had beaten and choked her."

"*Wait.* They rejected her because *he* abused her?"

Madison nodded.

"*That's* criminal."

"I agree. But it's legal. Some states still consider spousal abuse a pre-existing condition and deny coverage to the victims."

"Un-fricking-believable!"

Madison said, "So's this *insured* woman's story. She underwent laparoscopic surgery for a growth her gynecologist thought might be ovarian cancer. Her insurance agreed and paid for the $15,000 surgery. But four months later, her insurance changed its mind and sent *her* the $15,000 bill."

"*Why?*"

"Because many years earlier, she had a "dysfunctional uterine bleeding" episode. Her doctor said it was just an early period. The insurance company called it a preexisting condition and denied her claim."

"Don't lots of women have an irregular period at least once?" Ellie said.

"30% do. But she had to pay the bill. Maddening, right?"

"So's insulin," Ellie said. "A weekly dose in Canada costs $21. Same dose in US costs diabetics $450."

Madison nodded. "We may do a commercial about a diabetic woman, Laurie. Over the years, Laurie had to sell her home, her belongings, her car, furniture, and even give away her beloved dog to afford her increasing insulin prices. She calculated for her insulin alone, she will need close to $7 million dollars to keep living until she's seventy—if she pays out of pocket. Welcome to America!"

A nearby table broke into *Happy Birthday* for a young teenage girl who squealed when her mother handed her a new iPhone.

As Madison sipped coffee, Ellie turned, looked across the street, and froze.

"*He's back!* The man in the van! He's aiming the camera toward our window."

Madison panicked and leaned over the table to see out the window. From her angle, she couldn't see what the man held.

"Maybe a camera," Ellie said.

"Back away from the window, Ellie!" Madison feared it might be a weapon.

"Where's Gabriel?"

"Guarding the restaurant entrance."

"I'll go tell him," Madison said."

"Wait—I'm coming."

SIXTY-EIGHT

Margaret Mayo walked into MayMay's room and saw him still sketching something for Special Agent Stanford.

A man's face.

Her savant son's gifted memory recalled much more than numbers. MayMay also had savant *visual* memory: the talent to *draw* anything he'd seen with stunning accuracy. His drawings covered his walls. Magnificent Victorian homes, buildings, DC's National Cathedral, the Lincoln Memorial, the Vietnam Veterans Memorial, a Prague synagogue, his cousin's collie, and his best email friend, a fellow savant named Gavin in Michigan.

She pointed at MayMay's sketch. "Is that one of the men who hired you to watch Ellie?"

"Yes. The man called B." He grabbed a dark-brown pencil and colored in B's eyes.

"What's that?" she pointed to a spot on B's neck.

"A mole. He has another smaller mole on his left wrist."

"Is that C's face?" she pointed to another sketch.

"Yes."

"Your sketches look almost finished."

"Almost."

"Can I call Agent Stanford so he can come see them now?"

"Okay. Will you be with me when he comes?"

"Of course, my son, like always."

* * *

Fifteen minutes later, Stanford and McCall hurried into Mrs. Mayo's house. She led them back to MayMay's room where Stanford saw him sketching on a large art desk.

"So, you're drawing the faces of B and C?" Stanford said.

"And their clothes," MayMay said.

"May we see them?"

"Sure. They're for you."

"Thank you."

Stanford looked at the drawing of B and was amazed at its precise detail. B's eyes, nose, and mouth looked almost photographic. B looked exactly as Ellie described him. The body was tall with an average build. And the clothes were precisely the style and colors she said. MayMay showed him C's sketches. Again, they matched Ellie's description.

"These are terrific, MayMay," Stanford said.

"Thank you."

Stanford took out his iPhone, photographed the B and C sketches, emailed them to Ellie, then phoned her.

Ellie picked up the call as she and Madison walked into the Tosca lobby.

"Ellie," Stanford said, "MayMay just sketched B and C. I've emailed them to you. Take a look?"

"Hang on."

Seconds later, Ellie said, "My God—the sketches are like photos. That's B and C!"

"Great. We'll send them to our people," Stanford said. "We'll also try to run them through our new face-rec software. Maybe get their names."

"And I'll BOLO them to all DC police officers," McCall said.

MayMay said, "I hope the sketches help you and Ellie catch the mean men."

"I'm sure they will, MayMay."

"If you remember anything else about these men, just let us know right away," McCall said.

"Okay." MayMay smiled.

Stanford and McCall left and headed back to FBI headquarters.

"I want MayMay as an FBI sketch artist," Stanford said.

"I saw him first," Detective McCall said, smiling.

"Joint custody maybe?"

* * *

In the Tosca lobby, Madison and Ellie saw Agent Gabriel on the phone. He hung up and walked over to them.

"Good lunch?" he asked.

"Great. Except for an uninvited guest," Ellie said.

Gabriel's eyes narrowed with concern. "Who?"

"I looked out the restaurant window and saw a man in a black van aiming what I thought might be a telescopic camera at me or at Tosca's. He was in shadows but reminded me of B in MayMay's sketch."

"I just saw MayMay's emailed B sketch," Gabriel said. He quickly barked commands into his phone.

"Did you see what the man was wearing?"

"Black sweatshirt, hoodie down."

"Did he realize you saw him?"

"I think so, because he put the long-lens camera down fast and sped away."

"You think it was a long-lens *camera?*"

Ellie paused. "Maybe, maybe not."

"Do you know what brand van?"

"No, but black."

"Two-year-old Toyota Minivan," Madison said. "We just used one in a TV commercial."

"Anyone else in the van?"

"Not that I could see," Ellie said.

Gabriel looked outside. "Wait here while we clear the area outside in case he's waiting for you."

Four minutes later, an FBI Suburban pulled up at the Tosca entrance. The FBI driver signaled Gabriel it was safe to come out.

They hurried out and got into the Suburban.

"Where to?" Gabriel asked.

"My office in the Russell Building."

SIXTY-NINE

Donald Bennett unlocked the lower drawer of his desk and grabbed his ringing burner phone. Caller ID read *Reverend Smith,* his DC police informant.

Bennett answered. "Reverend."

"Detective McCall just ID'ed the two guys MayMay sketched as B and C."

"How?"

"From MayMay's sketches."

Bennett again grew angry that Archie had used MayMay to guard Ellie Nelson.

"Who are they?"

"B is Bucky Turnstead. C is Carmine Barollo. Cops sent out BOLOS on them. Cops have their recent addresses and know the bar they frequent. A beer joint named *Ale Mary's.* Probably collar them within forty-eight hours."

"Fuck!" Bennett squeezed his Montblanc pen so hard he bent the gold clip. "Archie should never have allowed MayMay to work on anything. MayMay's visual recall is as accurate as a Canon Mark IV."

"I saw his drawings. Incredibly precise," Reverend Smith said.

"What if Archie mentioned my name to B and C and MayMay overheard?" Bennett said.

"No indication he did."

"But it's possible. When you have B and C in custody, give them the Last Rites."

The Reverend cleared his throat. "Last Rites costs a lot extra. Like double."

"Amen!" Bennett said, hanging up.

Bennett stared out his massive windows at the panoramic view of Washington DC. The sun reflected off the Capitol Dome, the Washington Monument, and the Lincoln Memorial. Maybe the best view in DC. He'd earned it and enjoyed it for years.

But not for much longer.

The FBI tasted red meat. They were closing in. It was only a matter of time before they connected the dots that led to him ... and even to the Guardian.

Solution: eliminate the dots fast. Destroy all his anti-USMed communication to the Guardian and others *before* the police showed up with a search warrant.

He turned to his iMac and logged into his private numbered account in Caribe Bank on the island of Nevis. He checked his balance and smiled. He then logged onto his three banks in St. Kitts and smiled again. Total bank balances: ninety-seven million dollars. A decent nest egg to live comfortably on. And sheltered from the greedy IRS tax vampires. Plus, his stock holdings were over fifty-three million.

It was time to disappear and enjoy those millions. He'd earned them.

He looked around his Paragon Buildings where he'd spent two decades tripling the size of the company. The company meant nothing to him. Bricks and mortar. He had no emotional attachment to them or the employees. He was only attached to the hefty salary and bonuses the company rightly bestowed on him.

Time to live a little. Reinvent himself. Get the stomach-shrinking surgery. Little nip and tuck. Go on the new miracle beef diet. Lose a ton. Screw beach bimbos. Introduce the new svelte Don Bennett to the world!

He called his pilot, Chuck, and gave him his flight plans. Then he turned to leave, cramming cashews into his mouth as he hustled out the door.

* * *

Ellie and Madison worked in Ellie's Senate office. Ellie sat at her dad's big mahogany desk, Madison at a small side desk.

Madison realized working together helped them both. Ellie learned how to prioritize the major USMed healthcare benefits for all Americans, while Madison learned how to best communicate those benefits to Americans.

But Madison feared the man in the black van was still hunting Ellie … and that any moment the assassin's tiny red target dot might appear on Ellie's forehead like in the movies. Ellie needed protection until after the USMed vote.

Gabriel protection.

Madison saw him walk into the office and over to Ellie's desk.

He said, "No luck yet finding B. Or the black van from the restaurant. We're still checking CCTV on the streets."

Then he paused. "Ellie, we fear the van guy aimed more than a long-lens camera at you. Some rifles can be camouflaged to look like long-lens cameras."

Madison swallowed hard, thinking Ellie may have literally dodged a bullet.

The door opened and Estelle walked in, smiling.

"Desmond Arrington, Director of USMed Promo Group, just called. He got some more PAC money for USMed."

"Terrific!" Ellie said. "We need it. Paragon Pharmaceuticals just gave even bigger donations to some Congress members. We're in a bidding war."

"Against enemies with unlimited funds," Madison said.

SEVENTY

Donald Bennett unlocked the hidden compartment in the massive walk-in closet of his 9,000-square-foot French Provincial mansion in prestigious McLean, Virginia. The sprawling chateau was nestled among nineteen acres of terraced gardens that sloped down to his private spring-fed lake.

He reached into the closet and grabbed his pre-packed suitcase and a leather satchel stuffed with eighty thousand dollars. Pocket money for a few days. He took his three passports, each with a matching set of driver's licenses and credit cards.

He phoned his pilot again.

"My Gulfstream ready?" Bennett asked.

"Wheels up in two hours. Already fueled. Start pre-check soon."

"My flight plan?" Bennett said.

"Filed."

"I'll see you at Reagan in an hour."

They hung up.

Now the hard part, Bennett thought. *Tell the Guardian I'm leaving.* It's the right thing. *My only choice.* Better for him too.

Bennett grabbed his burner and dialed. The Guardian picked up on the first ring.

"What now?"

"Stanford and McCall visited me *again!*"

Long pause. "Why again?"

"They suspect someone here at Paragon hired MayMay to guard Ellie Nelson at the cigar shop."

"Do they suspect *you?*"

"No. Archie."

"But Archie is dead."

"Yeah, but they looked at me like I'm the guy who ordered Archie to abduct Ellie."

The Guardian said nothing.

"They'll get a warrant to search my emails," Bennett said. "See if I ever communicated with Archie. Which I did. See if I hired MayMay in the past. Which I did. See who else I communicated with, like you. Which I did. So I'm deleting every fucking record of all our subject matter and all our communication. They won't know I ever contacted you."

The Guardian paused. "Do they have a search warrant yet?"

"I'm sure they're getting one now."

The Guardian said nothing.

"So I'm leaving the country for a while," Bennett said.

"Makes sense. When?"

"In a few hours."

"First, make me a UBS flash drive of all communications between you and me, and you and Archie. Hand the flash drive to me in the Delta Sky Club at Reagan Airport in an hour."

* * *

The Guardian sat on a bar stool at Delta Sky Club. In the bar mirror he saw Bennett walking up behind him, looking worried. His puffy pink face glowed with sweat after squeezing through thick crowds of travelers.

He waved Bennett into the bar stool beside him. Bennett plopped down, obviously exhausted by the walk through the airport. He scanned the room, probably checking to see if he recognized anyone, then seemed to relax a bit.

"Bartender takes forever," the Guardian said. "I ordered your Glenfiddich." He nodded at the drink in front of Bennett.

"Thanks," Bennett said, wiping sweat from his brow, and stuffing salted almonds in his mouth.

"Where you flying?" the Guardian asked.

"I'll be in Miami for a day. Then in Buenos Aires. Haven't decided my final destination. I'll let you know."

"Use a burner."

"Always."

"You have my USB flash drive?" The Guardian asked.

Bennett pulled out a thumb-sized flash drive from his coat pocket. "This has everything—all our relevant two-way communication, and Archie's. The originals are all deleted. My personal hard drives have also been destroyed."

The Guardian nodded, took the flash drive, examined it briefly, then stuffed it deep in his pants pocket.

"What does the FBI know about the Nervochok deaths?" Bennett asked.

"Only that it kills fast. That's all," the Guardian said. "They can't figure out *how* it gets into the bodies."

"So, we can still use it."

"And will. The doctors think someone *sprays* it in ... but the security cameras don't show anyone get close enough to spray the victims. So the scientists and cops are going apeshit because they can't discover how."

"They'll never fucking discover how," Bennett said.

"Even if they do, they'll never tie it to us. The trail leads to the Russian KGB," the Guardian said. He checked his watch and stood up.

"I've got a meeting at the Capitol. And you've got a plane to catch."

"My Gulfstream leaves when *I* say!" Bennett smiled and sipped his whiskey.

"Be sure to phone me from Buenos Aires. Tell me your final destination. How to contact you," the Guardian said.

Bennett nodded.

They shook hands and the Guardian walked toward the *Delta Sky Club* exit and merged into a gang of rowdy businessmen backed up like a logjam in a clogged river.

He hid behind an alcove wall and looked back at Donald Bennett in the bar. The unfortunate Mr. Bennett. A brilliant businessman. A ruthless cost-cutter and profit builder. And a rock-solid defender of their common goal, protecting the present healthcare/pharma systems at all costs. The perfect partner. For years, he'd done everything well.

Then he let Archie hire MayMay to guard Ellie Nelson. A fatal mistake. Which led the cops to Archie … and then to Bennett … and perhaps eventually to *me,* if I don't eliminate my link to Bennett.

Buenos Aires, or anywhere else, was no escape for Bennett. The police would extradite him back to the States where his lawyers would bargain with the cops to cut a better deal—*for which Bennett would cough up my name in a heartbeat.*

So there's only one final destination for Donald Bennett.

The bar stool he's sitting on.

He turned and watched Bennett. Right on cue, the fat man gulped the rest of his drink.

Thirty seconds later, as expected, Bennett grabbed his chest, slumped forward, and did a hard face-plant on the mahogany bar.

He'd be dead in three minutes.

SEVENTY-ONE

In Ellie's congressional office, she and Madison worked on new social media programs.

Estelle walked in.

"Ellie, you have a visitor."

"Who?"

"Mr. Barrett Leazer from PharmUSA. He has a very important proposal for you."

"Marriage?" Madison said.

"One can hope," Ellie said, laughing.

Estelle smiled. "Mr. Leazer says he'll only take two minutes. And the proposal would achieve a goal your father and you worked very hard for."

"Which goal?"

"He didn't say."

Ellie looked at Madison who shrugged a why-not?

A minute later, Estelle introduced Barrett Leazer to her.

"Well, now. Tall, young, impeccably fitted three-piece-suit ..."

He ran slender fingers through his glossy brown hair and adjusted his squarish, dark-framed designer glasses.

"First of all, congratulations, Senator Nelson."

"Thank you. This is my colleague Madison Parker."

"Nice to meet you both," he said.

"So you have a proposal?" Ellie said.

"Well ... yes, but I was told to share the proposal exclusively with you, Senator."

Leazer smiled at Madison.

"No problem," Madison said. "I have calls to make."

Madison took her phone, walked out of the room, closed the door, then something warned her to leave it open a bit.

Who is this guy? The guy in the black van? Is Leazer a hit man?

No. The Rayburn security guards screened everyone entering the building for weapons.

Still ...

Madison leaned close to the door so she could hear their conversation.

"Senator," Leazer said, "we know how committed you and your father were to stopping the physical abuse of women."

Ellie nodded. "For good reason. One in three women experience physical violence from someone close to them. Each day, twenty thousand women call domestic violence hotlines."

"And that's precisely why we at Pharma-USA would like to offer you a major program to help abused women."

She waited.

"Namely, the establishment of a network chain of ten national shelters for abused and battered women. We'd like to name them *The Nelson Centers*, in your father's memory. First Center in Indiana, of course."

Ellie was stunned. "What a wonderful idea. More abuse shelter centers are urgently needed coast to coast."

"We agree."

"And after your interim term in the Senate ends, we'd actually like *you* to consider heading up the Nelson Centers Corporation. Your litigation experience with abuse cases, your healthcare experience, and your legal expertise are the right stuff for the CEO. All at a very handsome annual salary with bonuses."

The program, the CEO title, and the generous money offer overwhelmed her. She realized the offer might be the perfect career move after her interim Senator job ended.

"I'm honored and flattered, but why me? What would I have to do for this honor? As they say in DC, what's the *quid pro quo?*"

"Well, you might find that a tad uncomfortable." "Why?"

He paused. "We'd like you to reconsider your vote for USMed. We'd like you to vote against it."

Ellie felt like she'd been slapped. Not voting for USMed, or even abstaining, betrayed everything her dad and she had worked for.

"Mr. Leazer, your offer is very flattering. More shelters are badly needed. And yes, dad and I worked hard for more."

Leazer nodded and flashed his perfect white enamel teeth.

"But we worked much harder and longer for USMed. He dedicated his career to USMed. He died for it. And I promised him I'd continue his work. So I—"

"—but our latest vote count suggests USMed will be voted down in the Senate, even *with* your vote for it. So your vote *for* USMed would be wasted." He raised his eyebrows in hope.

Madison wondered if his projected Senate vote count was more accurate than theirs, which had them winning the Senate vote by two votes.

"But even if that happens, Mr. Leazer, I still can't vote against USMed."

"But the Nelson Centers are a sure thing. Your father would be very proud of them. I'm certain."

"He would," she said. But he'd be even more proud of USMed's universal healthcare coverage for all three hundred thirty million American citizens. Bottom line, USMed would save millions more lives than ten abuse shelters would save. So I must vote my heart. *For* USMed."

He looked disappointed. "Is that your final answer?"

"Yes."

"Well, if you change your mind, just contact me at this number."

He handed her a gold-embossed card with his name, title, and phone numbers.

"I will. And who knows, Mr. Leazer, if USMed passes, maybe we'll find a way to fund your abuse shelters."

He nodded but didn't seem convinced.

Leazer shook her hand and left.

Madison came in and smiled.

"You made the right decision."

"You heard?"

"His voice carried like an auctioneer."

Ellie asked, "Do you think his proposal was really about abuse shelters?"

"I think it was mostly about bribing you to vote against USMed."

* * *

"No deal," Barrett Leazer said.

"Why?" the Guardian asked.

"She's carrying out her father's last wish—voting for USMed. She won't budge."

"I assumed it would be a difficult sell. Almost a futile offer. But we had to try."

Leazer nodded. "So we need another way to stop her vote." Leazer said.

"We have one."

"Which is—?"

"—better if you don't know," the Guardian said, hanging up.

One second later, the Guardian's phone rang: an informant. He picked up.

"Another Congressman has turned down our usual generous healthcare donation."

"Why?"

"He accepted an alternative donation from one of the new *pro*-USMed PAC sources. He called it a no-strings-attached donation."

The Guardian grew enraged. Donations from these new well-funded no-strings PACS were jeopardizing pharma and healthcare's long-held financial control over Congress members.

"Anything else?"

"Early this morning, another *anti*-USMed Senator said he might vote *for* USMed."

"Why?"

"Ellie Nelson persuaded him."

The Guardian took a deep breath. His eyes went out of focus, and he hung up. Ellie had to be stopped, specifically for her influence over other voters.

The vote was soon – probably within forty-eight hours.

Trillions of healthcare dollars were at stake. *Trillions!*

To protect that, USMed had to be stopped and destroyed so America's present profitable healthcare systems continued to flourish.

The Guardian decided it was Luca Rizzo time. His work was immaculate. Like his crime scenes. No traces. No fingerprints. No DNA.

The Guardian made the call.

Luca picked up.

"It's me," The Guardian said.

"Talk."

The Guardian gave him the two target names. "Their photos, detailed schedules, and locations are in your draft folder. Your fee will be in your Caracas account within thirty minutes. Each target must be handled in a different way before Congress votes on USMed."

"My pleasure."

SEVENTY-TWO

After her Senate committee meeting, Ellie reviewed the USMed legislation until she felt comfortable with each detail. She then focused on other issues important to her Indiana constituents: increasing jobs in auto and components manufacturing, life sciences, medical devices and pharmaceuticals, truck and bus bodies, information technology, and agribusiness.

She'd met leaders of each industry and promised to help improve their global competitiveness.

She dialed Madison but got bounced into voice mail. She tried to leave a message, but Maddy's voice mail was jammed full.

She stepped into the hall to see if Gabriel was heading back from picking up their lunch. He wasn't. Her staff assistants were also at lunch.

Suddenly, she was alone in the hall.

Scary movie alone.

And then she wasn't alone.

At the far end of the long hallway, a tall man with Mr. B's body shape hurried in her direction. Too far away to recognize his face.

Her lizard brain kicked in again. She rushed back into her outer office, shut the door, and locked it.

Who's paranoid?

But paranoids only have to be right once, she reminded herself.

She phoned Gabriel. No ring. She saw why. Her phone was dead. No power. She rechecked that she'd locked her office door.

She heard the man's footsteps getting closer.

They slowed outside her outer office.

Then stopped.

She withdrew to her inner private office and locked the door.

Her outer office door handle rattled.

* * *

In Stanford's FBI office, he and Madison still tried to identify the boss who ordered Archie Braun to abduct Ellie.

Madison thought Bennett probably did. Archie, B, and C seemed to report up to Bennett. Stanford agreed, but he also suspected Bennett reported to someone. The top guy.

They re-watched a video of a disguised Archie entering Bennett's Paragon building on two earlier occasions. But Paragon records still said no department hired Archie. And they found no direct communication link between Archie and Bennett online. So why did Archie wear the disguise to Paragon? Simple. He didn't want to be recognized.

Madison knew companies occasionally hired thugs like Archie to break legs. And sometimes necks.

Stanford's phone rang. He answered, listened, looked stunned, shook his head, and hung up. He stared at her for several seconds without speaking.

"What?" Madison said.

"Donald Bennett."

"What about him?"

"He's dead!"

Madison's mouth fell open.

"Dropped dead seated at the Delta Sky Club bar in Reagan National Airport! He was chatting with the guy beside him. After the guy left, Bennett watched the bar TV, sipped his drink, munched some nuts. A minute later, he collapsed face down on the bar."

"What happened?"

"Doctors suspect heart attack or stroke. Bennett was a 300-pounder, heavy smoker, heavy drinker, heavy eater, and light exerciser. He was in lousy health. But the tox reports will tell us more."

Madison wondered *if the guy seated beside Bennett at the bar poisoned him?*

"Why do I think he got Nervochoked?" Stanford said.

"Me, too."

"Who was the guy seated beside him?"

"No idea. Maybe Bennett's big boss. The boss who fears we're connecting too many dots from Archie to Bennett. And from Bennett to him."

"Probably an industry contact," she said.

"Bennett's connected to every major industry contact, every heavy breather, every CEO player in the healthcare and drug industry. Literally hundreds. The bartender says he and the guy next to him chatted like good friends. So let's focus on Bennett's close friends."

"Who might be his enemies," Madison said.

"Agreed."

Stanford's phone rang. He answered, listened, shook his head. "That's a surprise. Call me later." He hung up.

"The lab rushed Bennett's preliminary tox test."

"And ... ?"

"Bennett died from cyanide poisoning."

Madison was surprised.

"Cyanide kills fast," Stanford said.

"In his drink maybe?" Madison said.

"Probably."

"By the guy seated beside him?" Madison said.

"Or the bartender. They're reviewing video now."

"Can we watch it?" Madison said.

"In about two minutes."

SEVENTY-THREE

Madison and Stanford watched large screen video of the Reagan Airport Delta Sky Club.

She watched Bennett sit on a bar stool beside a seated man … even though there were many other empty stools. Bennett greeted the man, shook hands, chatted as though he knew him.

The other man had a beard, sunglasses and a *Yankees* baseball hat pulled down in front, yet something about him seemed vaguely familiar to her. But she had no idea what, or who he was, or where she might have seen him, or even *if* she'd seen him.

She watched the two men talk.

"Was Bennett's drink waiting for him when he sat down?" Madison said.

"Let's find out," the technician said.

He rewound the video to when the first man arrived at the bar. He sat down and ordered a drink. He made a couple of phone calls, hung up, then ordered a second drink. The bartender brought him the second drink. Then the man moved the drink over in front of the empty bar seat beside him, the seat where Bennett would soon sit. The man received another phone call, talked briefly, hung up, then he grabbed his newspaper.

"Now watch him," the technician said.

The man raised his newspaper in front of the new second drink. His hand moved behind the newspaper.

"He just did something to that drink," Madison said.

"Just in time," Stanford said. "Look, Bennett's behind him walking toward the bar!"

Madison saw Bennett hurry straight into the bar and plop down on the stool next to the seated man.

"Bennett chats with him," the tech says. "Now watch Bennett."

Bennett takes something small from his coat pocket and hands it to the first man. The man looks at it, nods, and stuffs it in his pocket.

"What was it?" Madison asked.

"Looked like a USB flash drive. A thumb drive. We'll get a close-up later."

The men chat some more, then a minute later, the first guy checks his watch, stands up, shakes Bennett's hand, and walks away.

Bennett watches TV for a couple minutes. He checks his watch, chugs down his drink, puts money down, and starts to stand. But he pauses, wobbles and sits down fast.

"Watch!" the tech said.

Bennett's body froze, then his head slammed down hard on the wood bar.

The bartender ran over apparently shouting, "Is there a doctor here?" He dialed the airport Emergency Medical Unit.

A gray-haired man rushed over to Bennett, checked his pulse, and started CPR. A minute later, the airport Emergency team arrived and worked hard to revive Bennett.

Six minutes later, they shook their heads and pronounced him dead.

"So, who was the guy sitting next to Bennett? The guy that left?" Stanford said.

Madison said, "No idea. But again, something about him seemed oddly familiar. The beard, glasses, and hat are throwing me off."

"Remember where you saw him?"

"No. Maybe Ellie will recognize him."

"Let's get her over here."

"I'll Skype her over to us. It's faster," Madison said.

"Do it!"

Madison Skyped Ellie into their discussion.

"Can you see us?" Madison asked.

"Yes. Fine."

"Here's the video of the man at the *Delta Sky Club* sitting next to Donald Bennett," Stanford said. He held it up to Madison's phone.

"I see it," Ellie said.

"The man seemed vaguely familiar to me," Madison said.

Ellie watched, then paused. "Me, too, kinda. But his hair is wrong."

"It's a hairpiece," Stanford said. "See the stitching above his ear? And why wear dark sunglasses in a dark bar?"

"And why," Madison said, "does the guy meet Bennett in Reagan Airport with hundreds of security cameras and potential witnesses?"

"To stop Bennett from leaving the country," Stanford said. "He planned to fly to Buenos Aires."

Madison nodded. "Where'd the guy who dropped something in his drink go?"

"Let's check the video."

Six minutes later, video showed him walking out of the airport, but wearing a different hat and a blue coat. He got in the back seat of an older gray Chrysler minivan and drove off. The van's license was in a shadow and mostly unreadable, except for a letter A and a number 6.

Stanford said, "We'll see if our Motor Vehicles records people can identify gray Chrysler minivans with the A and 6 in those same positions."

"I sure I've seen this man," Madison said. "but I have no idea where."

* * *

"So who'd want to kill Donald Bennett?" Madison asked Stanford.

"Maybe hundreds of executives he fired," Stanford said.

"Maybe thousands of relatives," Madison said.

"What relatives?" he asked.

"Relatives who lost family members because they couldn't afford Bennett's outrageously high-priced prescription drugs ... drugs that could have saved their relatives' lives – while Bennett awarded himself huge bonesus."

"Bennett also had executive enemies in Paragon," Stanford said.

Madison remembered *her* executive enemy. A woman who tried to have her killed soon after Madison inherited Turner Advertising from her father a few years ago. Madison's friend warned her about the smiling vipers surrounding her, but she didn't take the threat seriously enough. As a result, Madison was almost decapitated by an assassin at a Dutch windmill. Seconds later, the spinning windmill beheaded her assassin.

The door opened and Agent Kate Carras walked in holding a flash drive in her hand. "Here are some key executives who had serious problems with Bennett. His major enemies. All would be happy to see him dead."

Carras loaded the flash drive and opened the document.

"Meet Trevor Gunther, CEO of Kalterburn Pharmaceuticals. Gunther claimed, quite correctly, that Donald Bennett stole Kalterburn's pain-mediation formula and marketed it under the Paragon brand. Gunther sued Bennett but lost. He despises Bennett."

"Meet Seymour Burch, CEO of *Burch Drugs*. He claims Donald Bennett bribed an FDA official to not approve Burch's dementia drug. But the FDA official denied that the bribe occurred. In fact it did. Burch sued Bennett but still lost. Burch swore revenge.

"And lastly, meet Nate Ryan, the CEO of a major pharmaceutical consortium. Bennett hired away six top opioid scientists from Ryan's company. Ryan sued, lost, became so enraged he put up huge billboards with Bennett's picture, and the words: DON BENNETT - OPIOID DRUG LORD.

"What about Bennett's executives *inside* Paragon?" Madison asked.

"Two aggressive EVPs clearly want his job."

"Enough to kill for it?" Madison said.

"Business is war." Carras shrugged.

"Are you checking Bennett's office calls?" Madison asked.

Carras nodded. "Mostly normal business. But his secretary says he used several burner phones for private or personal calls."

"Where are the burners?"

"Missing."

SEVENTY-FOUR

The Guardian answered a call from his Congressional informant.

The informant whispered, "Congressman Scott Sanderson is switching. He'll vote *for* USMed."

"But he got elected by campaigning *against* it. How do you know he's switching?"

"His good friend, a Congressman, told me."

"Why's he switching?"

"His voters tell him they can't afford fast-increasing healthcare prices. Also, he says the new USMed commercials are persuading thousands of them to tell him to vote for it."

Guardian felt his rage burn.

"So what do you want me to do with Sanderson?" the informant said.

"Nothing. I'll take it from here."

They hung up. The Guardian read his file on Sanderson. He knew the guy had a family and kids, had actually met them before. An idea formed in his mind. He made a call and learned more information.

He then took a different burner phone and dialed.

After four rings, Luca Rizzo picked up.

"Yeah?"

"Another Congressman is flipping."

"Who?" Luca said.

"Scott Sanderson, Iowa."

"You want I should do him like I done the last guy?"

"No. We'll use leverage."

"What kind?"

"His ten-year-old daughter, Trish. She attends Capitol Mount School. Take her, then we'll phone the Congressman and explain what he should do if he wants to see his daughter again."

"Where do we grab her?"

The Guardian said, "Where her school bus lets her off. She gets off alone. Walks the last block home. Take her, put her in a van, and drive her to the cabin."

"Who calls her old man?"

"I do," the Guardian said.

"*When* do I take her?"

"This afternoon. She gets out at 3:20."

"I need pictures, name, addresses, details. *FAST!*"

"They're already in your special draft folder."

"She got health problems? Special med needs?"

"No," the Guardian said, not knowing or caring if she did. "Call me when you have Trish."

* * *

Fifth-grader Trish Sanderson smiled at the *A* on her math test. *A's* meant she could go to softball camp this summer.

The Capitol Mount School buzzer rang. She and best friend, Jessica, ran outside and climbed into their school bus. Jessica couldn't stop giggling.

"What's so funny?" Trish asked.

"Mr. Thompson."

"What about him?"

"Snot keeps dripping from his nose onto his history book!"

"Conner and Cody bet money *when* the snot will drop."

"I saw two drops *splash*," Trish said, "but I feel sorry for Mr. Thompson."

"Me too."

"Let's put some Kleenex on his desk."

"Okay."

Minutes later, the bus stopped at Trish's street.

She got off and walked toward her home a block away. Her phone pinged. She saw cousin Nettie texted her.

As she started to text back, a van stopped beside her. A large man jumped out, smiled, and grabbed her. She started to scream, but his giant hand covered her mouth.

He lifted her into the van, another man shut the door, and the van drove off. The van was dark inside, but she saw three big men staring at her.

Trish was terrified. She'd heard what happens to young kids snatched off the streets. The first few hours were the most important for the police to rescue her. After that, her chances were not so good.

But she was a fast runner. Maybe she could escape.

One man grabbed her phone, opened it, took out the small flat battery, and tossed it out the window. Another man grabbed a damp washcloth and put it over her nose and ... seconds later, she felt herself falling asleep.

SEVENTY-FIVE

The Guardian checked his watch. It had been two hours since Luca abducted Scott Sanderson's daughter Trish and driven her to the forest cabin northwest of DC.

Luca told the Guardian she woke up from her chloroform-induced sleep, and was now awake, sitting in a chair.

The Guardian watched Trish in the chair via his CCTV cabin link. She looked frightened, but not hysterical, as she read her schoolbook. He remembered her. Cute kid.

The Guardian grabbed his burner phone, adjusted his ProVoice device to a distorted deep-throated male, and dialed her father, Congressman Scott Sanderson.

The phone rang several times. Obviously, Sanderson was letting it ring, hoping the FBI would trace the call. Wasted time. Tracing this call would lead them to a convent of retired Dominican nuns in Adrian, Michigan.

The call was picked up. "This is Scott Sanderson." The Guardian heard his voice tremble. "Your daughter is beautiful and intelligent."

"Have you hurt her?"

"She's fine."

Sanderson took a breath. "If you hurt her, I will find you and—"

"—you're not in a position to threaten."

"I ... Will ... Find ... You!"

The Guardian paused, impressed by the man's rage.

"I don't have a lot of money," Sanderson said.

"I don't want money."

Sanderson paused. "What *do* you want from me?"

"Your courage."

"For what?"

"To stand up for America."

"How?"

"By voting *against* USMed."

Sanderson paused. "But USMed *is* smarter healthcare for all Americans."

"False argument, Congressman. USMed will destroy our present, smooth-running, highly-efficient healthcare system."

"If it's so efficient, why are so many people declaring bankruptcy because of it?"

"Who cares about them?"

"I do."

"Go right ahead and care. But our little tête-à-tête just ended."

"Why?"

"Because it's time for your big decision."

Sanderson said nothing.

"If you vote *against* USMed, your daughter will be returned within twenty-four hours untouched and in mint condition, and—"

"—suffering post-traumatic stress and nightmares!" Sanderson said.

"She'll get over it. But ... if you vote *for* USMed, your daughter will be placed in one of Bangkok's brothels for people who like kids. Some are disease-ridden. Of course, girls her age, with her blonde hair and blue eyes, are highly desirable. Bottom line, sadly, you'll never see Trish again. Do you understand me, Mr. Sanderson?"

Sanderson whispered a curse under his breath.

"Understand, Congressman?"

"Do you understand—if you do this, or hurt my daughter, I ... will ... find ... you!"

"I'm not concerned."

"You should be."

"It's been fun chatting, Scott, but now it's decision time. Let me know *now*. Vote for USMed, and she's off to Bangkok tonight. You'll never see her again. So ... how will you vote?"

Long pause. Sanderson whispered, "Against."

✱ ✱ ✱

"A Congressman's ten-year-old daughter was kidnapped in DC." Agent Stanford said to Madison and Ellie in the FBI video room.

Madison stopped breathing, thinking how terrified the young schoolgirl and her parents must be.

What if someone kidnapped our little Mia?

Madison's heart slammed against her chest. She'd chatted with Mia hours ago, and as always, hearing her squeaky two-year-old voice brought joy and peace to Madison's soul. Knowing she was with Kevin's mom made the separation so much easier. Still, being far away from her always hurt and always made her feel a little guilty.

"Who's the girl?" Ellie asked.

"Congressman Scott Sanderson's young daughter, Trish."

"Oh God ... " Ellie lowered her head.

"Has he heard from the kidnappers?" Madison asked.

"I don't know."

"Sanderson was for USMed. Has he switched?" Ellie asked.

"No idea."

"Let's find out," Agent Stanford said. He punched the speaker, dialed the number, and it was answered after five rings.

"This is ... Scott ... Sanderson."

His voice hesitated a bit, Madison noticed.

"Congressman, this is Special Agent Tim Stanford with the FBI in DC. A neighbor informed police she believes your daughter was abducted off a street near your home today. Is that correct?"

Long pause, deep breath. "Yes ..."

"We'll do everything to get her home safely to you."

Sanderson said nothing.

"Did you hear from her kidnappers yet?"

Another long pause. "Yes."

"What exactly did they say?"

"They said if we involved the FBI, we'll—"

"—never see your daughter again?" Stanford said.

"That's what they said."

"Their standard threat, Congressman. My phone call to you can't be tapped. They won't even know we're involved."

Sanderson said nothing.

"Did they ask you to pay a ransom?"

"No."

"Did they ask you to *do* something to get your daughter returned safely to you?"

A deep breath. "Yes."

"Did they ask you to vote against USMed?"

Madison knew they did.

Sanderson said nothing. "I'm still considering my vote."

"Congressman, I believe they kidnapped your daughter to *force* you to vote against USMed. The people are ruthless. They've already murdered people to defeat USMed."

Sanderson paused. "I'm still thinking about my vote."

"I promise you, we can *invisibly* monitor their calls to you. And trace them without their knowing it. We can also search for your daughter. We have drones and satellite that might track where they took her after she got off the school bus. We can greatly increase the chances of returning your daughter to you and your wife."

Long pause. "How can I be sure your agents will be completely out of sight?"

"We've done this many times. Successfully."

Congressman Sanderson paused. "I have no choice but to trust you."

"It's the smart thing."

Deep breath. "Please save our daughter and bring her home."

Then he hung up.

Stanford said, "If we don't find his daughter before the vote, he'll vote against USMed ... to save his daughter."

"I would too," Madison said.

She turned and stared out the window at the DC skyline.

"Meanwhile, how can we warn Congress members to be on the lookout for Nervochok attacks if we don't know *how* the attacker attacks?"

Stanford shrugged.

Madison said, "Can we put a guard with each of the five hundred thirty-five Congress members."

"Possible, but crowded," he said. "That puts over a thousand people in and around the chambers. On top of that, they'd have to fit in with the staffs and hundreds of daily visitors to Congressional offices. It could get very overcrowded very fast."

Madison nodded. "And maybe we should station another five hundred guards around their homes."

Stanford nodded, got a text message, and said, "There's no time to organize all this protection."

"Why?"

"I just got word the House of Representatives is ready to vote on USMed—later today!"

Madison said, "Any chance the House can be persuaded to delay the vote until we sort all the best way to protect members?"

"The FBI suggested that yesterday. Both House and the Senate polled their members and 86% refuse to delay the vote. They say, the President, and all Americans, have waited too long for this USMed vote."

SEVENTY-SIX

The Guardian reviewed the latest vote estimates. His sources said USMed would lose by two votes in the Senate. And lose by three in the House. Both estimates were within the margin of error.

He didn't like margins of error. He liked margins of certainty. Numerical assurance. Because members of Congress couldn't be trusted. They connived, deceived, denied, and lied.

He mostly worried about those who say they'll vote *against* USMed, but plan to vote *for* it—because they secretly received large campaign donations from these new *pro* USMed PACS. Some Congress members collected money from both *anti*-USMed groups *and* from *pro*-USMed groups.

And time was running out. The USMed vote would begin within hours in the House.

To be certain USMed was defeated, he would eliminate another Senate pro USMed vote.

She deserved it.

* * *

"The House *has* to pass it!" Ellie said.

Madison nodded.

In Ellie's office they watched C-SPAN as the House of Representatives started voting on USMed.

"The Speaker of the House feels it should pass," Madison said. "But several cable news channels, including CNN and FOX, predict the vote could swing either way. It's too close to call."

Ellie felt partly responsible. "I should have persuaded more voters."

"You were locked in closets!"

"Look—the roll call's starting."

On TV the House clerk banged the podium, called the House to order, announced the bill, and began the alphabetical roll call vote.

Minutes later, Ellie heard, "Mr. Campbell ... "

"I'm worried about Campbell," Ellie said. "Rumor is someone offered to pay off his huge family debts—if he voted against USMed."

"I heard that too."

Congressman Campbell stood up, paused, looked at the TV camera, and defiantly shouted, "AYE!"

Madison high-fived Ellie. "If he was bribed, I hope he gives the bribe money it to a charity."

The House clerk said, "Ms. Denton ... "

"NAY!" she said.

After several more Congress members voted, Ellie asked, "What's the score?"

Madison checked the C-SPAN Roll Call tally board. "We're down three,"

They had hoped to be ahead by one at this point in the roll call. Three down was a lot of ground to make up.

Ellie was worried.

"Ms. Nuñez ... "

"AYE," Representative Nuñez said.

Many more Congress members voted, and Ellie saw they were still two behind and fast approaching the middle of the alphabetical roll call.

"Mr. Paulsen ... " the clerk said.

Ellie watched Paulsen turn and smile toward her, then say, "AYE." He'd been a close friend of her dad.

"Ms. Petite ... " the clerk said.

"NAY," Petite said.

"Mr. Sanderson ... "

Ellie said, "Sanderson's ten-year-old daughter, Trish, was kidnapped to force him to vote against USMed. But an FBI drone tracked the kidnappers to a cabin. This morning at 4 a.m. an FBI HRT team rescued Trish. She's fine and back home."

"*AYE!*" Sanderson shouted as though speaking to her kidnappers. Loud applause broke out through the representatives and galley.

Ellie checked the remaining votes. Only a few more votes, but still two down.

"Mr. Smothers ... "

"AYE," he said, smiling at Ellie.

"One more to tie," Ellie said.

"Ms. Whitten ... "

"AYE!" she said.

"Tied," Ellie said, her heart pounding. "This is it. The last vote."

"Ms. Yardley ... "

Vera Yardley paused, smiled and said—"*AYE!*"

Applause exploded in the chamber and gallery.

"*That's 118 AYES! A simple House majority!*" Madison said.

"*The House passed USMed!*" Ellie shouted.

Thunderous applause rocked the House chamber and balcony. Madison hugged her.

"And now it's up to the Senate," Madison said.

Ellie nodded, but quickly grew concerned.

Late word was that the Senate still had a number of unconfirmed votes. Passage was not looking good.

SEVENTY-SEVEN

Clearly frustrated, Stanford shook his head, then rubbed his tired, red eyes.

Madison knew he'd been working thirty-seven straight hours without sleep and worried he was fading.

She grabbed a file with the victims' phone call lists ... the calls they made the day they died. She kept moving her finger down the last fifty calls for Senator Jonathon Nelson. As expected, most calls were to fellow Congress members and some were from personal friends.

She ran her eyes down the call list of Senator Clete Ruskin who died sitting in his cottage. Again, most calls to and from fellow Senators.

Next, she checked the call list for Senator Woodwillow who died in his office. Similar calls to and from colleagues.

As she scanned the phone number list for Wendy Shuman, something caught Madison's attention. The last four numbers of a call to Wendy ended in *8476*.

I just saw 8476.

She checked Senator Nelson's calls. One ended in *8476.*

She checked Senator Woodwillow's phone list and saw another call ended in *8476.*

She checked Clete Ruskin's list—another caller's last four numbers: *8476.*

Her heart started pounding.

Quickly, she checked LaTisha Darnell's phone calls. Another *8476* caller. *What's going on?*

Were these *8476* calls soliciting support from the Congress members for some political cause?

No, she realized. *Because the 8476 Caller ID names are all different. Also different are the first six numbers of each 8476-phone number.* Each caller had a different caller name, and different numbers, except for the last 8476 numbers.

Her heart pounded. *What the hell is all this?*

These Nervochok victims all received a call from a phone number ending in 8476.

One victim's 8476 Caller ID said: *Geriatric HealCorp.* Another 8476 Caller ID: *Financial LTD.*

Senator Nelson's 8476 Caller ID: *National Institutes of Health.*

Another 8476 Caller ID read: *MedStar DC Hospital.*

Another 8476 Caller ID: *The White House.*

Another 8476 Caller ID: *National Security Committee.*

And all victims answered the calls. Some talked or listened to the caller for a bit.

Were these callers real people? Or Robocalls? What did they say?

Did the 8476 calls trigger some device in the victim's room that unleashed Nervochok?

"Agent Stanford!" Madison said, waving her hands at him.

Stanford hung up. "You found something?"

She nodded. "I think so."

"What?"

"How the Nervochok attacks the victims."

SEVENTY-EIGHT

Ellie grabbed her briefcase and smiled at Gabriel waiting at her apartment door. Having him close by, protecting her, watching over her the last few days, gave her a much better sense of security … and an even better sense of him. They'd shared their backgrounds over fast-food desktop lunches and a couple of slow tablecloth dinners. They got to know each other.

And she liked what she got to know. A lot.

And he seemed to like her.

But she knew FBI agent rules required him to maintain a professional relationship with his assignees. Avoid an intimate, personal relationship. She sensed he might be holding back because of those regulations.

But I, his sweet new assignee, have no regulations to hold me back.

His eyes said he was interested in her. Did his eyes see she was interested in him? More than a little?

They approached his FBI Chevy Tahoe, and he opened her passenger door like a chauffeur.

"Madam Senator, your carriage ... " he said with a slight bow.

"Carriage? Indeed, Special Agent."

They drove into medium traffic. She was excited. Within hours, she'd vote for a law that could finally bring healthcare coverage to *all* Americans.

She'd also vote for her father.

Gabriel turned onto Massachusetts Avenue heading southeast. Traffic got heavier and crawled down to ten miles per hour.

"DC traffic," he said. "GPS indicates H Street is also slow as molasses."

"Like Congress?"

"Congress is *parked!*" Gabriel said, laughing.

She laughed too. He made her laugh a lot, she noticed.

Magically, traffic eased up and soon they were racing along at thirteen miles an hour.

Ellie noticed a Nissan van pull up beside her. The driver and passenger wore their hoodies up. Why up on a hot, humid day? They glanced over at Ellie, then looked away. Seconds later, she caught them staring at her again. *Why?*

They were creeping her out fast.

She turned to tell Gabriel—

—when suddenly Gabriel's Tahoe raced ahead ... his hands flew off the steering wheel ... *the car was driving itself!*

Ellie's mouth went dry. "Gabe—what's—?"

"*—something's driving this car! I can't steer—*"

The Tahoe somehow steered itself around a slow car, then down a narrow street.

Ellie and Gabriel watched in total panic.

Gabriel tried to strong-arm-steer it to the curb but couldn't budge the wheel.

"Someone hacked into the Tahoe. They're *driving* it!"

"Hit the brakes!"

"There are none! I have no control!"

Ellie saw the guys in the van behind their Tahoe. They were smiling at her.

Ellie's heart pounded.

The Tahoe raced up to 60 mph on a narrow street, barely missing a moving van and a woman jaywalking between cars.

Ahead, Ellie saw a big vegetable truck parked. Not enough room to go around it. They were going to crash into the back end.

"Turn the key off!" she said.

"Can't. Key's in my pocket. But may—"

Gabriel reached in his pocket, grabbed the key, and threw it out the window.

The Tahoe engine turned off immediately.

But the heavy SUV's momentum coasted fast toward the vegetable truck. He tried to steer around it. Couldn't.

They would smash into it.

Gabriel pulled Ellie into his arms and threw his body between her and the dashboard.

The Tahoe slammed into the open end of the vegetable truck. Glass shattered, wood crates splintered, vegetables splattered everywhere.

The airbag exploded against her cheek as her head banged against the side door panel hard.

And then she saw nothing.

* * *

In the white Nissan van, Kurt Schick fist-bumped Jack Miller after the Tahoe crashed into the vegetable truck. They turned down a side street and left the area.

"Your fuckin' device actually *worked*," Miller said as he turned down another street.

Schick closed his laptop. "Fuckin'-A!"

"How?"

"I hacked into the Tahoe's Wi-Fi. Turned off the factory settings. Inserted mine and took over driving their Tahoe! The crash will stop her from votin' … and maybe from breathin'."

"Can you hack my bitch ex-wife's Jeep?" Miller said.

"Yeah, but it'll cost you big time!"

SEVENTY-NINE

In his DC laboratory, Dr. Gorman looked at Madison and Special Agent Stanford.

"Madison, you're saying Nervochok victims received a phone call ending with 8476?"

"Yes. But each 8476 call had a different Caller ID name."

"And you think that 8476 phone call probably triggered the Nervochok device located in the victim's area?"

Madison and Stanford nodded.

"Our tech team agrees," Dr. Gorman said. "*And* we think we found the triggering device in each victim's room or area. Let's test it here now."

Gorman led them down a hall into a spotless mini lab. Overhead LED lighting bleached the room brilliant white. They walked over to a large workbench. Dr. Gorman pointed at the objects on it.

"We suspect these devices."

Madison couldn't believe what she was looking at.

Four USMed iPhones.

"Next to these four USMed iPhones I'm placing this brand-new Apple iPhone we just bought at an Apple Store. As you can see, all the phones look identical."

"Each Nervochok victim had one of these free *USMed* iPhones with them when they died. Let's test one now. Please put on masks and gloves." He pointed to the boxes of masks and gloves.

Madison put hers on.

A lab assistant walked over to the bench. Using a tiny tool, she pried the backs off the four USMed iPhones. Then she pried the back off the new Apple iPhone and placed it next to the four USMed iPhones.

"Let's compare them," Dr. Gorman said.

They studied the inside components of all five phones.

Madison thought they all looked identical. Why wouldn't they? They were all iPhones.

"Look closely at the brand-new Apple *store* iPhone we just bought," Dr. Gorman said. "Inside, on the top left, is the phone's camera and LED flash. On its right side is Mic #2, and the headset jack. That big flat thing running the length of the phone is the lithium-ion battery. To the left of the battery are the micro-SIM tray and the flash memory. At the bottom is the microphone opening where we speak into the phone."

"Now please look at the *USMed* iPhones' battery area. Everything is the same, except between the camera flash location and the Mic #2 location. There we see something different—a small gray unit in each of the four USMed iPhones. Do you see the units?"

Madison and the others nodded.

"But in the new Apple-store iPhone we do not see that small gray unit."

"What's the unit do?" Madison asked.

"We're about to find out," Dr. Gorman said. "Kim, please put the cover back on Senator Ruskin's phone before I dial the same 8476 number that was dialed to him. Everyone, please tighten your face masks."

Everyone did.

Dr. Gorman reached in his pocket and took out his own iPhone.

"Okay, I'm now dialing the same phone number ending in 8476 that someone dialed to Senator Ruskin's USMed phone minutes before he died. Keep your eye on his phone, the one on the far left."

Madison stepped back as though Ruskin's phone might explode.

Ruskin's phone began to ring.

Dr. Gorman's gloved finger reached over and pushed Ruskin's *ACCEPT* button.

Madison heard the call connecting.

Then, she couldn't believe her eyes. A fine gray mist-like powder puffed out of the ear slot on Ruskin's phone.

Dr. Gorman's finger quickly punched the OFF button to stop more mist seeping out. He nodded to Kim who pried the back covering off Ruskin's phone and looked inside.

The lab went graveyard quiet.

"There!" said Dr. Browner, pointing. "See it?

The dust-like mist is still seeping from the small unit beside the lithium battery. The mist flows out through the phone's ear slot into the victim's ear canal! Then flows deeper into the ear, the back of the nose, the eustachian tube and respiratory system as they talk. The USMed phone ear slots were enlarged to permit more Nervochok to pass through into the ear quickly."

Madison moved closer and saw the tiny gray mist particles.

"Everyone stay back!" Dr. Gorman said. "That's very likely Nervochok."

Madison stepped back and held her breath.

"Kim, where's my Proengin?"

KIm handed him a hand-held device shaped somewhat like a Dustbuster.

"This Proengin AP2C chemical-nerve agent sensor will tell us what the gray particles are."

He turned on the sensor and moved its funnel opening very close to the dusty particles still flowing from the USMed phone's ear slot.

Seconds later, the Proengin detector flashed red.

Madison saw the luminous red readout:

DANGER: NERVOCHOK.

EIGHTY

"Back away from these Nervochok particles," Dr. Gorman said.

Madison took three steps back, tightened her facemask, and held her breath.

"As you just saw," Dr. Gorman said, "calling the 8476-phone number triggered Senator Ruskin's USMed phone to release the Nervochok mist particles from its storage unit in his phone. When he answered the 8476 call, he triggered the Nervochok to escape out through the phone slot and into his ear. As he talked or waited for the caller to say something, the Nervochok flowed into Ruskin's inner ear canal and then deeper into his airway passages. By the time he hung up, Nervochok was deep in his lungs and respiratory system, shutting down his ability to breathe. It was too late. He was dead within a couple of minutes. Same with all the other Nervochok victims."

Stunned, Madison stepped farther back from the phone. "Who got these free USMed phones?"

Stanford said, "I think many pro-USMed Congress members and some aides got them. The phones were gifts. All phone bills paid."

Madison said, "Senator Nelson warned that someone or something we thought was good, was not. Like a wolf in sheep's clothing. Maybe he suspected the group giving out the free USMed phones."

"Who gave the phones out?" Dr. Gorman said.

"I think some *pro*-USMed charity group," Madison said.

Gorman said, "If we get a list of who received them, we can warn them."

"*Oh my God!*" Madison sprang to her feet, horrified.

"What's wrong?" Stanford said.

"I think *Ellie* has her father's USMed phone! The phone that killed him! Estelle gave it to her because her phone was taken by her abductors."

"Call Ellie!" Stanford said.

Madison called Ellie's father's USMed phone.

She didn't answer and her voice message box was full. Was she already at her Russell Senate office? She said she was going in early. From there, she planned to walk over to the Senate to vote on USMed.

She called Ellie again. No answer.

She called Ellie's office, praying an aide picked up.

No one did.

EIGHTY-ONE

M ayMay dialed Agent Stanford's phone number from memory.

Stanford picked up.

"Hi, MayMay."

"Hi. You said to call if I remembered something."

"Yes."

"I remembered Archie telephoned another man."

"Who?"

"A man called Mr. Bennett."

Stanford shot his arm in the air and took a victory lap around his chair. "Bennett? Are you sure?"

"Yes."

"That's very helpful."

"Archie *whispered* to Mr. Bennett."

"About what?"

"He whispered, *I got your special gifts.*"

"What kind of special gifts?"

"Archie did not say. Another time Archie phoned a man he called Desmond."

Stanford thought he'd heard the Desmond name recently but couldn't remember where.

"Spelled D-e-s-m-o-n-d?"

"I guess so."

"What's his last name?"

"The first part was Arri ... I could not hear the rest."

"But you heard ARRI?"

"Yes. Archie told Desmond Arri ... that he delivered their *special gifts*. The gifts seemed very important to them."

"Why?"

"Because Archie whispered so low, like they were discussing big secrets."

Like secret USMed phones that kill people, Stanford thought.

"Anything else you remember, MayMay?"

"No."

"Thanks, MayMay. You've helped a lot."

"Good."

They hung up.

Special Agent Stanford stared at the name MayMay gave him: D-e-s-m-o-n-d.

Stanford thought he'd heard the name somewhere in the last two weeks. But who said it?

If Archie did what Desmond said, maybe Desmond was the big boss. How many Desmonds in DC? Did Ellie know any?

He dialed Ellie's number to make sure she got the warning about her USMed phone.

She did not pick up, so maybe she got the message and that's why she wasn't picking up.

He phoned her bodyguard, Agent Gabriel Allen. He didn't answer either, and his message box was full. Stanford sent a text.

No response. Not good. Gabriel was required to be reachable 24/7. And he hadn't left a voice or text message. Very unlike him. Stanford grew worried. Was Gabriel in trouble? Were they both in trouble?

Stanford would call him again in a couple minutes.

Meanwhile he turned to his computer and typed in *Desmond Arri* and hit enter.

The screen lit up with some possible names:

Desmond Arristoelus
Desmond Arrissian
Desmond Arritson
Desmond Arrington
Desmond Arriteque
Desmond Arritia

Stanford tapped on *Desmond Arristoelus*: the guy owned a Greek restaurant in San Diego. *Desmond Arrissian* worked in a Chevy assembly plant in Michigan. *Desmond Arritson* owned an exotic reptile shop in Naples, Florida.

He tapped on *Desmond Arrington.*

Bingo!

Arrington was the Chairman of a large pharmaceutical and healthcare conglomerate headquartered in DC. He'd been a former CEO of a major drug company and two national hospital chains for many years. A Pharma heavy breather. And the only Desmond Arrington in the DC area.

This had to be the Desmond that Archie phoned. Did Desmond ever phone Archie? Did Desmond call Donald Bennett?

Stanford phoned Special Agent Kate Carras. But again, was bounced into Kate's message box. He left a message asking her to get a search warrant for Desmond Arrington's phone records fast.

"Where the hell is everybody?" he shouted.

EIGHTY-TWO

In MedStar hospital, Ellie pealed open her left eye and stared into a blindingly bright penlight held by a tall red-haired nurse with thick glasses that made her eyes big as marshmallows. Her nametag said Brigette.

"How many fingers am I holding up?" Nurse Brigette asked her.

"None," Ellie said.

"*What?*"

"That's your thumb."

Nurse Brigette laughed. "Call CNN! A Senator with a sense of humor! Can you open *all* of your pretty blue eyes, Senator?"

Ellie opened them wide. The nurse checked them, her vital signs, then smiled again. "You're lookin' good. And you're livin' lucky as hell, Senator."

"What happened?" Ellie asked.

"You were in a car accident. Smashed into a big vegetable truck. EM rescue guys said you looked like a Caesar salad. Thought the squished tomatoes in your hair were bits of brains. Scared the bejesus out of them."

Ellie remembered the accident. She was afraid to ask the next question. "How is ... Special Agent Gabriel...?"

"Bruised shoulder and a head bump. Same side as yours."

"Is he awake?"

"Yep. Been waiting for you to wake up. I'll tell him."

"Thank you."

Seconds later, Gabriel walked in. His head and wrist were bandaged, but otherwise he looked fine. He walked over to her bed and they smiled at each other.

"Thank you for saving my life," she said.

"Thank you for saving my job," he said.

"How?"

"By staying alive. The Bureau gets really snippy if the person we're guarding croaks."

"Gee-that's strict?"

"Yep." He leaned over and kissed her cheek.

"Hey, isn't that against regulations?" she said.

"Can't remember. Head injury. You also have a forehead bruise. I better fix that too." He kissed it.

"You should have more head injuries," she said.

He laughed and started to kiss her again but froze as Nurse Brigette walked back in the room.

"Keep goin'," Nurse Brigette said, laughing. "I've seen all ten commandments broken in hospital beds."

* * *

Forty minutes later, after a heated discussion with their doctors, Gabriel and Ellie signed their *Discharge Against Medical Advice Forms* from MedStar Georgetown Hospital. The doctors made them promise to call if they felt dizzy or nauseated.

Despite her car crash bruises, Ellie felt pumped up. "No way I'll miss voting for USMed!"

"No way, I'll miss guarding you." Gabriel said.

They stepped outside and got in a Yellow Cab.

They headed toward her Senate office in the Russell Building. From there they would walk over to the Senate Chamber for the USMed vote.

She was excited. USMed was the most important bill she would ever vote for. Her father lived and died for it.

She would vote *AYE* for him and forty-four million Americans who now have *no* health insurance.

But the vote count was too close to call.

She grabbed her USMed phone. The police found it in the wrecked Tahoe. But the phone had zero power. Luckily their taxi had a charger, and she plugged her phone in. Gabriel's phone was destroyed in the car crash. A colleague would bring him a new phone at the Capitol.

The taxi was moving along nicely.

A minivan pulled alongside her and Ellie tensed up until she saw the soccer mom driving kids.

Chill, she told herself.

"How'd those two van guys grab control of your Tahoe?" she asked.

"Hacked in through the Wi-Fi computers and took over driving."

"Maybe I'll take the bus from now on."

"Save me a seat."

* * *

They arrived at the Russell Building, passed through security, and hurried down to Ellie's office.

"I need a face transplant," Ellie said, "Or at least to hide my bruises." She grabbed her makeup bag.

"You look swell," he said.

"Can you say swollen?"

He laughed and she headed into the nearby restroom. She looked in the mirror. The Bride of Frankenstein stared back at her. She put a fresh Band-Aid on her forehead cut. Her bruised cheek felt better but was an ugly purple green beneath her makeup. She applied more makeup, used eye drops to clear the redness, then glossed her lips. She combed through her unruly dark-auburn hair, happy that brain chunks and tomato stuff didn't fall out.

She had planned to have her hair blown out earlier for a CNN and FOX interview about her father after the vote. No time for hair now.

Back in her office, Gabriel smiled. "You look like you!"

"Thanks to you." When his body protected hers in the crash, he might have saved her life. When he kissed her in the hospital, he might have *changed* her life. She hadn't felt this way since Liam. Feared she never would again. But now there was hope.

"You ready to go cure American healthcare, Senator?"

"More than ready, Special Agent."

And *special* is the right word, she thought, drawn once again into his gentle eyes and warm, fun personality.

"What are the current chances USMed passes in the Senate?" he asked.

"Last I heard we might have a two-vote advantage. *Might!* But we never know. The count keeps changing every hour. So every vote is critical."

Gabriel nodded. "I would vote for USMed."

She smiled. "Good. But why?"

"First, I believe it's the American thing to do. Our government is sworn to protect American lives, right?"

"Right."

"In war they protect our lives from our enemies, right?"

"Right."

"Diseases are also our enemies. Our deadliest enemies sometimes. Our government should also protect our lives against serious deadly diseases."

"Agreed."

"Also, I heard you say thirty-nine million Americans have such *lousy* health coverage they can't afford the outrageously high co-pays. Government should fix that."

"You running for Congress?" Ellie said.

"Don't tempt me."

"But some Americans *love* the present healthcare systems," Ellie said.

"Who?"

"The top healthcare executives. The heads of pharma ... and managed healthcare ... and pharmaceutical sales ... and hospital chains ... and the ambulance companies have mind-blowing bonuses. Did you know the ambulance industry makes more money annually than Hollywood's entire movie industry?"

"Incredible," he said. "Speaking of which I just read about the bonus the executive got for merging Aetna with CVS?"

"How much?" Ellie asked.

"*Five hundred million dollars!* For one executive. Wonder how many thousands of poor families his bonus could have provided health care for?"

Ellie looked stunned. "Welcome to US healthcare, where the rich get richer and the poor get sicker. And sometimes die."

Ellie checked her watch. "We should probably walk on over to the Senate. It's almost Show Time!"

He nodded.

She grabbed her purse and folders, and they headed toward the tunnel that would lead them to the Senate Chamber.

She smiled at Gabriel.

And he smiled back. They were a team. She felt like holding his hand *now*, holding on to him, because after the vote, she would not be in danger, would not need a bodyguard, and he would probably be reassigned to somewhere like Grinder Switch, Alabama, chasing moonshiners.

Somehow, she had to find a devious way to keep him as her bodyguard *after* she voted.

Maybe a real threat would show up.

EIGHTY-THREE

E llie and Gabriel walked down to the underground tunnel that led them over to the Senate Chamber in the US Capitol Building. She'd been cooped up so much in the tiny janitor's closet, the cigar room, and the hospital room, she wanted to *walk*. Actually, she wanted to *jog* over … but her last jog ended with thugs abducting and drugging her.

She, Gabriel, and a few other Senators started walking over. Right on cue, reporters appeared and started hounding them like a pack of jackals, barking questions about her abduction and escape.

She noticed Gabriel watching the reporters for any who moved too aggressively toward her. When one reporter thrust her long-handled mic to close to Ellie's mouth, Gabriel gently pulled her mic back.

A reporter shouted, "Senator, are you going to vote like your father—for USMed?"

Ellie smiled. "Yes. It was his major goal. And mine."

"Do you think it will pass?"

"I think it will be close, but I'm very hopeful."

"Senator, have your kidnappers been captured yet?"

"They were identified but are still at large."

"We're you physically attacked?"

"Just locked in a room."

"Senator, did you feel sexually threatened?"

"Were you bound and gagged?"

"Were you attacked as a woman?"

The questions were getting personal. She remembered a trick her father used. When reporters flooded him with personal or unwanted questions, he pulled out his phone, pretended to take a call, and kept walking and talking to a fake caller.

Ellie pulled out her phone, pretended to take a call, and kept walking, talking to a dead phone.

But some reporters continuing firing questions at her.

* * *

Fifty feet behind her, Desmond Arrington, wearing tinted glasses and a full beard, walked with a pack of noisy reporters swarming around Ellie and the other Senators.

Perfect time, he thought.

He pulled out his phone, opened his Favorites, and selected the phone number ending in 8476. He would now send the number to Ellie's USMed phone ... the same phone that eliminated her father ... and would eliminate her.

And most importantly, eliminate her USMed *vote!*

Desmond dialed the number.

* * *

Ellie pretended to talk on her phone, when suddenly it started ringing. She'd heard that phone reception in the senate tunnel was sometimes hit and miss.

She answered. "Hello?"

She heard ... *hissing ... crackling ...*

"Ellie ...?"

"Yes ... *hissing ...* "

"It's Governor Wilson ... just calling... *hissing* ... to wish ... good luck ... USMed."

"Oh, thank you Governor ... *hissing ... crackling* ... has a good chance in ... *hissing* ... Senate. Like it passed ... *hissing ... clicking* ... in ... House."

"... by a simple majority ... *hissing* ... 218 out of 434."

"Yes ... *crackling* ... but we'll take a slim win ... *hissing* ... in Senate. The President has ... *hissing* ... promised to sign ... *hissing ... clicking* ... when it lands ... his desk."

"That's terrific news!" ... *hissing.* "Good luck, Ellie!"

"Again ... *crackling* ... thank you ... for this opportu ... Governor."

"... Indiana thanks you ... Senator."

EIGHTY-FOUR

Madison's pulse pounded against her temples.

She still could not reach Ellie.

"The vote starts any minute. We've *got* to warn her!" she said.

"I just called her again," Stanford said. "No answer. You sure she has the *same* USMed phone that killed her father?"

"Positive. She told me Estelle hand-delivered her father's USMed phone to her. Ellie's abductors had taken hers. What about Gabriel?"

"I tried his phone. It's dead. No ring."

"I'll try Ellie again now." Madison's fingers trembled as she dialed. She listened and hung up.

"No answer. Her voicemail's full. And she didn't respond to my text. She must have powered off."

Madison felt her stomach tighten. "I heard Senate Security requires Senators to surrender their phones before they enter the chamber. So if she has to surrender her phone, she'll be safe, right?"

"Not today," Stanford said.

"Why?"

"She doesn't have to surrender her phone for today's vote."

"Why not?"

"They're only required to surrender their phone when the Senate session involves confidential or national security briefings. For those confidential briefings they're required to leave their phone, tablet, and laptop with Security outside the chamber. Then pick them up after the briefing."

"So, since USMed is not a confidential or national security session," Madison said, "they can bring in their phones?"

"I believe so," he said. "But they still can't make calls or answer calls or take pictures during the session. If they get caught talking on the phone, or taking pictures, they can get reprimanded or fined."

"I'll try phoning Ellie *again* ... "

She dialed, waited, shook her head.

"Can you try Agent Gabriel again?"

Stanford dialed, waited, and shook his head. "Still nothing. I still think something bad has happened to both of them."

"Have they both been abducted?" Madison said.

* * *

Desmond Arrington saw Ellie still talking on her phone. A real call? Or pretending to keep reporters from harassing her?

It didn't work. A few reporters kept barking personal questions.

Arrington again pulled up the 8476 number on his phone.

He dialed it to her USMed phone.

He heard hissing and clicking as his call started to connect to Ellie's phone. He hated the lousy phone reception in the Congressional tunnels. The Capitol's sophisticated electronic systems seemed to screw up his connections and reception when he needed them most.

* * *

Ellie pretended to be talking on her phone as she and Gabriel took the elevator up to the level of the Senate Chamber floor. When they got off the elevator, another pack of reporters swarmed her.

She heard a real phone call coming in.

She picked up. But again she heard heavy hissing, click, and crackling ...

"Hello...?"

Hissing ... "Ellie ... thank God!" Madison shouted.

Buzzz ... *hissing* ... "Madi ... barely hear ... *hissing, cracking* ... are you in ... gallery?" ... *clicking ... hissing.*

"Ell ... turn ... *pho—*"

"Madi ... can't ... hear ... wha—?"

"... tur ... pho ... "

... *buzzz ... hissing ...*

"But ... *static ... hiss ...* 'xpect impor ... call ... got take!"

* * *

Desmond cursed. Another fucking call cut in ahead of his, and she answered it—blocking his 8476 call. He'd hoped to handle her *before* she reached the Senate chamber.

Not a problem. He'd handle her inside the chamber. Senators could take their phones into the chamber today for a special picture-taking dispensation – but only *after* the historic USMed vote. He call her before she voted.

A vote that Ellie Nelson's will miss due to her unfortunate fatal emergency.

* * *

A reporter shouted, "How do you feel about casting the USMed vote your father would have cast?"

"Honored."

Gabriel paused at the door to the Senate Chamber. "Ellie, I can't go in the Chamber. But don't worry, Senate Security people will take over. You'll be fine. I'll meet you right here after the vote."

"Sounds good." *If I'm not safe in the Senate Chamber where am I safe?*

She stepped into the Senate Chamber.

* * *

Desmond watched Ellie walk up to the entrance of the Senate Chamber where security guards checked Senators as they arrived.

"Good luck, Ellie!" a Senator shouted.

She turned and thanked him, then walked into the chamber, and headed toward her seat, looking relieved to escape the reporters.

Desmond walked up to the Senate gallery security guard and handed him his gallery pass and cell phone and entered the gallery.

In his coat lining he hid a pre-programmed burner phone that he would use to call her 8476 number.

He walked over and sat in his reserved gallery seat. He looked down and saw Ellie sitting at her desk below. She was checking the AYE-NAY buttons on her electronic voting panel. She chatted with Senators who stopped by, obviously congratulating her for surviving her abduction and maybe today's car crash. The lucky girl smiled at everyone.

But her luck had run out.

* * *

Ellie looked up at the gallery. She scanned over where Madison should be sitting in her reserved seat. But she wasn't there. Probably stuck in DC traffic.

She opened her compact and made sure her forehead bandage wasn't oozing yucky bloody gunk. It wasn't. As she put the compact back in her purse, she felt her phone. She saw Madison had called again, but her earlier call had so much static it was impossible to understand what she sounded so concerned about.

Ellie dialed Madison to find out.

But the call bounced her to Madison's voicemail. It was full.

* * *

Seated one hundred twenty feet above Ellie, Desmond Arrington reached into his coat lining and felt his hidden burner phone. He glanced at the illuminated 8476 phone number. It was ready to send to Ellie's phone again.

When she answered, she wouldn't survive long enough to vote.

And if she did not answer *this* time, no problem. He'd programmed his burner to keep redialing the 8467 number every ninety seconds until she answered.

He knew the USMed bill would fail by at least two votes, three with her demise.

USMed would be stillborn.

He hit *Send* ...

He heard his call connecting to her phone.

He watched her reach for her phone.

Game over.

Desmond stood up to leave. He didn't need to watch her gasp, choke, and strangle in her own vomit. He'd known Ellie since she was in college. Smart kid. But like her father, she wanted to destroy America's healthcare by giving everyone basically free health insurance. How ridiculous? How insane was that? If people don't pay for their healthcare, they deserved to be sick. Why should those who worked hard for their health insurance support those who did not?

He stood, left the gallery, picked up his regular phone from security, then walked toward the Capitol exits.

* * *

Ellie heard her vibrating phone again. A call coming in. Caller ID said: *White House*. The same *White House* call she'd missed minutes earlier? Who would call me from the White House? And why *now*? It made no sense. Should she answer it?

The Speaker was approaching the podium. All senate seats looked filled. The clerk would start the roll call voting any second now.

Ellie started to answer the call, then remembered the senate rule that she could not receive calls on the floor.

She also remembered Madison's frantic call. She wasn't sure what Maddy was saying. It sounded like she might have tried to say something her about her phone. But what? And why?

And this was a call from the *White House*!

She started to answer it ...

... as the gavel banged down on the senate podium three times—loud as firecrackers.

"The Senate will come to order!"

* * *

Desmond walked out of the Capital Building and headed down Constitution Avenue.

His driver, Leland, blinked the Mercedes lights three times. Moments later, he jumped out and opened the back door for Arrington. Desmond got in the back seat, took off his fake beard, and sipped the Glenfiddich Leland had prepared.

They drove off toward the BWI Airport where his Learjet awaited him.

In a few hours he'd be in sunny Bermuda. Minutes later, he'd be sitting on the balcony of his villa, sipping the island's famous Dark 'n Stormy cocktails, and watching the orange sun melt into the blue Atlantic.

EIGHTY-FIVE

The Senate clerk slammed the gavel down hard three times.

Now is the hour, Ellie knew.

"The Senate will come to order!"

Mumbling and whispering stopped.

Everyone … Senators in the chamber, and visitors in the gallery … went graveyard silent. The moment had arrived.

Ellie felt her heart pound faster.

The alphabetical roll call of the Senators was starting. The Clerk read the first name.

"Mr. Allen … ?"

Ellie watched Mick Allen push the AYE button.

"Mr. Alperton … ?"

Alperton pushed the NAY button.

"Mr. Bannister … ?"

Ellie watched her friend Bannister push the AYE button.

"Mr. Benston ... ?"

Benston pushed the NAY button.

"Ms. Considine ... ?"

Ellie watched Laura Considine, the attractive young Alaskan Senator, vote AYE.

"Mr. Conti ... ?" Laura's fellow Alaskan Senator had been against USMed, but Laura persuaded him to vote "AYE."

"Mr. Daniels ... ?"

He pushed NAY.

"Mr. Davis ... ?"

Davis pushed the NAY button.

"Mr. Dunston ... ?"

"NAY."

"Ms. Edwards ... ?"

"AYE."

Several more Senators voted. The score was now tied.

"Senator McCue ... ?"

Senator Don McCue pushed the AYE button. But his fellow Senator Meacher pushed the NAY button. McCue gave him the subtle finger and the gallery applauded.

The gavel slammed down loud.

"Mr. Moberly ... ?"

Steve Moberly, her distinguished fellow Indiana Senator, said, "AYE!"

"Ms. Nelson ... ?"

Here we go, Dad ...

Ellie took a breath, hit the AYE button, and tied the vote. Again, applause erupted in the galley. She looked up and saw some Hoosier pals applauding.

But many more Senators still had to vote.

Moments later, Ellie heard "Ms. Stevens ... ?"

Then she watched her close friend, Senator Haley Stevens, from Michigan, wave to her, smile, and push the AYE button.

The Stevens vote put USMed one vote ahead.

Ellie's phone vibrated in her pocket. A call was coming in. She thought she'd turned the phone off.

"Mr. Newton ... ?"

"NAY."

Ellie looked at caller ID and saw the *White House* calling again. *Who* at the White House? And why *now?* It must be important. But why me? Should I answer?

Again, she remembered what sounded like Madison's possible concern about the phones. Was she trying to say—*don't answer calls?*

But calls from the *White House?*

Maybe ...

* * *

Desmond Arrington stared out his limousine window at fast-moving traffic on I-295. He was nearing BWI Marshall Airport and listening to his radio reporting the USMed voting. So far, USMed was losing by two votes. As he knew it would be at this stage in the roll call.

He rechecked the remaining voters and relaxed. In minutes, the Senate would defeat USMed.

He allowed himself a smile. He had the majority of the remaining USMed votes in his pocket. He'd earned them through persuasion, donations, bribes, arm-twisting, and the occasional, but necessary, funeral. A few funerals were more than justified to preserve America's present, perfect, profitable healthcare systems.

* * *

Ellie blinked. She couldn't believe her eyes.

Madison, Stanford, and the Senate Sergeant at Arms were running down her senate aisle toward her.

What the hell are they doing?

Her phone vibrated. She looked at it. White House. Again.

Madison arrived at her desk, looking terrified. "Ellie, where's your phone?"

"There!" She pointed at her purse. "It keeps vibrating every few minutes with the same White House call."

"Thank God you didn't answer."

"Why? Who's calling me from the White House?"

"Nervochok."

"*What?* Maddy, what the hell's going on?"

"If you answer that call, the phone will release Nervochok into your ear."

Ellie's face went chalk white. She felt like she'd been kicked in the stomach.

The Sergeant at Arms and Agent Stanford took her phone and placed it in a metal container.

"We're removing the phone from Senate now!" Stanford said.

"I'll fill you in later, Ellie," Madison said as she left with Stanford and the Sergeant at Arms.

Ellie watched them hurry from the Senate like they were carrying a bomb. She was terrified by what Madison told her.

Am I trapped in a crazed USMed nightmare?

After the ruckus at Ellie's desk quieted down, the Speaker banged the gavel to continue the final few votes on the USMed bill.

"Mr. Vernardin … "

Senator Vernardin said, "NAY."

Ellie smiled, then checked the roll-call total. The vote was tied. Not good. Just three more votes.

"Mr. Williams …?"

Here we go, Dad.

Senator Williams pressed AYE.

"Mr. Winstone …?"

Senator Winstone dramatically whomped the NAY button.

Tied again.

Now the last vote.

The *deciding* vote.

"Mr. Wonn-Denofsky ...?"

This was it, Ellie knew.

The Senate hushed graveyard quiet.

Senator Jerome Wonn-Denofsky's vote would decide the future of healthcare in America.

Wonn-Denofsky looked over at Ellie ... clearly remembering her father's decade-long campaign to pass USMed. He smiled at her and she smiled back.

He gave her a thumbs up and said, *"AYE!"*

Cheers exploded in the floor and gallery.

The electronic board recorded his *AYE!*

USMed PASSED!

"Congratulations, Dad!" Ellie whispered.

She exhaled, wept, and rested her head in her hands.

* * *

Desmond Arrington stepped from his limo carrying his eleven-thousand-dollar crocodile carryon. He strolled through the entrance to BWI-Marshall Airport, the smaller airport near the Baltimore Washington Airport.

He always used BWI, an executive airport. Easy in ... easy out. Easy security. No riffraff. No fat sweaty people seated beside him. No crying babies. Takeoff when *he* wanted.

In *his* Learjet 75.

He walked into the check-in area and nodded to his steward.

"Takeoff ready, Karl?"

"When you are, Mr. Arrington."

Karl took the carryon and they walked down the hallway toward the departure gateway.

The Guardian nodded at Toni Faye, his busty blonde stewardess, who looked like she was smuggling balloons. She winked at him.

And he smiled back. Toni Faye served up coffee, tea, vodka martinis, and on occasion herself.

He tried to check the final USMed vote info on the phone, but the airport's electronics always screwed up his iPhone's Internet reception. He would celebrate the good news on his jet's big-screen TV.

He stepped out on the tarmac and saw his co-pilot standing in the jet door. Seeing Desmond, the man nodded and turned back inside and headed toward the cockpit, probably triple-checking the weather as usual.

Arrington reached the aircraft steps, paused and looked around the airport one last time. Chances were that he would not be back here any time soon, maybe never. Chances were that the police would eventually track his connection to Donald Bennett and Archie Braun.

Not a problem.

He had six passports—over eight hundred million dollars in offshore banks—and luxurious villas in Bermuda, Caracas, and Rio awaiting him. And most important, he had VIP friends in non-extradition countries.

He entered his Learjet, turned to go sit in his comfy brown leather seat, and froze.

A man sat in it.

The tall handsome man stood up and smiled. "Always wanted to sit in a plush executive-jet seat. Far more comfortable than those skinny cheap seats I ride in. Hope you don't mind."

Desmond Arrington did mind.

The man flashed his FBI badge.

"I'm FBI Special Agent Tim Stanford."

"Do I know you?"

"No. But you're about to."

"Why?"

"Desmond P. Arrington, I'm arresting you for conspiracy to commit the murders of Senator Jonathon Nelson, Senator Ellie

Nelson, and Senator Clete Ruskin, and others to be named. You have the right to—"

"—I want my lawyer, Darrel Cedrick, *now!*"

"So do we. In fact, we're arresting Mr. Cedrick as we speak, for aiding and abetting various felonious activity, obstruction of justice, and additional felony charges. He'll be arraigned tomorrow morning."

Stunned, Arrington looked around. His pilot and co-pilot and curvaceous Toni Faye stared at Agent Stanford like he was stealing their Sugar Daddy. Which he was.

Special Agent Stanford looked at the pilot. "Time to save fuel, Captain. Mr. Arrington won't be flying right now."

"At what time can we take off?" the pilot asked.

"Think decades."

EPILOGUE

"Who knew?" Kevin said.

"Knew what?"

"That aliens landed on the Potomac," Kevin pointed toward the river.

Madison turned and smiled at the long, wide, glass-covered luxury dinner-cruiser.

The newly christened *DC Potomac Palace,* a glamorous, all-windows river cruiser that really looked like a *Star Wars* spaceship. It offered passengers many breathtaking views of the Washington skyline, the Jefferson Memorial, the gleaming Washington Monument, the Georgetown waterfront, and much more … as they cruised the moonlit river and wined and dined on gourmet cuisine.

Walking beside Madison and Kevin were Ellie and Gabriel ... far more awed by each other than the *DC Potomac Palace.*

They all boarded the cruiser and stepped inside the dining area where Madison saw the rest of their USMed Victory Team seated at long, elegant tables.

The four of them settled in at a table with Tim Stanford and his wife, Mack McCall and his wife, Special Agent Kate Carras and her partner, Drs. Browner and Gorman and their spouses, MayMay and Mrs. Mayo.

Minutes later, after cocktails, the cruiser eased away from the dock and glided out into the river.

Ellie said, "I like this stretch of the Potomac much better than the stretch near Bealls Island."

"Why?" Stanford asked.

"At Bealls Island B and C planned to toss me in the Potomac with a concrete block around my neck."

Stanford nodded. "We just tossed B and C in the slammer with thirty-year concrete sentences around *their* necks."

Everyone raised their glasses and toasted their sentences.

Soon, the waiters brought everyone's first course. Madison tasted her lobster bisque and felt like purring. Kevin chomped on jumbo scallops and grinned his approval. The main courses followed. Madison had pan-seared Pacific salmon. After a couple of bites, they looked at each other and knew why the *DC Potomac Palace* got five-star reviews.

Madison smiled at MayMay's plate of three thick cheeseburgers.

"This food and the rocking ship may put me to sleep," Madison said to Kevin.

"Say goodnight to Abe first."

"Who?"

He pointed behind her.

She turned and saw the bright-white lighting on the white-marble Lincoln Memorial made Abe even whiter than white. She noticed Abe's eyes seemed to follow hers as the *DC Potomac Palace* cruised past.

She suddenly realized something. Giving all Americans much better health insurance for a better life wasn't nearly as momentous as abolishing slavery, but she thought Abe would approve of USMed.

"By the way," Stanford said, "the two felons, Schick and Miller, who destroyed your USMed commercials at Turner Advertising and hacked into Gabriel's Tahoe, each got thirty-five years for attempted murder. Plus ten more years for assaulting Mary Alice, your agency cleaning lady. Also, your employee, Waylon, was found guilty of aiding and abetting Schick and Miller."

"We also nailed Luca Rizzo," Detective Mark McCall said.

"Who's Luca?" Ellie asked.

"The guy who killed Archie and a biker in the alley. He also kidnapped the ten-year-old daughter of Congressman Scott Sanderson. Trish is fine. Luca got life without parole. His fellow thugs got thirty years."

"How'd you catch Luca?" Ellie asked.

"*Days of our Lives,*" Stanford said.

"What?" Ellie said.

"Luca is obsessed with the show's star, the actress who plays Chloe Lane. Kept stalking her. We collared him twenty feet from her home."

The waitress brought deserts.

All conversation stopped as everyone spoon-licked their way through Triple Chocolate Mud Pies, chocolate and strawberry cheesecakes, profiteroles, and Key Lime Sublime.

As the *DC Potomac Palace* sailed past a tall office building, Madison pointed it out to Special Agent Stanford.

"That's Desmond Arrington's corporate headquarters," she said.

"Not for long," Stanford said. "A few hours ago, a jury found Desmond Arrington guilty on seven counts of Murder One, plus abduction of Ellie, the kidnapping of Sanderson's daughter, and more assorted felonies too numerous to mention."

"What's his sentence?"

"Eternity. Plus three life sentences without parole."

"Oh no," Ellie said.

"What?"

"He'll miss our wedding!"

The group laughed.

Madison was delighted that Ellie and Gabriel had set their wedding date. As her matron of honor, Madison was looking forward to helping with Ellie's fun decisions about her dress, bridesmaids' dresses, and reception.

And after those big decisions, Ellie had a couple more. First, whether or not to run for Senate *after* her interim term expired.

And second, whether she might accept the president's offer to head up the legal team consolidating the numerous healthcare plans under the big USMed nationwide umbrella.

Madison sensed Ellie would relish that assignment to help implement her father's dream.

Ellie tapped her spoon against her glass.

"Hey everybody … thank you for being here and for all you've done to bring USMed healthcare coverage to *all* Americans. Because of you, men, women, and children will not suffer and many will not die for lack of healthcare. So, thank you again. And remember, when our next flu season comes along, get your shot. It's free, under USMed."

Everyone drank to that.

Ellie sat down and Kevin whispered, "Don't forget *your* flu shot like you did last year."

"I won't. Let's just hope it's not the Spanish Flu type," she said. Fortunately, that type of pandemic only happens every hundred years or so."

"The Spanish Flu hit in *1918*," Madison said.

"This is January 2020. You saying we're overdue."

"Maybe."

Madison heard the TV announcer say, *"Breaking News."* She saw the large-screen TV report about a new virus emerging somewhere in a city called Hunan, China.

Thank God it's so far away, she thought.

Know anyone who might enjoy reading...

Available at:
Amazon.com
mikebroganbooks.com
Bookstores

ISBN: 978-1-7338037-3-1   print

ISBN: 978-1-7338037-4-8   ebook

ISBN: 978-1-7338037-5-5   ebook

Also by Mike Brogan

CAR WARS

Madison Parker is excited. She just won a large advertising account for a revolutionary new car. It will transform driving.

Competitive car companies can't begin to compete with it.

But one competitor decides to do something about that – something that will likely cost lives of Madison and many others.

Available at:
Amazon.com
Or 800-247-6553
MikeBroganbooks.com
Bookstores

ISBN: 978-1-7338037-0-0

Also by Mike Brogan

BREATHE

Doctor Nell Northam is abducted by men and forced to help them launch a weapon of mass destruction. The President asks his top security advisor, Donovan Rourke, to save her and stop the attack.

But when Donovan and Nell are finally ready to stop it – they realize they've been set up – and that thousands of Americans are just seconds from dying.

Available at:
Amazon.com
Or 800-247-6553
MikeBroganbooks.com
Bookstores

ISBN: 978-1-9980056-7-6

Also by Mike Brogan

KENTUCKY WOMAN

As an infant, Ellie Stuart is adopted by a poor, but loving parents in Harlan Kentucky. When she's sixteen, they die in an accident, leaving her completely alone in the world. In college she searches for her birth parents with the help of a law student, Quinn Parker.

But as she gets close to finding them, an assassin tries to kill her and Quinn. When she finally discovers why – it may be too late – and Ellie and Quinn have to run for their lives.

Available at:
Amazon.com
Or 800-247-6553
MikeBroganbooks.com
Bookstores

ISBN: 978-0-9846173-9-5

Also by Mike Brogan

G8

Donovan Rourke, a CIA Special Agent, learns a man named Katill will assassinate the world's eight most powerful leaders at the G8 Summit in Brussels in just three days. The President asks Donovan to handle the security. Donovan agrees ... but reluctantly. His wife was murdered there, and he blames himself.

In Brussels, Donovan works with the European G8 Director, and a beautiful translator named Maccabee. They learn that Katill has penetrated the G8's billion-dollar wall of security - and that they're too late – as they watch the world leaders walking into Katill's deathtrap.

Available at:
Amazon.com
Or 800-247-6553
MikeBroganbooks.com
Bookstores

ISBN: 978-0-9846173-0-2

Also by Mike Brogan

MADISON'S AVENUE

First, Madison gets a frightening phone call from her father. Hours later, he's dead. The police say suicide. But Madison suspects murder. She inherits his agency – and his enemies.

When she and her new friend Kevin zero in on the executive behind her father's death, they realize an ex-CIA hitman is zeroing in on them.

The story whisks you from executive boardrooms - to the white sand beaches of the Caribbean - to the high hopes and low cleavage of the Cannes Festival – and to a world where some take the phrase bury the competition - literally.

Available at:
Amazon.com
Or 800-247-6553
MikeBroganbooks.com
Bookstores

ISBN: 978-0-692-00634-4

Also by Mike Brogan

DEAD AIR

Dr. Hallie Mara, an attractive young MD, and her friend, Reed Kincaid, learn that someone has targeted many men, women and children to die in ten cities across the U.S. in a few days. But because Hallie has no hard proof, the police refuse to investigate.

Then Hallie and Reed unearth proof, something far beyond their worst fears. And as they zero in on the man behind everything, he zeros in on them.

Midwest Book Review calls DEAD AIR, "a Lord of the Rings of thrillers. One can't turn the pages fast enough."

Available at:
Amazon.com
Or 800-247-6553
MikeBroganbooks.com
Bookstores

ISBN: 1-4137-4700-0

Also by Mike Brogan

BUSINESS TO KILL FOR

Business is war. And Luke Tanner is about to be its latest casualty. He overheard men conspiring to gain control of a billion-dollar business using a unique strategy – murder the two CEO's who control the business. The conspirators discover Luke has overheard them and kidnap his girlfriend. He tries to free her, but gets captured.

They escape, only to discover that the billion-dollar business is *his* company. And that it's too late to save it.

Writer's Digest gave BUSINESS TO KILL FOR a major award. They called it "The equal of any thriller read in recent years…"

Available at:
Amazon.com
Or 800-247-6553
MikeBroganbooks.com
Bookstores

ISBN: 0-615-11570-5

About the Author

MIKE BROGAN is *Writers Digest* award-winning author of BUSINESS TO KILL FOR, a suspense thriller *WD* called, "the equal of any thriller read in recent years."

His DEAD AIR thriller also won national awards, as did MADISON'S AVENUE.

His years in Kentucky gave him a unique perspective in writing KENTUCKY WOMAN ... as did the amazing, but true story that inspired him to write it.

And his years living in London and Brussels, narrowly escaping terrorist bombs twice, gave him the background to write G8 and BREATHE.

In his recent suspense thriller CAR WARS you read how the newer cars we drive are basically computers on wheels ... and thanks to Wi-Fi, car computers can also be hacked ... *even while you are driving them.*

His latest suspense thriller, CAPITOL MURDER, reveals how far some people will go to prevent more affordable comprehensive healthcare legislation for all Americans.